1

Finding Grace on the Red River

By Bob Nelson

Homeroom, A Shelter From the Storm

Finding Grace on the Red River

(Notes from the Red River Symphony)

Hope on the Red River

(More Notes from the Red River Symphony

Coming this summer)

Finding Grace on the Red River

(Notes from The Red River Symphony)

A Novel

By

Bob Nelson

Dedicated to

Bryan and Paige whose support equals my gratitude

and

My Sunday School class who consistently inspires me.

Cover design by Rob Nelson

Published by Lily Borne Publishing

ISBN-13:978-0692360521

"The thing is," he said. "We all live life like we are driving a car on an expressway-speeding along."

"Is that the thing?" she said.

"But, we don't experience it that way, you know?"

She shook her head. "I have no idea what you mean."

"Well, it's like we see life through a rearview mirror ... and a distorted one at that."

She nodded.

"Memory does not serve us so well. It is warped and dis ... disjointed."

"Yeah, we don't always remember things the way they happened."

"Or even in the right order. Insight doesn't flow logically, but haphazardly."

She thought for a few seconds. "Insight is a product of a random, distorted, rearview mirror."

"What a concept: Life through a fuzzy, out of focus, rearview mirror."

On the Road with Officer Britt and President Nixon

August 9, 1974

Somewhere, Oklahoma

About 45 miles from the Red River

Clark Bradley, in a gesture more habit than anything else, brushed a strand of his shoulder-length hair from his bearded face – an imaginary gust of wind on a scorching Texas day. He was standing next to a Volkswagen bug that, at one time, had been blue yet was so sun-stained and dirty that it was impossible to discern the true color. It was just as hard to see any patch of skin in his mane of hair. He looked right and left, then back and forth before squatting down to the same level of his petite companion.

"Well, kiddo, it looks like we're going to have to hike a little bit. The car is all broken. We're going to have to leave ol' Bernie at this here gas station."

"In the car hospital?"

"It's a garage, Hope. I know you are only 5 years old, but you know what a garage is; there is no such thing as a car hospital. I'll just get some of our stuff out of the backseat."

"Where we going?" she asked while stretching her T-shirt.

He pointed across the highway and down the road.

"Aggh," she gasped. "That's not *too* bad. It's only about a thousand miles. And it's only about 300 degrees. It is *Okrahomie*, you know."

"Sorry."

"I don't wanna go. It's too far."

He sat all the way down. "Hmm, I see what you mean. It does look like a long way … to walk, I mean. What do you think we should do? If we just sit here, it's gonna get really boring and not any cooler. The gas station is really stanky and dirty and no fun whatsoever. I thought we could get something to eat over there and wait for a bus – Greyhound stops there. At least that's what the mechanic fellow said. I don't know. What do you think? Got any better ideas?"

She stared at him and then looked at her tiny Birkenstock sandals that matched his. "I guess that sounds like a good idea, Daddy. It'll be a'venture."

"How did one 5-year old get to be so smart?"

"I got it from Mom."

She laughed and he sort of chuckled. It was a well-rehearsed routine, often repeated, but still true. He gathered some things together from the backseat of the car and stuffed them into a backpack.

"Don't forget the guitar," she said as if he needed a reminder.

"But first …" he said as he held up the suntan lotion.

"What is that?" she said suspiciously.

"Suntan lotion."

"It's all yucky and slimy especially that white stuff on my nose. Don' make me, Daddy," she started to whine and was working her way into a full-fledge cry.

"I know you don't like it." He dropped the tube down to his side. "But the way I see it, if you don't put it on, by the time we walk across the highway and across that giant – it must be 200 miles long – parking lot, you'll be all sunburny and hurtin' and *that* won't be any fun. Now, it seems to me, that the slathering it on – as bad as that is – might be better, I mean, you know, in the long run. I mean, what do you think?"

She looked at him – first up to his eyes, then down to his hand holding the sunscreen, down to his sandaled feet, and back up to his eyes. "Could you make the slathering into a game?"

"Pobably."

So, he rubbed it on her arms and tickled her and rubbed on her face and made her laugh until she shouted, "All right! I'm all slathered up. Stop it already!"

He grabbed her and hugged her. "I'm going to give you a big kiss on your slimy, slathery forehead."

"I love you, Daddy."

"I love you even more."

He stood up and tied his hair back into a ponytail. He looked down the road. He figured a good 20- or 30-minute walk. He slung the backpack on, picked up the guitar case with his left hand, and held out his right hand. "You stay close and hold my hand. This road has lots of traffic and I don't want to take any chances with precious cargo."

"OK, I will 'til we get in the parking lot."

"No, Hope. Even then, until we get in the actual restaurant."

She looked at him and knew he was serious but more importantly, she trusted him, "All right."

They took off walking alongside the road, crossing carefully when they got to the parking lot. He was completely vigilant, constantly turning his neck to see if any trucks were approaching. He was confident that he would hear anything in plenty of time to respond, but he didn't relax or take her safety for granted. She, for her part, took her cues from him and was as watchful as he was. She didn't try to dart away or dance or play. But, when they were safely in the parking lot, maybe 15 yards, she began to sing, "The water is white I cannot get ober it and neither habe I wings soes I can't fly. Build me a boat and both shall float my lob and me. Is that right, Daddy?"

"Close enough." How, he marveled, did a 5-year old girl get to be so smart? The answer, of course, was as simple as Hope said. Her mother, Grace, was the most intelligent women he had ever met.

Just before they arrived at the front door of the truck stop, Hope asked Clark, "Where are we?"

"We are on the north side of Somewhere, Oklahoma."

"How much further?"

5

"I think it is a little more than a hundred miles." *But it might as well be a thousand,* he thought.

As they reached the door, he noticed a sign in bold letters:

NO HITCHHIKING AND NO LOITERING

ALLOWED ON THE PREMISES!

When they stepped in, the first thing to greet them was a refreshing breeze from the air conditioning. They both turned to each other and just smiled. Hope closed her eyes, raised her arms, and slowly turned a circle letting the breeze hit her from every angle while Clark scanned the environment. It was a fairly large truck stop, but not the busiest time of the day. To the right were some racks of merchandise and snack food. To the left, there was a diner of sorts with a few booths and a counter. "This is what passes for a restaurant in Somewhere, Oklahoma," he thought to himself. There were three people sitting at the counter and a couple at a far booth in the corner. They were all staring at Clark and Hope. Everywhere Clark looked, he saw cowboy boots, plaid short-sleeve shirts, jeans, straw cowboy hats, and hair cut so short the scalp looked sore. *The hippie and his little girl just invaded the Redneck Paradise Lounge,* he thought, but knew better than say aloud. To fade away anonymously into a booth was not a practical option no matter how much he wanted to do so, and Clark knew that the next few minutes were crucial to his well-being and, more importantly, for the safety of Hope. Invisibility was clearly not an option, so the next best play was cordiality and politeness. "It sure is hot and that is one long parking lot. Our car broke down on the highway, and we had to leave it at the Texaco station," he directed his remarks to no one in particular and to everyone

6

at once, then he broke into his biggest most friendly grin, but everyone just turned away from him. He sensed some sort of reprieve. At least they could sense that he was no threat to them, he thought. He sat down in the booth closest to the door in case he needed to exit quickly. He had Hope sit with her back to the rest of the diner so he could face everyone with his back was to the doorway. The waitress came up to them and he continued to be as friendly as possible, "Could we have two glasses of water, and Hope, how would you like a milkshake? You do have milkshakes, don't you?" he asked the waitress.

She only nodded.

"Hope, I think a milkshake would be refreshing after that long walk. What do you think?"

"Can it be strawberry? You always get chocolate."

"Sure. You've got strawberry?"

Another nod followed by a perfunctory, "Is that all?"

"For now. No, wait, I need some change. Can you give me some quarters? I need to make a phone call." He pulled out his wallet and offered her a five dollar bill.

She took the money, returning with 20 quarters. He made sure he thanked her profusely and loudly, although it was clear that she, and everyone else wanted nothing to do with him.

"Look, Hope, you sit still and be good ... be very good. Drink your milkshake when it comes. I'm going to be right over there." He pointed at the phones in the back of the store, "You'll be able to see me. But, I don't think these people are

7

going to be very nice if you or I make them mad. I've got to make some phone calls to see how … what we're going to do next."

When he came back to check on her, maybe 15 minutes had passed. By then, the milkshake was nearly gone and a visitor was sitting in the booth where he had been sitting – a policeman. Clark had some experience with the law, and it enabled him to assess the situation. If the policemen had been a state trooper or a Texas Ranger or even from the sheriff's office, he would probably be investigating to get an explanation for this unlikely traveling companions – a hippie and a 5-year old girl. Was Hope a kidnap victim? But, Clark feared that a small-town policeman was probably out to harass the only hippie he had ever seen close-up; he was going to make damn sure his town was safe from a hippie invasion. At another time in another place, Clark would have felt confident that he could avoid a confrontation; he was usually good at that. But, today, here, he was not so sure. He had done nothing to warrant police attention except look different, have hair too long, be unshaved, and stir an ignorant response in the cop.

Today, he was with Hope, and concern for her took precedence over any desire to confront authority; prudence trumped morality. He knew he would have to tread delicately and that the next 30 seconds were crucial. "Be personal, but not phony," he thought so he looked at the nameplate.

"Officer Britt. Can I help you?"

Britt ignored Clark's efforts of politeness. "You play the guitar?"

"No."

8

"Yeah, I know. Your daughter told me you didn't. Good thing you didn't lie and try to tell me you did. So, what's in the guitar case?"

"A guitar. My wife's guitar."

"Where is your wife?"

Clark was not pleased by the questions. He didn't feel that it was any of Officer Britt's business, and he really did not want to share the information with him. He squirmed in his seat, hesitated, and thought better about refusing to answer, "My wife is deceased."

"That means she is dead," Hope spoke up as she continued to slurp the last of the milkshake. She was indifferent to the presence of the policeman. Clark kissed her on the top of her head.

"What's in the backpack?"

"Nothing very significant."

"I think I'll search it."

"I wish you wouldn't."

"My mommy is in the backpack," Hope chimed in with a loud slurp of the milkshake. She spoke in an innocent way, but it had a stunning effect on Officer Britt.

"Hope, why don't you go look at that rack of magazines and comic books on the other side of the store and see if there is one you would like me to read to you. Stay where I can see you." Clark picked her up, swung her around, and watched her run off. "I don't like to talk about these things in front of her.

Her mother's ashes are in an urn in my backpack. We are headed to Dallas to give them to my mother-in-law. Hope's grandmother."

"Dallas, huh?"

"Actually more like a suburb ... a really a small town north of Dallas. Nettie, Texas."

Britt just nodded.

"If I searched the backpack and the guitar case, would I find any marijuana?"

"You would not."

"I think I will have to take a look for myself."

Clark nodded. He handed the backpack across the table to Britt. He knew Britt would search, but he also knew he had to tell him about the urn before he discovered it himself. Britt, for his part, had to ask about any drugs before he searched because if he did find anything, the fact that Clark had lied would elevate the crime above simple possession to resistance. He finished the search and passed the backpack back to Clark.

"What are you doing in our little community? You know it is illegal to hitchhike."

"Yes, I do know that, and to loiter also. I am doing neither. My car broke down and I left it at the garage – the Texaco station down the road. I came in here to see if I could catch a bus, but the next one is tomorrow afternoon. I just called my mother-in-law and made some arrangements. Someone from her church is coming to pick us up, and should be here in about two or two and half hours. So, I'm just going to

10

get something to eat and chew really slowly while I wait for my ride. I'll try to keep my daughter entertained in the meantime."

"Sounds like loitering to me. I could run you down to the jail right now."

Clark knew that arguing with Britt would be the wrong tactic. The longer and louder he protested, the more resistance he would arouse in Britt. "Officer Britt, I think you could do that. Legally I think you would have every right to do so, but I sure hope you decide not to. I'm thinking mainly for Hope. She has had a rough life and I would rather not add a night with strangers while her father is in a jail for vagrancy to her resume. I can guarantee you that we are not going to cause any problems."

"Well, Mr. Clark Bradley, at the office they are currently checking your name for any arrest warrants. If everything checks out ... but if there is a problem, I'll be back to talk to you."

"I understand," Clark said and nodded his head up and down. As Britt left, he stopped at the register, talked to the waitress, and looked in Clark's direction.

For the first time, Clark was nervous, maybe even a little frightened. He did have an arrest record. Would Britt's check reveal his three arrests? Each had been in a different state, none had been for a felony, but perhaps worse in this environment, he had been arrested for participating in civil rights marches. How would the people in the truck stop have responded to him had they known of his history? How would Officer Britt have responded? Clark really did not want to know;

11

he just wanted to slink out the door quietly and leave – to disappear. Sometimes, invisibility seemed very attractive.

"Daddy I don't want any of those books. They're all about people getting ready to take a bath."

"What? Baths? Oh, I'm sorry honey, I sent you to the wrong type of magazines. I don't think they have any children's books. But, I tell you what. Let's color in your book and then we'll get something to eat. Want to?"

She nodded her head up and down furiously. Coloring was one of the things she loved to do the most. Clark pulled from the backpack a coloring book and some crayons and, together, they selected a picture. Most girls her age would have been coloring in a Barbie coloring book or some Disney fairy tale book, but Hope liked to color dinosaurs. She and Daddy would take turns coloring. Sometimes, she tried to stay within the lines, but she also liked to add objects to the picture, and make up stories to explain her new pictures. Clark would do the same and soon each picture was a jumping off place for a journey of pure imagination and fantasy. Today, however, Hope was tired and the coloring was simply coloring, but it enabled her to talk to Clark and ask questions. Today, she picked a picture of a Tyrannosaurus Rex standing over a fallen Stegosaurus.

"What is Granny Wheels like?"

"She's very nice. You will like her. I know she loves you very much."

"But, what is she like?"

He could tell that she was asking more than he had told her, more than he was prepared to tell her, and more than he could tell her. "I've only met her once. She came out to stay with us when you were first born. Mom wanted some help when she came home from the hospital with you. She was very sweet to me and to your mother. She couldn't hold you enough. She would just beam and smile whenever she held you. I think seeing you made her the happiest I've ever seen anyone."

"Why didn't she ever come back to see us?"

Clark wasn't sure how he could explain everything to Hope and, yet, he never wanted to be the sort of father that kept things from her. "I think it was really hard for her to travel and get around in San Francisco."

"Because she lives all the time in that high chair?"

"A wheelchair. And, yes, that made it difficult for her to come out to visit you. But, she always kept inviting us to come visit her."

"And here we are." Hope didn't look up from her coloring.

"And here we are," he echoed. He didn't think he needed to add that he didn't want to come to San Francisco because it hurt too much after Grace died. Before Hope, Clark was not appreciated by anyone in Texas who knew Grace. As far as they were concerned, their beautiful, bright Grace went to the West Coast to college and Clark corrupted her and converted her into a degenerate hippie, probably a drug-soaked one at that. They would never believe that the truth was really more the opposite. Grace was more politically active than he was, at least as far as the anti-war effort went. As far as drugs, neither he nor Grace were very active in the drug culture. Grace had clarified all of this to Mrs. Wheeler when she visited at

13

Hope's birth. Still, the community of Nettie blamed him for her death, which only exacerbated his own sense of guilt. Hope had no idea how much courage it took for Clark to make this journey to Nettie. Mrs. Wheeler – only Hope called her Granny Wheels – recognized how hard the journey was, but neither she nor Clark were clear why he was coming to Nettie – what he hoped to accomplish. It was more than three years since Grace's death and, for two of those years, Mrs. Wheeler had been trying to get him to visit – pleading, begging, and nagging. The simple truth was he couldn't stay in San Francisco any longer – too many memories and too much pain. There was nowhere else to go. He was going back to Grace's home, a place he had never been before. But, it wasn't so much a visit that he was on but rather a pilgrimage.

"You hungry? 'Cause I'm feeling some hungries. What do you think, kiddo?"

"Yeah, I got some hungries, too."

"What do you want?"

"Cake and some pie."

He looked at her and cocked his head. She smiled and said, "Real food huh?"

"Hope, it is too early for sweets and you know that. I let you get by with the milkshake, but you need to eat something good for you."

"Cheese sandwich?"

"And a vegetable."

"Green beans. OK?"

He walked up to the counter and gave the waitress the order. He got a hamburger. They ate. He bussed the table for the waitress and left a nice tip. He walked Hope to the bathroom and waited for her. Then, they walked back to the booth and waited for their ride.

They sat quietly, staring out the window. Slowly, she started swinging her foot and kicking the table. "I'm bored, Daddy."

He knew how to end the boredom. "Once upon a time …"

She turned toward him with a face full of pure delight. There was nothing in the world she enjoyed more than "pretend stories" that they would make up together.

"Once upon a time …" he started again, waiting for her to do her part.

She picked up her cue perfectly, "Are you sure it didn't happen twice?"

"No, this story only happened once … upon a time …" It was a little game they would play. He would tell a familiar fairy tale, but with all sort of twists and bizarre details added. She would ask any distracting question she could think of, and he would pretend to get mad and confused.

"You always say that!"

"Be that as it may, once upon a time, there was this girl named Snow White."

"Why was she named that?"

"I don't know. Oh, yeah, because her skin was as fair and pure and clean as newly fallen snow. So there."

"What is snow?"

"Snow? You don't know what snow is? Well, I guess you wouldn't having lived in San Francisco all your life." He looked around the room. "Snow is like frozen rain – sort of."

"Huh? Her skin was like frozen rain? She sounds ugly and … wet."

"No, snow is like powder and it covers everything and makes stuff all pretty and white and pure and clean and …"

"Now you're lying to me."

"No, haven't you seen pictures at Christmas of the streets covered with white snow? So, she was called Snow White because she looked like that – all pretty and pure and clean."

"Why would anybody want to look like *that*? She must have looked like a ghost."

"No. Everyone thought she was really pretty. The wicked queen, who was really an ugly witch, was really jealous of her. In fact, the wicked queen had a magic mirror and she would ask it every night who was the fairest of all in the land. When the mirror started saying Snow White, the queen decided she had to put an end to Snow White."

Hope was quiet. She pondered the details of the story and thought about them. "How could the wicked queen think she was fair if she was wicked? And how did the mirror know that Snow White was fair? Did the mirror see her play checkers or something?"

"In once upon a time land, fair means pretty. The fairest in the land means the prettiest in the country."

"That's really stupid. Fair means you don't cheat. And the queen was an ugly old witch. She couldn't be pretty."

"She was the most beautiful in the land until Snow White came along."

"Was this a country of ugly people – the land of the ugly. That would make this a better story." With this, Hope threw herself onto the table, laughing.

Clark was laughing, too, but he continued to try to tell the story, "I think the queen had all the pretty women killed so that she didn't have any rivals. So, she had Snow White taken out into the woods where ..."

"Hansel and Gretel ate her?"

"Well," Clark said in mock protest, "that is the silliest thing I've ever heard."

"The Big, Bad Wolf was going to eat her, but Red Riding Hood saved her?"

"Who is telling this story? Do you want to hear it or not?"

"Daddy! Don't stop! What happened next?"

By now, Hope was standing on the booth, bouncing up and down. The rest of the customers in the restaurant were watching them and smiling. Some were laughing out loud. Everyone was captivated by the moment.

"Well, as I 'member it, she was saved by seven dwarfs."

With this Hope stopped, stunned. "What's a dwarf?"

"You know short people. Real short people," he made a gesture with his hands indicating a few feet in height.

"Smidgeons?"

"You mean midgets, and yeah, kinda like that."

She hesitated for a just a second before she collapsed onto the booth laughing hysterically. "Snow White and the seven smidgeons," she gasped between guffaws.

"Well, they were miners."

"Miners?"

"Yeah they would go off every morning whistling while they dug up diamonds and gold. Now, here is the interesting part. One day, the wicked queen showed up dressed like an old ugly witch."

"I thought she was an ugly witch."

"Well, she already had the wardrobe, you know. The clothes made it an easy change. She tried to get Snow White to eat a poison apple, but instead the wicked queen fell down and got a thorn stuck in her hand. It really hurt, but Snow White felt sorry for her, so she took the thorn from her hand. The queen felt so grateful she stopped hating Snow White and invited her to live in the castle with her."

"And they lived happily ever after."

"Not exactly. You see the queen really was wicked, and while Snow White was at the castle, she found a secret room and inside was … "

"Hansel and Gretel?"

Clark shook his head back and forth.

"Goldilocks?"

"No."

"Rumble-tiltskin?"

"Are you finished? You ready to hear what Snow White found?"

She sat down and nodded.

"Snow White found Prince Charming – asleep. He was under a deep spell. The wicked queen was his mother, and she wanted to protect him from all beautiful girls, so she put him under the spell. Well Snow White took one look at him and took pity on him. She bent over him and…"

When Hope didn't say anything, he realized that it was time to end the story. "She kissed him. The kiss broke the spell! Prince Charming woke and the wicked queen no longer felt a need to be wicked, and she became a kind queen. Prince Charming married Snow White and …" He raised his arms like a conductor of a band.

Hope and everyone around them all joined in together as he dropped his arms together in a giant crescendo, "They all lived happily ever after." Everyone laughed and Hope collapsed in his arms.

"Daddy, you are so silly."

"Some try. I succeed."

He gave her a hug, and they sat quietly, looking out the window waiting for their ride. A half hour later, their reverie was broken by a voice behind them, "Excuse me. Are you Clark Bradley? I'm your ride – Ralph Plymale."

Ralph was 6-foot-2-inches tall with hair that would not be called long nor short, but would be classified as well groomed. On the left, a clear straight part separated his hair into two distinct, well-maintained, and combed layers. He had on a short-sleeve shirt with wide stripes. It was well-pressed and starched so that the button-down collar and front of the shirt were not betrayed by any wrinkles. His pants were khakis, but just as pressed and wrinkle free. A wide white belt matched his loafers. Ralph looked like he was in his early 30s. *Obviously, a member of the right fraternity,* Clark thought. Clark shook his hand and said hello. "I really appreciate this ..." But Ralph's next gesture caught Clark completely off guard.

Ralph bent down so as to be at eye level with Hope, "This must be the famous Hope. I have heard so much about you! Your grandmother talks about you all the time. She can hardly wait to see you. I have a daughter, Meredith, just about your age, and she is really looking forward to meeting you and playing with you. Are you ready to ride in my car and go see your Grandma?"

Hope nodded yes, so Ralph continued, "Would you like to ride in the front between your Dad and me, or would you prefer to ride in the back and have the seat all to yourself?"

"Can I ride in the front, Daddy?"

Clark just nodded. He was impressed that Ralph had taken the time and effort to make Hope feel so comfortable and special that he had focused so completely on her. A tension left him and for the first time all day, he felt that he could relax.

They walked out to the car. Clark put the guitar and backpack into the truck, and Hope got into the front seat while Clark took his place in the passenger seat. The car was an Oldsmobile Cutlass, but the front seat did not have bucket seats; there was not much room, but enough for a little girl to sit between the driver and passenger. She leaned against Clark and was asleep by the time they left the parking lot. By the time they reached the main highway, Clark transferred her into the back seat where she could sleep lying on her stomach.

"I want to thank you again. I really appreciate you driving all this way tonight. You need any gas? I insist that I'll get you a tank before you drop us off."

"Don't worry about it. I've known Mrs. Wheeler a very long time, and there is not much I wouldn't do if she asked me. Besides. I was eager to meet Hope. You have quite a daughter there."

"Yeah, I know." Clark knew who Ralph was. He was Grace's ex-boyfriend and her first lover. The night of her junior prom, while he was a sophomore in college, she decided to lose her virginity in the back of his pickup truck. She provided the air mattress. He wasn't sure if Ralph knew much about him, or if

21

Ralph realized that he knew anything about Ralph's relationship with Grace.

"At that truck stop – they didn't seem to be too hospitable to me, if you know what I mean." Clark did not want to risk talking about Grace. "I guess they don't see many people like me, or they just don't like my type. I'll have to admit, I was a little scared. I wasn't sure what I was going to do if things got out of hand – you know, to protect Hope. Then, on the other hand, Hope's presence might have been the only thing that saved me."

"They probably wouldn't have done anything one way or the other, but it was probably a bad day for you to be there looking all hippie-like."

"How's that?"

"You know, because of what happened today. Lot of people around here took it real personal."

"What happened? I've been kinda out of the loop for a few days – haven't read a paper or seen a newscast or even listened to the radio."

"Nixon resigned. He left office today. Gerald Ford is president. Lord help us. Lot of people around here blame the hippies. People around here feel that Nixon was their president. Some of their anger was probably directed in your direction. I can't believe you didn't know."

"I don't follow politics much these days."

"I figured you would have been celebrating."

"There was a time that I would have, but I haven't been political in quite a while – a few years."

Ralph nodded. He drove in silence with the darkness of the highway occasionally punctuated by an oncoming car light. Finally, Clark broke the silence. "You know, I recognize your name. You were Grace's boyfriend in high school."

"Well, you have an advantage on me because I don't know much about you. How did you meet Grace?"

"We met at college – Stanford – during her fall semester of her sophomore year. I was in graduate school. I had been a math major as an undergraduate, but in graduate school, I was leaning more toward statistics and probability, maybe even psychology. I spent most of my time in textbooks and laboratories. At some point, I managed to look up and notice that I wasn't at all comfortable with our government's policy in Vietnam. It is true that Grace and I met at a protest march, but contrary to what some people in Nettie might think, she was much more politically active than I was. She was well read in economics, anthropology, and psychology. I was pretty much into numbers, but she made me feel like a schoolboy about people. She taught me and she radicalized me. I was attracted to her passion, I was drawn to her energy, I was mesmerized by her creativity, and I fell in love with the compassion she demonstrated for every person she contacted. Her energy was contagious, her mind so quick, so open. I've never seen anyone so full of life.

"Did the fact that you used to be Grace's boyfriend have anything to do with why you were the one who picked us up?"

"No. I don't think so. Maybe. Not really. I've been really close to Mrs. Wheeler. I do favors for her. I think I was the first person she asked. There would have been others had I said no. But, like I said earlier, I really would do anything for her. She helped me through some rough times in my life, not the least of which was when Grace broke up with me, and went away to college. But, that was not the last or the only time she has helped me. When my mother died, Mrs. Wheeler … healed me. That's what she does; she heals people. As far as I'm concerned, she is an angel. I do not know what I would have done without her. Besides, I was over Grace a long time ago."

"Somehow, I doubt that. No one gets over Grace."

"There's a lot of truth in that, but don't tell my wife," Ralph chuckled, but realized nothing that was said was funny to Clark. "I am really sorry. Grace was an incredible person, even in high school, and I can only begin to fathom your loss. Hope looks so much like her mother. When I saw her at that truck stop … it took my breath away. Her eyes and her smile – the similarity must be a great comfort."

"Sometimes it is, and sometimes it is unbearable." The following silence was much longer and when Ralph looked in Clark's direction, all he could see was Clark's reflection on the window. They rode in silence.

"How much longer? I saw a sign for the Red River in 20 miles; I guess we must be close." Clark finally asked.

"It's another hour or so." Nettie is really nowhere near the Red River. Probably 45, 50 miles past it."

"I just thought you must be close … you know Red River High School, Red River Lane."

24

"Lot of people think that, but … "

Clark sat in silence and twisted his head before he finally spoke up. "Why, then, is everything named after the Red River if you are nowhere near it?"

Ralph sighed. "There is an old joke about a little boy with a fishing rod. He sits down on the curb in the middle of the city and starts casting his fishing rod into the street. A man comes by and watches him. The boy makes three, four casts. Finally, the man says, 'Little boy, you caught many?" And the boy says, 'Yeah, you're the fourth.'" Ralph laughed.

"That's funny." Clark said and then he sat in silence. "It is a little short of hysterical, and I don't understand how it relates to the relationship between Nettie and the Red River."

"Well there is a creek – more like a ditch – that runs through the middle of Nettie and one of the founding fathers of Nettie use to call it the Red River. No one is sure if he was just wrong or if he was trying to con people. But, the name, as a sort of legacy, has lingered. I mean, the ditch isn't there anymore; there is a drainage ditch, but not much else."

"That is weird." Clark just shook his head. "That is really weird."

"Well, that is my hometown. We'll be there in maybe a half hour. I guess it's going to be Hope's bedtime and Mrs. Wheeler'll have to wait until tomorrow to play with her and spoil her. You have no idea how excited she has been since she heard you were coming. How long are you going to stay?"

"I don't know. I really don't have any plans. To tell you the truth, I'm not even sure why I'm coming here. Life just

25

wasn't working in San Francisco any more. It just didn't seem like the right environment to raise Hope. My heart wasn't in graduate school anymore. I had been teaching at a free school a couple of years ago, but free schools don't make any money … you know, by their nature. I found a hard time getting any job. It just seemed like the right time. Somehow, I thought it was important for Hope to see her mother's hometown and really meet her grandmother. I was hoping it would give me some sort of … closure. I don't even know what that means. I just felt it was something I had to do. You know what I mean?"

Ralph nodded his head, but said, "No, not really. It is really hard for anyone to relate to your situation. People just don't become widowers in their 20s. Single parents are usually female." There was a long pause, "But, you have to do what you have to do."

"Thanks." Clark liked Ralph because he was just being honest. Clark responded in kind, "You know, you're not really comforting me."

Ralph nodded, "If there is one thing I know is that grief is an individual thing. My mother developed cancer during my junior year of college, but it didn't get really bad until my senior year. I would come home every month the fall semester and then every weekend during the spring semester. I wanted to drop out and stay home, but my mother would not let me. Every Sunday, I would leave to go back to college, I would be crying by her bedside, and she would be pushing me out the door to return to campus – literally, at first, and then more figuratively. Finally, I would go dutifully and cry all the way back. And, every time I would return, she was weaker than when I left. She finally died two weeks before my last final exams. I am an only child – no father – so I made all the funeral arrangements. The extended family and the church were very critical of my decisions – a very quick funeral. I didn't miss any classes during this time. I drove back to campus and went through the motions, one step in front of the other, although I never felt like I was even alive at all – I was in some weird nether zone. The ultimate irony, I made all A's on my finals – the best I had ever done. I graduated, although I did not attend the ceremony. I went home, collapsed on my sofa, and did not move for two days. The only person who understood, supported me, and accepted me was Mrs. Wheeler. She came by with food. The first three days, she literally fed me. She continued to bring me food for two weeks, and never said anything. Then, she came in one day and said, "Ralph, it is time to get up and start living again." I got up and started living. I needed those two weeks. I mean, I felt like my life had ended; they might as well have buried me. You know what I mean?"

"Yeah," Clark's voice was almost a whisper, and Ralph sensed the sincerity.

"I don't know what I would have done without Mrs. Wheeler. I mean, she saved my life. She provided the energy that kept me going until I could function on my own. The next fall, I met Gloria and we started dating and finally married a year and half later. Now, we have Meredith, who is the same age as Hope, and I feel like none of that would have happened if Mrs. Wheeler hadn't come by and fed me. Like I said, she healed me. She does that. I'm not the only one."

"When did you stop grieving?"

"I don't know that I have. I just started living again. I still hurt."

27

Clark liked Ralph and he appreciated Ralph's openness and honesty, but Clark was not as free with his feelings as Ralph. There was a long silence before Clark responded. "I just wish I could take a deep breath. It's like … I'm always holding my breath."

Ralph swallowed. "Someday. You will. It will get better. Someday."

"That's what they say."

Clark shook his head back and forth and rolled his head. "We need to change the subject, lighten up or this last half hour is going to be the longest ride of either of our collective lives."

"Well, when you are right, you are right."

"Whatever happened to Mr. Wheeler? Grace was always vague about him"

"Well, I don't know everything, but as I hear it, her husband, Jimmy Wheeler, inherited a ranch with a lot of land and a few head of cattle. They say that, during the war, he was quite the dashing soldier, a decorated officer. That's when they met and wed. Things went downhill for him after the war. He lost the cattle in an anthrax epidemic. He never got back on his feet financially. I guess the final straw was the accident when Mrs. Wheeler broke her spine – some sort of riding accident involving a motorcycle as well as their horses. He never forgave himself, and he started drinking. He finally drank himself to death.

"You know, a lot of people around here blamed you for Grace becoming a hippie and all that, but Mrs. Wheeler straightened them out – at least most of them. I mean, I knew the truth. Nobody ever made Grace do anything she didn't want to do. That girl was immune to peer pressure."

"You're right about that." Clark wanted to change the subject. "Tell me about Nettie."

"Not much to tell." Ralph rubbed his chin. "Nettie is a small town, about 1,200 people. But, all of them work somewhere else. I suspect Dallas will keep moving north and someday Nettie will become a suburb. We have a good school district, and the school board is progressive and forward-looking. We have plans to build new high schools whenever the population dictates so that none of the schools become too large."

"What do you do for a living?"

"Funny you should ask. I'm the principal at the senior high school in Nettie – Red River High. It's kinda funny about the name, like I said. One of the founding fathers made a mistake or a bad joke; either way, the name stuck. I kinda lucked into the position. A couple of years ago, I was promoted to part-time assistant principal, but still a classroom teacher. Last year, I was promoted to full-time assistant principal when the principal had a stroke. I was appointed as interim principal, but they liked the job I was doing. So, at the end of the year, they made the position permanent. I'm the youngest principal for a 2A school in the state."

"Congratulations."

"I think it has more to do with the fact that they would have to pay anyone else more than they pay me, but it is a good position with a good salary. You mentioned that you've taught and you were a math major in college. It just so happens, I am in desperate need of a calculus teacher; might even need an algebra teacher."

"I don't think so. All my teaching was at a free school with inner-city street kids, elementary age. I don't have any real teaching credentials."

"I can get you an emergency certificate – no problem. You would be doing me a tremendous favor. If you don't like it or if you are no good, you'll give me some time to find someone else instead of starting the year with an empty room."

"No. Thanks, but I don't think that ... it's just not me."

"Well, think about it."

"No." Clark didn't want to be rude, but Ralph left him no other choice but to be emphatic.

"OK. Sorry."

They sat in silence as Ralph turned off the highway made three more turns and pulled down a dirt path that had a wooden sign that read Red River Lane. The house was at the end of the path but, really, it was in the middle of nowhere – a field.

"Here we are," Ralph said.

The street, if you could call it that, was dark, with no streetlights, so it was hard to see the house clearly. A lengthy front yard with at least one tree, a car parked in a car port next to a walkway leading to a ramp up to the front porch, was all one could see of the outside of the house. The light from the inside radiating out was the most obvious feature. All the surrounding dark was pierced by the warmth of the light emitting from the front rooms. Mrs. Wheeler opened the door before Ralph's car had fully stopped, and she was rolling down the ramp toward them. While Ralph got the guitar and backpack from the truck, Clark lifted Hope gently from the back seat. She stirred and started to cry, but Clark soothed her, "It's all right, kiddo. We're here. You just go back to sleep. I'll put you into a bed. Go ahead and sleep." His voice was low and sort of singsong-like. Hope barely opened her eyes before closing them again.

Mrs. Wheeler wheeled herself up the ramp and noiselessly rolled across the floor to a room to the right of the living room. She opened the door and pointed to the bed. Clark took Hope into the room, laid her on her back, took off her sandals, socks, and shorts, and tucked her under the sheet. She rolled onto her stomach and was fast asleep. He left a crack in the door as he walked into the kitchen, which was on the left side of the living room. He sat down across the table from Mrs. Wheeler.

"Ralph leave already? I wanted to thank him and give him some gas money."

"He wouldn't have taken it."

They looked at each other. She was heavier than Clark remembered. Her hair was darker and short cropped, almost a page boy cut. There were a few hints of grey and Clark noticed the glasses she wore around her neck. Mrs. Wheeler put her hand to her mouth. She took two deep breaths. "It is so good to see you!" Her voice cracked, but she managed to hold back her emotions. "I have waited a long time to get you and Hope here."

He nodded but had no idea what to say. "Thank you. Hope is looking forward to getting to know you."

"And you?"

"You have always been very kind to me, and I really appreciate your hospitality." There seemed to be other words that needed to be said, but he wasn't sure what they were.

"You look exhausted. Let me show you your room. We can talk tomorrow. You need a good night's sleep."

"Thanks, you're right. I am very tired."

She showed him the room between the living room and the carport. A dresser, a desk, a small closet, and a single twin bed made up the complete inventory of the room. There was a door to the carport. One picture of Grace – her high school graduation picture – was on the dresser and the only decoration in the room. He slipped off his sandals, jeans, and shirt. He wondered if Hope was in Grace's old room. That seemed logical, but knowing Grace, she would prefer this room with her own door to the outside. He was probably sleeping in her bed. He wasn't sure how that realization made him feel – close to her or more empty. It made him question once again why he was here. What did he hope to accomplish? He thought to himself, *I used to be the kind of person who always made plans. But, now, it seems like I've forgotten how to make plans. Or, I can't seem to make myself care about plans. I can't seem to … I just don't know what I'm doing one day to the next. I came here to get healed for Hope's sake, or get her into a good environment until I do.*

Mornings had become the best part of the day for Clark because, when he first woke up, there was a moment when he thought that the last few years have been a nightmare and Grace was really alive. He relished those few moments and tried to make them last before reality would slip in and he would have to get up. The night was the worst part of the day, especially lying in bed waiting to fall asleep because his last thought at night was relentless: Grace is still dead.

"Love is too strong a word"

May 27, 2006

Red River High School, Nettie, Texas

About 50 miles from the Red River

Clark Bradley finished the last mark on the grade validation sheets, dropped his pen, lowered his elbows on his desk in front of him, and cradled his head with his hands. In the past, he would have reflectively flicked his hair, but it had been several years since his forehead had been invaded by anything resembling hair. Loss of hair was one of the few benefits of old age, he liked to think, or at least that is how he comforted himself – proof that he could rationalize practically anything. He leaned back in the chair, straightened the stack of papers collectively known as grade validation sheets, grabbed a lone sheet of paper on the side of the desk, and swiveled the chair around to inspect the room visually – one last time. Everything seemed in order. The desks were all aligned. No trash visible. All books shelved. Boards cleaned. He stood with his papers and headed to the office. After giving the validation sheets to the secretary, he asked if he could see the principal, Charles Miller.

The secretary said, "Yeah, he was busy earlier, but I think he's free right now. Better jump in before he gets a phone call."

Clark stepped into the office. Mr. Miller was sitting behind his large mahogany desk with his back toward the doorway as Clark entered. "You got a minute?" he asked as he sat down in the chair in front of the desk deciding the answer for Miller.

Miller swirled around in his chair to see who was asking. "Just about one minute. What can I do for you?"

He was as pleasant as always and an outsider would never have noticed the subtle tension between the two of them. Clark had little respect for Miller as an educator or administrator. They could barely tolerate each other, but both were as professional as possible and were always polite in their exchanges. Clark certainly missed the mutual admiration and respect he shared with Ralph Plymale, but it had been five years since Ralph retired. Red River High School had a reputation as an excellent academic school, and a large part of that reputation was built on Clark's achievements in mathematics, and Clark always recognized that his success had been directly related to Plymale's influence. Plymale always let Clark teach. Miller, he felt, over-administrated.

Miller, for his part, did not trust Clark. Miller tended to see popular teachers as the enemy – not to be trusted, too willing to sacrifice "academic rigor" for popularity. Still, even Miller had to admit that Clark was very different. Clark did not try to be popular; he did not court students. He was just naturally on their side most of the time. Basically, he was just simply anti-authority. Clark trusted students more than he trusted principals. Clark could often be a thorn in Miller's side. Most teachers are rather docile, and follow the policies of the principal. If Clark was ever passive and cooperative, he outgrew the trait long ago. He would question every policy before he would agree to follow it. However, Miller could not argue with Clark's results. The man could teach. He was selected the District Teacher of the Year 15 years ago and could earn it every year if that were possible.

Clark stood before Miller and handed him a piece of paper. He said, "I am retiring."

Miller looked at him not knowing what to say. Words seldom failed to come to him, but he wasn't prepared for this, and he did not know what to say. "I … I … really … is there anything I can say to get you to change your mind?"

"No. It is time for me to retire."

"I hope I haven't done anything … Red River High will not be the same without you. I'm not sure that you are replaceable."

"Everyone is replaceable."

"I'm not sure."

"I guess you'll find out."

"I'm serious Clark. I know you've always had a kind of love/hate relationship with administrations here at school."

"Love is too strong a word."

He let what he said hang in the air for a few seconds before continuing, "It has nothing to do with you or the school. It is just the time for me to retire. It is a personal decision."

"Clark, I think you will really regret this decision." Miller said. "You don't have this kind of obligation to her. You shouldn't make this kind of a sacrifice for her. She is only your mother-in-law."

Clark stared at Miller then he stood, turned, and walked to the door.

Miller talked to Clark's back as he stood in the doorway, "What are you going to do? Are you just going to nurse Mrs. Wheeler the rest of your life?"

Clark stood still for several pregnant seconds, "I think I'll learn to play the guitar."

And it was all over – 32 years of teaching, a profession, a career, and a way of life – over. "Well," he thought. "I did come to Nettie for closure."

Compassion and a Bowl of Clam Chowder

October 17, 1968

San Francisco, California

1760 miles from the Red River approximately

Sometimes, it rains. Even in San Francisco, sometimes it rains. Generally, Clark had found the weather in San Francisco to be the least unpleasant aspect of the community. Usually the weather was pleasant, and if the nights were cool during even the warmest summer days, they were still tolerable. It did not rain often, but it was not unheard-of. Seldom was there a torrential rainstorm like there was this morning – very heavy rain that was not going to let up for the entire day. A good day to sleep in, a bad day to be out and about and, yet, he found himself out – in a coffee house/sandwich bar. He noticed that the usually crowded streets were nearly empty. All of the customers were wet to varying degrees, and even he had a drenched raincoat that he hung on the wall as he got a cup of coffee and proceeded to sit down facing the back of the room. He scanned the small crowd – no one he recognized, and he was about to disappear into the newspaper when he saw her across the room.

She looked horrible. Everyone else looked like they had come in from the rain; she looked like she had been swimming fully dressed in the ocean. Her long hair was flattened against her head and shoulders. Her coat – a beige trench coat – was no longer protecting her from the wet and cold, as it was as wet and cold as the weather itself. Her jeans and tennis shoes were wet enough to be discolored. He recognized her from several anti-war protest meetings he had attended. He did not know her name but had been impressed when she spoke at the meetings – intelligent, articulate, and self-assured. He was attracted to her independence and intellect. Additionally, she was physically attractive. Her eyes were bright, her smile, and every gesture seemed so open and somehow sensuous. Her most noticeable characteristic was her hair – long, beautiful brunette hair that glimmered in the light. Except for today. He had to admit, she did not look attractive today; more like a drowned cat.

He was caught off guard when she walked briskly across the room toward him as if he was her destination. There was no hesitation as she approached him. She knew exactly what she was doing and what she wanted. Indeed, she radiated self-confidence.

"You really want to buy me a cup of coffee," she said as she sat down opposite him.

"No," he responded. "I think I want to buy you a bowl of … " He cocked his head sideways and looked her over and then looked at the menu over the snack bar. "… clam chowder. You need a bowl of clam chowder, with crackers – oyster crackers."

"And a cup of coffee," she added.

"And a cup of coffee. Of course."

He turned and got the chowder and the coffee. She started to take off her coat, but a glance in the mirrored wall made her realize that her blouse was soaked and revealed more than she felt comfortable exposing. He returned with the order. She turned her sole attention to them for several minutes before she responded to him. "I should introduce myself. My name is Grace."

"I am …"

"I know who you are: Clark Bradley. You are a legend around here. I mean in the anti-war movement. You marched with King – you were arrested. When you walked into our meeting, half the group almost peed in their pants. We all worship you. We've marched and protested around here, you know on campus, but you, you have been out there."

"I haven't done much. I've been impressed by your speeches and your work. I've wanted to talk to you."

"You should have. Why didn't you?"

"I never really had the opportunity," Clark was beginning to feel uncomfortable in some strange way.

"Last month, in that rally at the Hall," she spoke between slurps of soup and sips of coffee, "when everyone was planning the protest for the coming months, and some of the speakers were planning to harass the returning vets, I was really impressed by what you said. I mean, you didn't say much, but what you said was powerful. It was perhaps the most … "

"We shouldn't be against the soldiers even if we are against the war. We can't forget that if we are against the war it is because we are *for* people, and soldiers are people. We just can't forget that. Right or wrong, they did what they did because they thought they were fighting for us … you shouldn't insult them for that." He spoke with little conviction in his voice as if he had no confidence anyone would believe him.

"You don't speak a lot, but you say a lot." She took a large mouthful of cracker. "You know what I mean."

He nodded. "Actually, I have no idea what you mean."

She began to shiver as she spoke. "Well, it's like …"

"Grace, I don't know if you noticed or not, but you are shivering, and I think this conversation can wait. I don't know what your plans are, but my apartment is right around the corner, and I have some dry, warm clothes you could put on. We could talk and you wouldn't have to shiver."

She stared at him.

He thought about saying more, but didn't. If she needed more reassurance, he probably could not provide enough.

"OK," she finally nodded. "But you don't know how much I need what you are offering."

"It's up to you."

She nodded and stood up. They left together.

A trip that usually would take five minutes in the kind of torrential rain they were experiencing was somewhat shorter as they did not try to avoid puddles; getting wetter was impossible. They reached Clark's doorway and climbed the indoor stairway to his apartment.

When they entered the apartment, Grace looked around at his apartment which was quite large and nicely furnished. There was a bedroom to the side, a large living room with a sofa and a love seat, and a kitchen with a table and four chairs. The stove and refrigerator were quite modern and the shelves very neat and presentable. There was even a laundry room off behind the stove and opening onto a porch in the back. Two large bookcases – full – were on either side of the living room

41

and a large expensive stereo player with a tape deck occupied the wall facing the bedroom and living room.

Clark disappeared into what appeared to be a small pantry to the side of the kitchen but, in reality, was the laundry room. "This is not the apartment of a typical graduate student," she said.

He handed her a pair of sweatpants, a sweater, some socks, and a towel. "I guess I am not a typical graduate student," he said. "You can change in the bathroom while I change in the bedroom."

He resurfaced first, moved to the kitchen sink, and poured some water to start some coffee. She emerged from the bathroom with the towel wrapped around her head. "I feel so much better," she sighed.

"Not to mention drier."

"I can't believe how … nice your apartment is. And the view of the street – stunning."

"And I can't believe you used the word stunning in a sentence."

She smiled. "Would you like for me to finish making that coffee for us?"

"Probably not."

"What?"

"It is all but done. It just has to percolate for a minute or two. Why don't you sit on the sofa while I pour the coffee and serve it? You don't need sugar or cream, right?"

The coffee finished. He poured two cups and turned to deliver hers, but she was asleep on the sofa. He found a pillow, gently placed it under her head, and covered her with a blanket, making sure her feet were covered. He stared at her for several seconds watching her sleep before he turned away.

He looked at his watch. He had two classes, but he figured he could miss them both. He took his textbooks from his bookcase, opened a notebook, and prepared to spend the rest of the day reading and taking notes. He stretched and drank the cups of coffee. Later, he went to the bathroom. He took her wet clothes, put them in the washer and later the dryer. It was not that he didn't notice the girl asleep on his sofa, but he didn't want to stare at her. He turned his back to her for most of the afternoon. He respected her privacy. He did not impose his growing attraction. He would wait for the waking Grace to continue the relationship.

For her part, Grace sort of woke up twice. The first time, she was lying on her side and opened her eyes just enough to see Clark sitting at the table with his back to her. She could tell he was reading. She rolled onto her other side and went immediately back to sleep. Later, she woke up and didn't remember where she was. She didn't really want to get up, but she felt apprehensive. When she rolled over, she saw Clark still reading, and she remembered him. Suddenly, she felt comfortable and safe. She allowed herself to relax and fall asleep, and she did.

Grace slept heavily all day. When she finally woke up it was evening. She rolled over and looked at Clark. He was still sitting at the table although a dish with remnants of a sandwich and an empty class revealed that he had eaten a lunch of some sort. He was listening to his headphones connected to his stereo. She wondered if he had been sitting there the whole time, and she wondered how long the whole time was. She noticed darkness outside the window, so she guessed that it was late in the day.

She turned on her side and stared at him. Who was this man with whom she'd just spent the whole day? His hair was kind of dirty blond, neither light nor dark. It was neither long and shaggy nor short and neat – somewhere between Bohemian intellectual and fraternity conventional. He was tall and somewhat lanky, but from this angle, his shoulders looked broad. He looked like a college student, slightly older than most, intellectual and aloof. Yet she had seen him at the anti-war protest meetings, and he was talked of by others in hushed tones. He had marched in the early civil rights marches with Dr. Martin Luther King Jr.; it was said that he had been arrested in Mississippi and Alabama. He had paid some dues. Others spoke of him with reverence and respect. He was some sort of a legend on campus, although the reasons were a little unclear to her.

"Thanks," she finally said although she had to repeat three times, progressively louder each time before he heard her through his headphones.

"You're welcome," he said as he turned toward her and took his headphones off. He held up the album cover: "Blonde on Blonde" by Bob Dylan. "I figured you might not appreciate waking up to Dylan."

She nodded. "That's true, but not what I meant. Thanks for letting me sleep here today. I guess the term 'crash' was coined for times like this. Thanks."

"You're welcome."

"I really needed to sleep."

"I thought as much."

"Well, thanks."

"No problem."

She looked awkward like she wanted to say more without saying anything else. "I was exhausted I'm dealing with a lot of … shit. I needed some rest … you know, undisturbed sleep. Don't know where I could have gotten any. Thanks doesn't really cover it."

He stared at her, pondering what to say next. "Really, it was no problem for me. I was glad to help you out."

At first, she just stared at him, not moving. Then, a singular tear appeared in her eye and started the journey down her cheek. Neither he nor she moved. Slowly, he moved closer to her until he was sitting next to her on the sofa. He opened his arms in a gesture without moving any closer – he did not want to risk invading her space. She hesitated, and then buried her head in his shoulders. At first, she stayed there motionless, and then she began to cry and sob. She clutched him and cried violently and uncontrollably. She shook and sobbed hysterically, losing her breath two or three times before she finally stopped. She pushed herself back from him, "I'm sorry." She was wiping her eyes and still trying to catch her breath. "I'm not usually like this … I don't cry."

"It's all right. This shirt has been wet before. You know, I bet you are really hungry. I mean, a cup of clam chowder will only go so far. How about some supper?"

She had composed herself enough; the tears stopped and her breathing returned to normal. "Do you want to know why I was crying?"

"Do you want to tell me?"

"No. Not really."

"You do not owe me an explanation; you don't have to tell me anything ... until and unless you want to."

"Thanks. I just don't feel like talking."

"OK."

"Why don't you let me fix you some dinner?" She offered. "It would be the least I could do after taking up your couch all day."

"I would love that, but my kitchen is not congruent with food preparation if you want something edible. You know what I mean? You catch my drift?"

"Congruent with food preparation. Who talks like that? You don't have any food – is that what you are trying to say?" she said.

He nodded. "I ate the last of the bread for lunch, a cheese sandwich." He stood up and waved his arms energetically. "However, you know what they say about housing – location, location, location. Within retching distance, there are more restaurants than one person can regurgitate from in a lifetime – Chinese, Italian, right around the corner, two doors down, some sort of ethnicity of unknown origin with a wholesome, we hope, familiarity with grease, yogurt, and olive oil. I can be back in the time it takes you to change back into your original clothes – dried and folded in yonder chair. I would point out – quicker if I get lucky."

"Italian sounds good."

"Pizza or pasta?"

"Pizza sounds wonderful."

"Wine or soda?"

"No wine for me."

"OK, pizza buffet around the corner, they have a pick six plan, you get six pieces of any type pizza on the buffet for the price of one pizza. I'll be back in five minutes." He jumped up and ran toward the door.

"Wait," she stopped him. "What do you mean quicker if you get lucky?"

He winked and disappeared out the door. It was closer to 10 minutes when he finally returned. He knocked on the door to make sure she was dressed and entered with a pizza box and a six-pack of sodas. "I got the equivalent of a large pizza with a variety of slices – pepperoni, mushrooms, sausage, and plain cheese. I'm sure there will be something you like," he displayed the pizza on the table and put some paper plates and cups on the table.

"It will be fine," she said as she made her way to the table.

"They make a pretty good pizza."

"It will be fine."

He poured some ice into the cups and tore some paper towel for the napkins. "Some pizzas are better than others, but as far as I am concerned, there is no such thing as a bad pizza."

She smiled and sat down.

"I know," he said. "It will be fine."

They ate in silence. Finally, after her third slice, she spoke, "This really is good pizza."

He nodded.

"I'm sorry I'm such a dud," she said.

"What do you mean?"

"I'm just not in the mood for … banter … you know … conversation."

He looked at her and nodded. "It's OK. Something is going on and you don't want to talk about it. You don't need to talk to me. I accept that. It really is OK." He lifted a slice of pizza. "If or when you want, we can talk, but I am perfectly content just to sit and eat pizza."

"Thanks," she smiled for the first time.

When they finished, he put the pizza crusts and paper towels in the garbage. He cleaned the table. He brought out his textbook and a notebook. "I have some work I need to do."

She stood up and looked around. "I guess I need to be going."

"No, no," he became animated. "That is not what I meant – not at all. You are welcome to stay here, to 'crash' as you said earlier. You can use my bed." He pointed to the bedroom off from the kitchen and living room. "I can sleep on the couch. The bedroom has a door, and I am going to be up late working. We both will be more comfortable. You look … you're still tired. Am I right? You'll feel better after a good night's sleep."

"Are you sure?" She hesitated, but everything he said sounded quite appealing to her. She was surprised that she hesitated, but she was even more surprised that she considered his invitation at all.

"Yes. Absolutely," he replied.

"I don't usually accept sleepovers with strangers," she heard herself saying. "But, thank you. I really appreciate this."

"No problem," he responded casually as he turned toward his books.

She walked toward the bedroom, but before she entered, she stopped and turned back toward him. "Why are you doing this? Why are you being so nice?"

He just looked at her and shrugged his shoulders. But, he could tell that his response was less than satisfactory to her. "Seriously, I have seen you around at many of the same meetings I attend, the same protests. We are kindred spirits, teammates so to speak. I just think teammates should help each other out. I would have done the same thing for anyone in the movement."

"Really?"

"Probably. Mostly. Yes."

She nodded and started to turn away.

"Grace," his words stopped her and she turned toward him. "I would have done the same thing for most of the guys in the movement. A few of them are jerks, but most of them are OK."

"Thanks," she felt relieved. "I needed to hear that. I'm not sure why."

"You can trust me."

She stood there. She didn't say anything. She raised her hand and waved good night, turned and went into the bedroom.

"Good night," he said.

The next morning, asleep on the couch, a blanket covering his head, feet exposed, Clark awoke to smell of bacon frying. He lowered the blanket and inhaled deeply. "That smells," he searched for the right word. "Decadent."

Grace was supervising the bacon while stirring a bowl of eggs, her back toward Clark. "Good morning," she said without turning around.

"I didn't think I even had any bacon," he said while stretching.

"You didn't. I got it while you were still sleeping."

"I have a theory about bacon," he spoke as he sat up on the couch. "Do you want to hear my theory?"

"Do I have a choice?"

"I can see it will be easy to be humble around you and, yes, you have a choice. I would not impose my bacon theory on you without your express permission."

She turned to face him as she put the bacon and eggs on the table. "OK. What is your theory on bacon?"

"Nothing smells better than bacon in the morning."

"That is some theory."

"No, no … that is not the interesting part. Here is the interesting discovery on my part. Are you ready?"

She nodded.

"The olfactory pleasure of bacon is in inverse proportion to the amount one participates in the production of said bacon." He pulled the blanket around him and sat down at the table victoriously.

"In other words – it smells best if someone else cooks it."

"That about sums it up. But, no kidding, thanks. I usually don't eat breakfast and …"

She looked around, "I could tell you don't, but I don't like to … I wanted to contribute. Breakfast I can do. It was my way of saying thanks for last night."

They ate in silence. When they finished, he made a proposal, "You cooked, so I will do the dishes."

She nodded her approval. While he collected the dishes and was washing them in the sink, she watched him. "You know," she said. "I have a theory, too."

"About bacon?"

"No," she shook her head. "About last night."

He turned and looked at her but then turned back to the dishes.

"Do you want to hear my theory?" she asked.

"Do I have a choice?"

She laughed. "I guess I deserve that."

He put the dishcloth down and sat at the table, "So, what is your theory?"

"I think you sensed how vulnerable I was yesterday – right from the beginning at the coffee shop – and your kind offer came from your sense of kindness, but ..."

"Wait, before you go putting your buts in there, I did not sense your vulnerability. Not at first. I sensed that you were wet. Wet is different. I mean later I sensed you were ... vulnerable, but that was later, not earlier."

"I stand corrected, but I don't like being vulnerable, and I do not want a relationship based on vulnerability."

"OK, I understand. I accept that. Whatever was going on does not define you, and I would not let it be the foundation of our relationship. I would not want it to be any more than you would."

"OK." She maintained eye contact while she spoke in a very serious tone. "Maybe I have trust issues, but I do not want to get burned."

"I told you, Grace. You can trust me. But, I do not expect you to believe me just because I said that. I figure I will have to prove it, and I hope you will give me a chance to prove it. I will not take advantage of your vulnerability. No, let me rephrase that, I will not try to take advantage of your vulnerability nor will I break your trust."

"OK," she said.

"But, Grace," he lowered his voice and tilted his head downward. "I have to tell you this. I think you need to know. This is like a warning, you know, like on the cigarette packs? Ready? I find you very attractive. I know that now is not the right time to act on those feelings, but some day, when the time is right, I will make my move."

She was silent and waited before she responded. "You have moves?"

"Oh, yeah. I have moves." He tilted his head down toward her and lowered his voice, "May I kiss your hand, madam?"

"Be still my beating heart." She stood up and moved around the room. "Can I stay here a few days while I figure things out? I'll do my share – cook meals and so forth."

"Sure. Stay as long as you need to, but don't say I didn't warn you."

"I'll take my chances. Are you sure? I don't want to impose, but I've kinda run out of options."

"Really, you will not be any imposition, especially if you do the bacon thing in the morning. We will work out some details on the chores."

"We will work out details. I refuse … I will pull my share of the load."

"OK."

A Motif

November 9, 1980, 6 a.m.

26 Red River Lane, Nettie, Texas

Clark opened the door into Hope's bedroom. She was asleep on her right side away from him. He sat on the edge of the bed and began singing in a whisper, "The water is wide, I cannot get over." He raised his voice slightly in volume, "and neither have I the wings to fly." Still louder, "But, build me a boat that can carry two, and ..."

"OK, Dad," Hope said. "I'm awake now." She stretched and turned to face him. "You know every day, you come in and wake me with that same song. Don't you think it is time I get my own alarm? I think I am old enough to get myself out of bed in the morning."

"Maybe, but then I would miss waking you, and I wouldn't get to see you in the morning. It would just be you and Granny until I got home in the evening. When you go to junior high, you'll ride the bus and I'll drive Granny and ..."

"I know. I know." She sat up in the bed. "It was really nice in kindergarten and first grade and so on, but now, I'm getting older, and I feel like you are treating me like a little girl. You know? I'm too old to have my Daddy waking me up every morning."

He nodded. "Especially with a song, huh?" He stood up. "OK. I understand how you feel. I can respect it. Things change. We'll get you a clock this weekend."

"Thanks." She watched him as he started to leave the room, and she didn't sense any hurt. "Why that song, Dad?"

"It was one your mother sang."

"Mom sang other songs, too."

"Yeah, but this song was important to us and it seems so … appropriate."

"Appropriate?"

He sang, "And both shall row, my love and I."

"I can play it on the piano."

"Really?"

"Granny says she will teach me how to play it on the guitar."

"I didn't know Granny knew how to play the guitar."

"She says she can do a little flat picking, whatever that is. She says she learned it when she lived in the White Trash Mountains of Virginnie. Sometimes, I don't know what she means when she says things."

He laughed. "Her family was from West Virginia and Kentucky. You might not always understand what she says, but I've found she almost always says something worth listening to."

"Dad – we can wait on that alarm clock."

"How about as a Christmas present?"

"Sounds good."

"Well, get dressed for school now."

"Everybody Goes to the Party, But Not Everybody Parties"

June 3, 1985

Nettie, Texas

Mickey could hardly wait for his shift to end. Normally, he enjoyed his work as a cashier at the grocery store. It was less than intellectually challenging, but he got to interact with a lot of customers and that made up for the routine. Mickey found the senior citizens really interesting and somehow admirable. He could only imagine what lives they had led. The middle-class housewives were either trying hard to curtail their own children or seemed bitterly alone. Either way, Mickey felt an affinity toward them. He liked to play with the little kids as much as he could, and most of the mothers seemed to appreciate his efforts. The smiles he gave to the more lonely women were always politely received even if they weren't particularly welcomed. There weren't many male customers, but the few who did come through his stand always seemed to recognize him from the football team and would ask him questions about the coming season or express some sort of support. Mickey was not exactly a football star except to those who really knew their football. He was a starter on the defensive line, hardly a glamour position. He was small for his position, but he was All-District, and he looked forward to an outstanding senior year. At spring football, the new coaching staff instituted a new defense with Mickey functioning as a linebacker from a down lineman position, and he anticipated "wreaking havoc" with several opponents from this new position. At any rate, in Nettie, Texas, being a starter on the high school football team was like being a celebrity even behind the checkout stand at the grocery store. If it was living in a bubble, it was a nice bubble, Mickey thought.

But, today was different. Today was the first Saturday of summer vacation and the first party of the summer. Mickey was not much of a party animal. In fact, he tended to avoid parties, but there was a good chance she would be at this party, and he hadn't seen her since graduation. They had both been junior ushers at graduation, and that was how he met Ashley, although he had certainly seen her all around school. She was a cheerleader with as much visibility as a football star. But, until graduation rehearsals, they had never talked to each other. She was the kind of beautiful that everyone admires from afar, but most guys fear because it is unapproachable. She had beautiful straight blonde hair that shimmered whenever she moved and her eyes were deep blue. The guys on the football team called her Barbie because she was shaped like a Barbie doll – large breasts and long, shapely legs. To Mickey, she was physically as close to perfection as a girl could possibly be. No one in the junior class had ever dated her. The few dates she had were all seniors and seniors from the year before, but none of them were serious relationships. Her parents would not let her have a boyfriend until her junior year and, by then, her beauty was too intimidating for her peers. Then there was also the religious thing. When Ashley wasn't at school, she was at church. Her father was a deacon at the church and she went to worship services on Wednesday and Sundays, but could be found at church other nights of the week serving on committees, choir rehearsal, or babysitting. She was very devout. All of the guys Mickey knew thought Ashley was unapproachable or unreachable. They put her on some sort of pedestal and did not know her as a real person.

At the graduation, Ashley and Mickey were to lead the seniors into the auditorium through the rows of chairs to the appropriate row and to their correct seat. Ashley and Mickey were responsible for making sure each row was the right length. One mistake could ruin the whole processional. Ashley began making up different scenarios of how they could subvert the system. She was very dry in her delivery and no one would hear her except Mickey, but he had a difficult time holding back his laughter. "What if we turn this group to the right instead of the left?" she would whisper to Mickey. She was particularly devastating in her reaction when principal Plymale gave his earnest speech on the necessity for solemnity for the march into the graduation. She had plans to have each row screwed up with students who would have no place to sit while other rows would have only two students in them. "Let's have this group walk backwards." She was going to have rows marching down into other rows, which would be marching forward. At one point, she had a plan where all the students would be standing in the middle of the room around two chairs. It was all very silly, and Mickey laughed, knowing they would not do anything of the sort, but also knowing that Ashley had stolen his heart. He saw a silly, spontaneous sense of humor that he found irresistible. Humor with incredible beauty, a combination he could not even begin to resist, and he certainly was not trying. So, he could not wait for his shift to end because they had made plans to see each other.

Ashley spent the morning at a cheerleading practice. The afternoon was spent teaching gymnastics to kindergarten age kids. She had time to stop by the church for choir practice and a quick prayer meeting for her youth group before coming home for supper. After supper, she showered and started getting ready for the party. In many ways, it was a typical busy day for her, but today was totally different. She had never gone to a school party before. Her parents were very strict and would not let her attend parties until she finished her junior year, and then only if she maintained her grades. She had all A's and had proven that she could be trusted by never having broken a rule or getting in trouble of any sort. They felt they could trust her to go to a party. They were very proud of her. She was popular enough among her classmates to be selected as a cheerleader, but she never compromised her parent's values. She was a paragon of morality. Ashley had a curiosity about parties. She wondered what everyone on the cheerleading squad found so rewarding about them, and she was eager to have the experience for herself, but if truth were known, she was really looking forward to the party for just one reason: Mickey would be there.

All of the dates she had in high school were pleasant experiences, but they were polite social events. Mickey was special. There was something in his eyes. When he looked at her, he saw her. When he listened, he heard her. No one else had ever made her feel the center of awareness. It started as the simple flattery of his laughing at her jokes, but it expanded to other topics, other moments. School had ended before their relationship had a chance to develop into anything, and that is why tonight was so important to her. It was the first chance they would have to be together and laugh and talk and … She couldn't think too much along these lines or she would blush. It was too early in the relationship to make more of it than there was to make of it. It was what it was. But, she hoped for something more, something unique. Other girls had boyfriends, why not her? Ashley was discovering that deep down below the cheerleader, below the choir singer, below the church attendance, at some primitive level, she was profoundly lonely. No one knew and she certainly never had expressed her feelings out loud, but she had a deep sense that she was missing something … something she did not know how to define or how to recognize. But, she felt strongly that Mickey could fill some void. Her feeling toward Mickey was new for her – intoxicating, exciting, oddly guilt-provoking, and very intense in a dreamy sort of way. The desire to see Mickey was irresistible, and she could hardly wait to get through her Saturday and get to the party.

Although the party wouldn't really start until everyone got there about midnight, the door opened at 8 or 8:30. Mickey showed up at 9 o'clock, not wanting to be the first one there, but hoping to be there early enough to greet Ashley when she would show up. He walked through the open front door and was surprised to see how many people were already there. *It must be because it's the first party of the summer,* he thought as he walked from the dining room into the living room to the kitchen, strolling from room to room saying hello to everyone he recognized – which seemed to be everyone enrolled at Red River High School the past three years. Buddy, the host, approached him. "Mickey, you ugly son of a bitch! What you doing here? You never party."

"Well, I couldn't miss your party, Buddy. I heard you hired a band, or was it Garth Brooks?"

"What? Garth Brooks?" Buddy looked around, agitated. "No, man … Oh, you're shittin' me. Man, don't mess with me. I'm too wasted. You want a beer? There's a keg in the back by the pool."

Mickey just glared at him.

"OK, OK. Stupid question. I think there's some water in the fridge, just for you."

"Buddy, you are starting pretty early, aren't you?"

"Look, Mickey. This is going to be my last party before I go to college, and it is going to be the best party. I don't even know what ... With any luck, I'll never remember it. I probably won't even be around for most of it. You know what I mean?"

"Yeah, I know what you mean. I just don't understand your way of thinking."

"Huh?"

Mickey left Buddy and walked into the kitchen and found water like Buddy said. He continued his stroll around the house into the backyard and the swimming pool area. That was when he saw her. She was standing with a group of three or four girls by the side of the pool with her back to him as he saw her. She turned sideways and he saw her profile. Seeing her took his breath away – literally. She had on leather sandals, blue jeans, and a white top. The sandals were composed of thongs of leather that had the effect of emphasizing the feet and making them look more pure – and just plain sensuous. The jeans were dark blue and form fitting, highlighting the contours of her athletic, muscular, and perfectly feminine body. The white top was silky and loose yet clingy, cut low enough to reveal a shoulder. As she stood sideways, the outline of her breast could be seen. Dumbly, he stood there, overcome by his own reverence. She lifted her left hand, sideways from his view, to reveal a drink, and she took a drink before she noticed him. Was that a beer? He blinked and came out of his reverie. She smiled at him and her face came alive. "Hello," she said.

Hello was all she said. Hello was all she needed to say, and his heart began to beat in some new rhythm.

"Hi."

Suddenly, they were all alone and everyone else at the party dissolved away.

"I didn't expect you to be here this early. Had I known, I'd have been out here sooner. Usually these things don't get started ..." He was still having trouble forming words and taking his eyes off of her.

"You know this is the first 'party' I've been to. At least, this is the first one where my parents didn't drive me to the door, and I didn't bring a gift. I wasn't sure when to show up. I hope I didn't seem too anxious. Seems like there are plenty of others here."

"You're fine, I didn't mean to make you feel ... " he said. "But, you'll see, there will be twice as many here later, and the serious drinking will begin. What are you drinking?"

"A wine cooler."

"Wine cooler?"

"Yeah. Is that bad?"

"No. No." He didn't know how to hide his disappointment, and he didn't know why he was disappointed or why he should be disappointed. He felt confused, which he was beginning to realize was a common feeling around Ashley. "I was just kind of surprised."

"What are you drinking?"

"Water."

"Water? At a party?

"I'm in training."

64

"At a party?"

"Yeah. Even at a party. I take my training seriously."

"Then, why would you come to a party?"

"Because ..." he stared at his feet and blushed. He couldn't finish his thought.

"Mickey," she sensed what he was going to say and saved him the embarrassment of saying it. "This is my first party ever, and I came because I knew you were going to be here, and I got here as early as I could because I couldn't wait to see you."

He looked up at her. They stared into each other's eyes before she spoke, "I wanted to drink something so that people wouldn't look at me like I'm sort of leper. They told me a wine cooler sort of tastes like Kool-Aid. Actually, it tastes like Kool-Aid mixed with lighter fluid."

He laughed. "We are probably the only people here not drinking beer. Probably."

She nodded, "You ever tasted beer? It is gross. I do not know how anybody could drink it."

"Yeah, it tastes like it looks."

"Nothing yellow ever tastes good."

He nodded and then shook his head, "What about bananas? I like bananas."

She conceded. "OK. Nothing yellow ever tasted good except bananas."

"Pineapples. Pineapples are good. They're yellow."

"OK. Pineapples and bananas – nothing else."

He nodded his head slowly, but she could tell he wasn't in agreement, "Vanilla ice cream is kinda yellow. And cheese – I like cheese."

"Can we get off the yellow already? I give up. You win," she laughed.

"Lemon can be good, too. Corn. How about corn?"

She burst into a belly laugh that was so loud, playful, and full of joy it drew the attention of everyone at the pool, especially the group of three sophomore girls sitting at a table directly across the pool. Hope Bradley was the first of the three to comment, "Mickey and Ashley – now there's a match made in …"

"I think they are a cute couple," Sarah interjected.

"It's not just that they are cute," Meredith looked at Mickey and sighed. "I think they are the perfect couple. I mean, they are the straightest straight arrows of the school. I bet you won't see them at another party all summer."

Hope countered. "How many more of these soirées are you going to catch us at? I know I don't plan on attending any more. I'm already tired of being the obligatory sophomore. And being hit on by juniors and seniors is not my idea of a swell time."

"Hey. It's still early. Things don't really get started until later, like midnight, I heard," Sarah said. "You'll see. It'll be fun."

"Right. I don't think being hit on by drunken juniors and seniors instead of sober ones is going to improve my assessment of this evening's festivities," Hope replied.

"Oh Hope, you are such a …" Sarah said, beginning to get angry.

"Yeah," Meredith chimed in. "Can't you ever just chill? Who says 'evening's festivities? Just have drink and relax. Let go a little."

"If I were going to get drunk, it wouldn't be here," Hope looked around. "And when I want to let go, it is not going to be where I'm surrounded by relative strangers who want me to dance with a lamp shade on my head, if you get my drift."

"Can't you ever forget that your father is a teacher?"

"What does that have to do with anything? That has nothing to with it. My father has nothing to do with my choices on this matter. There are lots of kids here who have parents that are teachers. I just look around, and all I see are these creeps that made junior high a living hell for me. I just know what I like, and this ain't really it."

"Let's face it, Hope. You don't like anything except playing the piano all day long." Meredith said.

"And all night," Sarah added. "So, why did you come anyway?"

"Because you both asked me to come, and I said I would and see what it was like. I'm thinking it is pretty lame. Are you having a good time? You want to stay?"

"Not really," Meredith dropped her head and looked down as if she felt guilty about admitting that she wasn't really having a good time.

"Well, I'd like to stay a while longer," Sarah offered. "Maybe an hour or so – and see if things get better …"

"Whatever better means," Hope interrupted.

"I just feel if we're already here, and if we've spent this much time…"

"OK," Hope responded. "But, if one more guy offers to show me the back seat of his car or a can of yeast excretion, I am out of here."

"Jeez, don't be so antisocial!" Sarah said as she punched Hope in the shoulder.

"Yeah!" Meredith agreed.

"I came here to meet guys," Sarah confessed. "You know as long as they're not drunk, or at least not too drunk to talk."

"Look … look at them." Meredith nodded in the direction of Mickey and Ashley, who were sitting cross-legged on the grass facing each other and talking. Sometimes, they would lean in toward each other and almost whisper and, other times, they would lean back and laugh. At one point, they grabbed each other's hands and held on. They saw Ashley reach up and stroke Mickey's cheek, but it was such an intimate moment that all three girls looked away.

Hope spoke, "You know as you look around this yard, there are several couples swapping spit and making out, but

Mickey and Ashley are the only ones who seem to be really into each other."

"That's what I want in a boyfriend. Someone who will take the time to get to know me," Meredith said.

"Someone who will look at me when I talk," Sarah added.

"It's called a relationship," Hope said.

Suddenly, a loud noise erupted from the house and the door banged open. Two guys were pushing and shouting at each other. Between them was a girl crying and screaming, trying to stop them. Even from a distance, the drunkenness of the two boys was obvious. The boy closest to the house managed to push the other, smaller boy out into the yard where he fell.

"Oh God! A fight!" shouted Sarah.

"Hell! A drunken brawl!" Hope said.

Everyone moved toward the two boys and circled them except Mickey. He jumped into the middle and grabbed the taller boy – the one still standing. He held him back and gently pushed him back into the house with the girl. He turned to face the other guy, who was crouching with a bottle of beer in his hand. Mickey stood as straight as he could and said, "Doug! Doug! What are you doing? You don't want to do this. Cheryl is not your girl anymore. It is not going to help anything by getting in a fight, especially with me. You're drunk. You need to go home and sleep it off. Tomorrow, you'll feel different."

Doug looked around at everyone. He stood up straight, shook his head back and forth and cussed everyone. Then, he sprayed the beer on Mickey. He threw down the bottle and staggered off through the yard, cussing and swearing, mostly inaudible, that everyone would pay for this. Mickey tried to brush the beer off his shirt, and then walked back to Ashley.

"I don't know about anybody else, but I'm glad I got to see the entertainment for the evening is over," Hope said sarcastically. "I have had enough of this. Let's get out of here."

It took another five or ten minutes to meander out through the yard, but Sarah, Meredith, and Hope final left the party. The last thing they noticed was Mickey and Ashley still sitting on the grass holding hands and talking. As they drove off, they did not notice the police car stopping in front of the house as they left.

Unwanted Flashbacks

August 23, 1965

26 Red River Lane, Nettie, Texas

Margaret Winston, Maggie as she once preferred to be called, had been married now for more than half of her life, so she had adjusted to being known as Mrs. Wheeler. Today, sunrise could not come soon enough; she was awake and too excited to sleep. She hoisted herself into her wheelchair and rolled into the kitchen. She stopped to look at herself in the hallway mirror. There was a time she took pride in her dark, thick wavy hair. Now she kept it short and straight. There was a time she took pride in her voluptuous curves, radiating sensuality. Now it was hard to tell where one body part started and another ended as she sat in her wheel chair—folded together as one large lump, at least in her mind.

She reached the coffee maker and filled the pot from the sink. This would be a much easier task if she were not in a wheelchair. She had managed to feed Grace every day and support her through high school. None of these had been easy for a single mother in a wheelchair. That they had managed was due to her salary as a school nurse thanks to the grace of one Owen Talbert.

She had been filling out papers on vaccination records and occasionally administering shots to the kindergarten enrollees in the downstairs office when the chemistry teacher burst into the office, hysterically shouting, "There's been a terrible accident in the chemistry class upstairs ... we need a nurse!" She took off running up the stairs, two stairs at a time. "What happened?" The teacher, a fortyish male was ashen in

71

complexion as he tried to explain, "Some of the boys were in the back of the room goofing around with chemicals. I told them to stop. They kept playing suddenly there was this loud pop, an explosion. I yelled at 'em and ran at 'em, but one of 'em … Jesus … one of them was laying on the floor clutching his throat … blood everywhere." By then, they had reached the room. Maggie saw immediately that only one person was hurt and he was lying on the floor motionless in a pool of blood with even squirts of blood shooting out of his neck. She pushed everyone out of her way and made a quick diagnosis – arterial bleeding, very dangerous, already loss of consciousness. She had to stop the bleeding. She looked around the room and could see nothing that would help. She took her fingers and could feel the artery pulsating and grabbed it with her fingers. That stopped the bleeding, but the boy was not out of danger. "Help me pick him up. Get him in a car and drive him to a hospital." She was very firm and decisive – no time for discussion.

Two of the classmates picked up the boy as she continued to pinch and hold the artery inside of his neck. By now, the principal was in the room, "The closest clinic is Dr. Como's office south of town, maybe a 10-minute drive."

"No," she said. "He needs much more help. He needs a major trauma center. We'll have to take him to Parkland."

"That will take you better part of an hour."

"You call the police for an escort. He'll be dead if we don't get him there faster than that. Call his parents. Look up his records. Find his blood type. He needs a blood transfusion as soon as possible. Call Parkland with all the info and warn them we're coming." She shouted all the orders as the three were carrying the boy down to the first big car in the parking lot, a

Cadillac owned by the principal who got behind the wheel and took off with the boy's head in her lap, her hand still pinching his artery. The boy lived. The boy lived because of Maggie's quick thinking. She had learned the technique in the army during the war. Her experience had saved the boy's life. The hospital staff praised Maggie's quick thinking and competent handling of the situation. There was no doubt that the boy lived because of her. The boy's name was Richie Talbert. Richie's father, Owen, was a very wealthy politician with a lot of influence at both the local and state level. His gratitude knew no bounds. From then on, he made sure that Maggie always had a job as school nurse in the school district. He saw to it that if there were ever any problems with training or accreditation, Maggie would be exempted. He even saw to it that she did not lose her job when she had the accident and became handicapped. The district was always extremely pleased with her performance. Her handicap was not a problem when it came to serving the community.

For Maggie, today was the payoff for all of her hard work. Grace was leaving for college! They had made it.

Some of the other mothers felt a sense of loss and grief to see their daughters going away to college. Even though most of them were not going any farther than Austin College in Sherman or North Texas State in Denton – both less than a hundred miles away. They would be home every other weekend if not every weekend. Some were going all the way to University of Texas in Austin or the University of Oklahoma in Norman, neither of which were more than 300 miles away. But, Grace was headed to Stanford University all the way in California, and Mrs. Wheeler could only feel a sense of triumph. Not only was it one of the best schools in the country, it meant that Grace was escaping Nettie, something that she had wanted to do for more than 20 years and had failed to do.

The coffee was done. She poured herself a cup and rolled onto the porch on the east end with the cup balanced between her legs. She looked out on the sun beginning to creep across the horizon. Nothing blocked her view. This was her quiet moment of the day. Her rest before the struggle – because every day was a struggle for her – this moment was pure bliss, enjoying the coffee and the sunrise. The only difference between now and the view the first day was the encroaching rooftops, which were getting nearer and nearer each year. Still, at this point, there was a large field between her and the first house.

On the porch looking into the rising sun, that first day, that first time she saw the view, that first week of her marriage. She woke before Jimmy, made the coffee, took it onto the porch, and surveyed her new home. From horizon to horizon, west to east, there were no neighbors as far as she could see. Far ahead to the south, she could barely see the hints of some rooftops, but in the dark of the sunrise, even they were more visual rumors than reality. On the right, the sun was beginning to crack the horizon. She shifted her weight onto her right foot and took a long drink of coffee, closed her eyes to soak in the rays and feel the pure contentment of the moment. Slowly, she became aware of Jimmy's hands gently touching her. She kept her eyes closed and leaned her head back as his hands slid up her gown to her breasts. Her breathing changed and a sigh escaped from her lips. He was kissing her neck and she felt his naked body pressing against her. She turned to greet his lips full and began kissing him passionately. Urgently. The coffee cup left her hand as he tried to enter her, but they ended up falling, alternately laughing and panting. Her back arched as he finally managed to enter her, she opened her eyes, and saw the sunrise completely fill the skyline as he finished. "Good morning," was all he said as he rolled onto his back.

"If this is going to be an every morning thing, we better make sure we never get any neighbors or that the ones we get are really open minded."

They both laughed.

She blinked and turned back into the kitchen thinking of the successes of the past four years. Grace was the school valedictorian, National Merit scholarship recipient, and had been accepted to Stanford. Grace would be able to know a world beyond the boundaries of Nettie, Texas. She would be able to grow beyond the cultural sameness and narrow-mindedness. She would experience new vistas and new adventures. Maggie knew these were all her hopes longer than they had been Grace's, but she knew they shared them nonetheless. Grace wanted out as much as Maggie wanted out. Mrs. Wheeler couldn't escape. Paralyzed legs do not seek new vistas or go on adventures.

Ralph and his mother were taking her to the airport, and Maggie promised them a big breakfast. She started mixing pancake batter and biscuits. Perhaps it was the sensuous experience of mixing biscuits or perhaps it was the lingering effect of remembering the first sexual encounter that first morning – whatever it was, she kept recalling brief images of sex from that first year with Jimmy.

Sex in the hayloft after a horse ride, in front of the fireplace, in the shower, Jimmy on top, she on top, standing up, or sitting on the big chair. A hunger too intense to satisfy. Then, one night, Jimmy came home from work, and decided that he should take his horse for a ride; it needed the exercise. When he came back from the ride – longer than usual – while Jimmy was brushing the horse after the ride, Maggie came out to the stable wearing only a blanket. Maggie put the blanket on the hay and lay on the blanket naked. He turned and went into the house ignoring her. She never felt the same. She never again felt as free or open. A door was closed never to be reopened.

Mixing the pancake batter brought her back to the present and the kitchen. She filled the pitcher with milk. She put several slices of bread in the toaster, but waited to turn it on. She cracked some eggs in a bowl and mixed in some milk to make the scrambled eggs. She threw the eggshells into the garbage and began beating the eggs faster and faster.

Jimmy shouting at her on the opposite side of the table. She was crying and yelling at him. She threw a fork at him, scraping his head and drawing blood. She ran to him and they kissed. Passionate, unreasonable makeup sex. A drunken Jimmy staggered through the door and fell against the table, scattering dishes and food across the floor. More images of him yelling at her. She screaming at him while he passed out at the table. Too many lonely nights waiting for him. Sometimes, he staggered through the door, sometimes a day or two passes. Jimmy was always mad. Once while drunk, he raised his hand as if to hit her, but he restrained himself. He always did, but she didn't. She hit him as hard as she could, breaking his nose. The next day, she told him he fell and hit the table, and he couldn't remember what had happened. He could never allow himself to admit that his wife beat him.

The eggs were done. Everything was ready. There was no reason to wake Grace yet; there was still plenty of time. She turned the wheelchair around and headed out onto the porch once again stopping to refresh her coffee. She stared into the sunrise. She often pondered about what went wrong with their marriage that first year. They started with so much promise. Even though they were so young and fresh from the war, they felt so much passion for each other, and God they were so handsome. Jimmy had a hard time adjusting to the loss of the cattle, but that wasn't enough. He had been poor before and lack of money wasn't going to be enough to ruin his marriage. For Maggie's part, she found Nettie incredibly repressive and narrow-minded. She had underestimated how hard it would be for her to settle down in a small town after the war. She could have done more to adjust. Dallas wasn't that far away, and she could have taken college classes. No, the single event that destroyed their marriage was when she rescued Richie Talbert and the fame it brought her. Until that moment, Jimmy had been a local hero with some medals from the war. But, after that, she was the hero – the local legend. Everywhere they went in Nettie, someone would say something or buy her a drink or point out her accomplishment. Jimmy could not handle living in her shadow. A man can only live like that so long before he has to do something, prove that he is a man. So, he started drinking and cheating. He wasn't limited to one.

Raymond started dancing with her. She had been at the bar drinking and enjoying the music with some girlfriends. If Jimmy could go out drinking so could she. At some point, she found herself dancing on the small dance floor entranced by the music. At some point, Raymond joined her, but she hardly noticed him; it was the music that transformed her. Swaying to the beat of the country songs from the jukebox, she was in a different place, a sensuous hypnotic state or otherworldly place. Raymond had his arms around her and they both swayed to the music. Slowly, in perfect harmony with the music, he kissed her; a long, warm sensual kiss that morphed into a passionate hot, wet kiss full of promise. The type of kiss that felt like the whole body was kissing through the lips. The type of kiss where two individuals became one entity. She stepped back with her eyes still closed. She finally opened them, and smiled, nodded, and walked back to her table to sit with her girlfriends. The kiss had the effect of sobering her. Still, she spent the rest of the evening more quietly, but she would look in Raymond's direction throughout the night. I am a married woman, *she thought,* but that was one exciting kiss.

She saw the Plymale car turn off the highway and kick up the dust as it turned down Red River Road. She wheeled through the doorway and rolled toward Grace's room. She maneuvered her wheelchair sideways so that she could knock on the door. "Grace, Grace, it's time to get up. The Plymales are almost here. Get dressed and help me with breakfast. You don't want to sleep late today."

Grace threw open the door. She was fully dressed. "Good morning." She turned to show her mother her outfit. "How do I look? You think this is all right for the flight?"

She was dressed in a light blue A-line skirt with a white blouse fully buttoned to the Peter Pan collar. A sweater of pastel pink was on her shoulders right under the gentle swirls of her hair. She looked like the perfect co-ed.

"I couldn't sleep. I've been awake for hours. I finished packing, picked my clothes, showered, and I worked on … I worked on a new song I learned. I'm going to play it for you and

Ralph and his mother. I'll play it right before we leave. It will be perfect. You'll see."

"You could have come in and helped me with breakfast."

"Yeah, I could have, but you'll like this song better."

Maggie smiled and turned her wheelchair back in the direction of the kitchen. She came to the ramp and, as always, she rolled back to get some momentum to roll up across the bump. "Grace, get the cups and saucers down for you and the Plymales. I'm gonna start the pancakes. You cook the bacon and sausage."

"Aw, Mom, I can't cook the meat. It'll splatter onto my white blouse. "I'll set the table. You cook the meat, please."

"Grace, you know how much I hate the smell of bacon."

"Mom!"

"OK."

Grace knew her mom hated to cook bacon, but she didn't know why. Grace didn't know about that day on the highway. She didn't know the details and how the smell of bacon brought back the smell.

First she woke to the smell of the burning gasoline and then the burning flesh. When she could finally see, she wasn't sure what had happened, but she knew she couldn't feel her legs and they couldn't move. She felt a trace of blood flowing down her face, but the first thing she recognized was Jimmy pulling her across the pavement and down the road. Maybe 20 yards away was Raymond's motorcycle on its side with Raymond on his knees, crawling toward them. She saw the puddles of

79

gasoline encircling the motorcycle and she saw the flickers of flames on the right side as it moved rapidly toward Raymond. She was aware that Jimmy was saying something, shouting something, but she never could understand the sounds he emitted. Raymond stood and burst into flames simultaneously. Sounds were coming from her. Then, standing there engulfed in flames, the motorcycle exploded and Raymond flew apart in every direction. She was aware of the surge of heat and sensed a spray of body parts hitting her before she gratefully fell into unconsciousness.

The bacon was sizzling in one pan on the front burner of the stove, and gravy was bubbling in the next burner. The biscuits were ready to come out of the oven. The toast popped out of the toaster, and the pancakes were flipped on the electric skillet next to the stove. Everything had to be close to the edge as Maggie did not have an extended reach form her wheelchair. She adroitly rolled back and forth from one appliance to the other. Grace set the table, poured some glasses of orange juice, and set the coffee pot on the table just as the Plymales opened the door and entered the kitchen.

"Good morning, Maggie. Grace," Blanche said as she pulled out the chair and sat down. "I can't believe you've gone through all this trouble. A roll and some coffee would have been enough. You didn't need to fix this big breakfast. Maggie, you just didn't need to go to all this trouble."

"Nonsense. I wouldn't have it any other way," Maggie responded. "You drive a daughter all the way to the Dallas airport, the least a mother can do is put a good breakfast before you."

"Hi, Grace." Ralph spoke so softly as to give the impression of intimacy to the statement.

"Oh. Hi, Ralph. Mrs. Plymale." Grace responded in a louder tone to distract any meaning from Ralph. "It sure is nice of y'all to take me to the airport. I really appreciate it."

"Shoot," Blanche chimed in. "It's no big thing. Seems only right for us to be the ones sending you off after ... everything. Hand me the salt and pepper, Ralph. Please."

Grace shot a sudden look at Ralph. She did not want her past relationship with Ralph to be the center of everyone's awareness. Blanche believed Grace would soon realize her mistake and come to some sort of change of heart. Ralph just wanted to deny that their relationship had ended, and Maggie was eager for Grace to grow beyond Ralph. There might have been an awkwardness and tension except that everyone in the room really liked and respected each other too much for too long to allow any distance to develop between them.

"Oh, goodness," Blanche spoke up. "Don't let this old woman say anything that makes anyone get all tense. I just blabber sometimes. But, you know, Grace, you and Ralph have a history, dearie, and your mommy and I go way back ... been best of friends since before either of you was here. I just wouldn't have it any other way, except we'd be the ones drivin' you to the airport."

"That's right, Grace," Ralph spoke out. "I wouldn't want anyone ... I want to say goodbye and I want you to know that things are all right between us ... with you going away ... and stuff."

Grace smiled at Ralph – that smile of hers that said more than words ever could. She nodded. She did not need to say anything. Suddenly, the door rattled open and Jimmy stood in the doorway.

"Good morning. You didn't think I was going to let my little girl go away to California without a proper going away hug and kiss?"

"Daddy!" Grace was always surprised to see him. She moved toward him and awkwardly gave him a perfunctory hug.

"Jimmy, have some breakfast." Maggie started putting some eggs, biscuits, and gravy on a plate.

"I don't want to interrupt anything …"

"Don't be silly," Maggie was busy wheeling around getting a fresh cup. "Here's some coffee. Grab a chair."

He reluctantly sat down. He nodded at Blanche. "Blanche, how have you been? Ralph, how are you doing?"

"We're fine." Blanche and Ralph both reflected an awkwardness that was as obvious as it was uncomfortable. No one knew how to treat Jimmy. No one knew how to label him. He didn't live with Maggie and Hope, but they wouldn't get a divorce. No one would see him for months at a time, and often when they did, he was too drunk to communicate with.

Grace either didn't notice, didn't care, or was immune to what others thought of her father or, most likely, she felt some combination of all three. Mainly, she felt indifferent to her father, at least consciously. She sometimes wondered if there was some hidden trauma she hadn't acknowledged. At any rate, everyone she cared for in Nettie was together under one roof. She sensed it would be the last time. This would be her last day in Nettie. She shared her mother's vision, her dream of escaping Nettie. She saw horizons much greater than provided in Nettie.

"Listen, while everyone is here, I've got a special song I learned last night. I practiced all night – a special version of a song. I want to play it for you now, now before ... while we are all here." Grace ran off to get her guitar.

"Is that a Martin Guitar?" Jimmy asked. "That is quite a guitar. How did you get that?"

"Only the best for my daughter," Maggie replied.

"How did you afford it?" Jimmy asked.

"I did some extra work at a vaccination clinic a few weekends."

Her answer seemed to disturb Jimmy.

"Is everything ready?" Grace asked Ralph.

Ralph nodded. He arranged a tape recorder on the middle of the table.

"This is actually an old song, but I just learned it last night. Here it is:

> The water is wide, I cannot get over
>
> Nor have I wings to fly
>
> But give me a boat that can carry two
>
> And both shall row, my love and I."

It was raining when Raymond appeared at her home. He drove up on his motorcycle and parked in the front yard. She saw him coming from the front window. She knew what he was there for and she was equally flattered, excited, and enthusiastic. When he parked, she walked slowly out to him, and he walked slowly toward her. When they reached each other, they embraced and kissed with an intensity and hunger that burned. They hugged and fondled and kissed and fell on the ground and devoured each other. The rain poured down on them, but as they ripped their clothes off and bit and licked, they rolled in the mud with an animal nature unaware of anything else except the spending of their own energy.

"I leaned my back against a young oak

Thinking it was a trusty tree

But first it bent and then it broke

Just as my love grew false to me."

At this point, Grace played a guitar bridge that was intricate and melodious and had the effect of causing everyone in the room to lean forward and listen even more intently to the lyrics when she began singing again. Grace, for her part, now began to make eye contact with each member of her audience before each line as if to communicate that the line was directed toward them. The first lines were directed to Ralph, and then Mrs. Plymale and her father.

"But love is gentle and love is kind

Gay as a jewel when first is new,

But waxes old and soon grows cold

And fades away like the morning dew."

Then last line was sung directly at her mother.

"The water is wide. I cannot get over

Neither have I the wings to fly

But give me a boat that carries two

And both shall row, my love and I."

Then Grace sighed. Blanche lurched for her and hugged her. Ralph had to turn his head and swallow, and Blanche spoke, "Grace, that was beautiful ... I ... I'm speechless, and that doesn't happen often."

Jimmy stood up and gave Grace a hug and handed her an envelope.

Grace opened the envelope and gasped, "That's a lot of money."

"You'll probably need some spending money in California."

"Thanks, Daddy."

They took off down the road and hit the highway out of town, Raymond driving the motorcycle and Maggie on the backseat with her arms around him. They were taking the curve onto the highway when they saw Jimmy galloping across the field toward them. Jimmy was riding his horse, but he had Maggie's horse with him, and he was riding at full speed. He would run into them at the curve. They were freighted because it wasn't clear what he was going to do. Another curve was ahead. Maggie's horse broke free and ran at the motorcycle. There was a crash. There was something wet on the surface – an oil slick – when Raymond hit the oil slick, he lost control and went into a spin. Maggie fell off, but Raymond skidded 20 or 30 yards with his legs pinned under the bike. Jimmy jumped off of his horse and ran to Maggie. They watched Raymond combust and explode. There was never an explanation for the flame that Maggie and Jimmy saw that lead to the explosion.

Grace turned toward her mother and made a sign of a three and silently worded hundred. Maggie smiled and nodded. She looked at Jimmy to say thank you, but he looked away to avoid eye contact. She didn't try any harder to connect with him.

"I just wanted to stop by and wish you well, but I got to go now," Jimmy said as he put his Stetson back on.

"Why don't you ride to the airport with us?" Grace invited.

"Nah. I've got things to do."

"I'm not going," Maggie added.

"Maggie, that's not it. I really have things to do." He walked out the door, waved goodbye from behind as he left, and was gone.

"Well, that was real nice of him to show up like that," Blanche said. "Let me help you clean up the table now, Maggie."

When she finally regained consciousness the first thing she noticed was the tubes going into her on her right arm. Dripping slowly, there was a clear liquid and a red one. She gathered that she was getting a blood transfusion as well as being fed intravenously. She looked around the room and began to get a sense of where she was and why. Jimmy was on the left side of the room. "Tell me this didn't happen. Tell me I've been having a terrible dream," she spoke to the ceiling.

Jimmy looked up, his eyes bloodshot. But, he didn't say anything. She knew everything was true. She kept staring at the ceiling closing her eyes and picturing the events. At the last image of Raymond exploding, her eyes flashed open. She took some sort of inventory; it did not take her long to realize that she had no feeling in her legs.

"Why? What were you trying to do?"

Jimmy dropped his head, "I don't know ... I just couldn't let you go away with him."

"Why? I wasn't leaving with him. We were going for a ride. I've always wanted to ride a motorcycle. Since when did you care what I was doing or where I was?"

"You are my wife."

"In name only. You just couldn't stand your wife having ... having a life beyond you. Not like I could do anything you haven't done a dozen times."

"I might not have been much of a husband, but what you two were doing was wrong."

"Did Raymond deserve to die?"

He just stared at the floor.

She spoke very directly and sternly, "You killed him."

"I didn't. I never hit y'all. I was backin' off. I was about to turn around when y'all spun out. I don't know what caused the accident."

"But, it wouldn't have happened if you hadn't come after us and jumped out like that."

He just dropped his head, and sat quietly for a long time before he whispered, "I know. I am so sorry. I didn't mean to hurt nobody."

"I know, but being sorry is not enough. You haven't been worth a damn since ... Jimmy, it shouldn't have mattered."

He just hung his head. "I know, but I couldn't let you ..."

"What? Have a job? Be respected?"

He nodded.

"You can't handle that people look up to me since that Richie Talbert thing," she said. "That's it, isn't it? That's the real thing. You were the big hero in the war, and now you can't handle your wife having some glory."

"Nobody wants their wife to be ... I feel like I'm a big nobody."

"Jesus, Jimmy. You make me sick."

"I'll make it up to you. I promise." He said. "You'll see. I'll make it up to you."

She just looked at him and shook her head. "It is not that simple; it is not that simple. Just leave me alone."

Jimmy left the room and Maggie spent the night alone wondering how she could go on.

Blanche started to help with the dishes but Maggie said. "Y'all leave the dishes. I'll get them later. You need to be going". She spun around in her wheelchair and carried a few dishes to the sink. "Now you get going. Ralph, you help Grace with her bags."

Ralph carried the two bags of luggage to the truck of the car, and Blanche got into the passenger side. Ralph sat in the driver's side and they waited for Grace. Grace scurried to the door carrying her guitar case and ran to the car putting the guitar in the backseat. The car started, but before it went three feet, Grace jumped out and ran back into the house.

"Mom! Mom! We did it." Grace spoke with a lump in her throat and tears flowing down her cheek. "This is your dream, too. But, it is so hard to say goodbye."

"You aren't saying goodbye. Not to me. You are saying hello to your future. You are taking all my dreams with you, and you are going to build your own dreams upon them. There is no sadness today! I love you and I want you to … take off – to grow!"

"I love you. No one, I mean, no one has ever had a more wonderful, less selfish mother."

Grace bent down to the wheelchair and hugged her mother. Then, she turned and looked around the house one last time before jumping into the backseat and riding off toward the airport.

The doctor walked in with two nurses. They began to read the charts and note things without saying anything. The doctor took Maggie's blood pressure. Finally, after checking all the vital signs, the doctor spoke, directing his remarks to Jimmy, "I have bad news and good news. When you dragged you wife across the pavement, it caused the spinal cord to snap completely. I am afraid she will be paralyzed from the waist down permanently. If there is a good side to the snap, it did not affect the part of the spine above the break." At this point, Maggie broke in, "Doctor, I am in the room. Could you talk to me? Are you saying that I will be ..." and as hard as she tried, as brave as she wanted to be, she faltered in facing the reality of her situation.

"Yes, Mrs. Wheeler, I am sorry to have to tell you this, but you are paralyzed from the waist down – permanently."

Tears filled Maggie's eyes, but she didn't say anything.

"However," the doctor continued, "the good news is that the accident has not affected the baby at all. There is no reason that the pregnancy cannot continue to a normal birth."

"Baby?" Jimmy and Maggie said in unison.

Maggie watched the car until it was completely out of sight, then she went back into the kitchen. She took the dishes off the table and piled them in her lap. She turned toward the sink, stopping to slide leftovers into the garbage. She put the rest of the dishes into the sink.

Maggie leaned back and rested. She was feeling satisfied. She was proud of the person Grace had become.

Maggie had finished nursing Grace and had put her into the crib for a nap when she turned and wheeled herself back into the kitchen. Jimmy was standing with his hat in his hand his eyes trying to avoid Maggie's.

His voice cracked as he spoke, "I ... I think I'm going to have to ... leave."

She nodded.

"I'm going to West Texas and work the oil fields. I'll send you my paycheck."

"You don't need to do that. Grace and I will be all right. I'm gonna continue as the school nurse. We'll be OK."

"No, I want to help. I want to send you the money."

"Jimmy, it's not going to make you feel any better."

"I ... have to ..."

"Jimmy, you don't have to leave."

"Yeah ... yeah, I do. I've tried staying here and helping you out as much as I can ..."

"And God knows you've tried drinking as much as you can."

He just put his head down and said nothing.

"Jimmy, the court ruled it was an accident."

"It was. It was an accident. I didn't mean to do anything."

"I believe you. I know. And Jimmy, I forgive you."

With these words, Jimmy shook his head back and forth, "It doesn't matter. Every day, I see you rolling about in that chair, picking Grace up and struggling to change her diaper, struggling to warm her bottle, wheeling her back and forth, every day. I know you have forgiven me, but I cannot handle your forgiveness."

"And every day, I see the pain you are suffering that I cannot heal, and I know I am the cause because I stopped loving my husband and made a selfish, silly decision. And worse, I know Raymond is still dead because of that decision. And I cannot forgive myself."

She looked away from him. "Maybe you do need to get away, at least for awhile. You can spend some time wildcatting, and maybe you will find it in yourself to forgive yourself if you don't have my presence shoved into your face every day. And I'll get busy with the job of raising our daughter, and maybe I'll be able to forgive myself someday. I'll leave your bed made and ready for you until Grace is old enough to need it. This will always be your home."

Jimmy stood and left. He didn't hug or kiss her.

The dishes were all done – washed, rinsed, and dried – and the pots and pans were soaking. Maggie poured one more cup of coffee, braced it between her legs, and rolled out onto the porch. She smiled. It had been a very long arduous battle, but Grace was going to school in California. She was escaping Nettie. Maggie felt successful as if she had accomplished her mission in life. She looked out on the porch. The sun was blazing down. It was going to be a hot afternoon. The landscape was busy with new houses; she did not have the solitude she once had. She had mixed feelings about the influx of civilization. Part of her liked having neighbors. She took a long drink of coffee.

She closed her eyes to soak in the rays and feel the pure contentment of the moment. Slowly she became aware of Jimmy hands gently touching her. She kept her eyes closed and leaned her head back as his hands slid up her gown to her breasts. Her breathing changed and a sigh escaped from her lips. He was kissing her neck and she felt his naked body pressing against her. She turned to greet his lips full and began kissing him passionately, urgently. The coffee cup left her hand as he tried to enter her, but they ended up falling alternately laughing and panting. Her back arched as he entered her, she opened her eyes, and saw the sunrise completely fill the skyline as he finished. "Good morning," was all he said as he rolled over onto his back.

"If this is going to be an every morning thing, we better make sure our neighbors are open minded."

They both laughed. She smiled.

"Suicide effects the way you see the world"

July 12, 1982

26 Red River Lane, Nettie, Texas

Hope hated when it rained. When the sun was shining, there was always something to do during the summer. She could ride her bicycle up the street to the right and eventually Meredith would come out and play even though she lived on the other side of the big field. Or, she could ride to the left and see Sarah down the street and around the corner. With Meredith, she could play in her backyard on the playhouse, but with Sarah, they might ride their bikes to the swimming pool or the library even though it was a long ride. Sometimes, they would go ride horses on the ranch just over the hill the past the street where Sarah lived. Sarah lived with her single mother and, most of the time, she was in day care in town or with a babysitter, but sometimes she was left unattended. Those were "adventure days filled with danger" as Meredith labeled them. Meredith sometimes would tag along with them, but she was more of a stay-at-home girl. Besides, being the high school principal's daughter gave her too much visibility to do much adventuring. Hope liked having fun with both girls, and she liked having choices, but when it rained, she just sat at home and was bored. This summer, she felt even more desperate because next year she would be starting junior high school and, somehow, she felt that it was important to exercise her choices before she lost them. Junior high seemed to be a big change element in her life. Fortunately, it didn't rain often, but today was one of those days.

She was kneeling in front of the bay window watching the rain trickle down the glass when Granny Wheels came in.

"Why don't you invite Sarah and Meredith over? I can go pick them up. You could have a tea party or play some board games I've got lying around … or something."

Those few words began a lazy, rainy summer day that would radically change Hope's life forever in a dramatic, drastic way. The day began with a simple Monopoly game, but Sarah and Hope quickly grew bored.

"Let's play Chutes and Ladders and Candy Land and Monopoly at the same time," Sarah suggested.

"Yeah, we'll put the Candy Land board before the Monopoly and the Chutes and Ladders after and use two sets of dice," Hope giggled as she rushed to set up the boards.

"This sounds stupid," Meredith, always the logical one, sounded skeptical.

"No, no. This will be fun," Sarah insisted.

"Mega-fun!" Hope exclaimed.

The game quickly escalated into an insane bout of rule-making that only Sarah and Hope understood. Meredith was constantly befuddled and frustrated.

"My turn. My turn." Sarah squealed. She rolled four dice: Four, three, five, and six. She was on the Chutes and Ladders board and moved forward eight spaces, and then back 10 spaces, which put her on a ladder to the top of the board.

"Wait. You can't do that. How can you do that?" Meredith questioned.

"It's the reverse even rule. I get to move backward on the even-numbered dice."

"Oh." Meredith seemed to accept the rule, but when she rolled her dice and tried to do the same thing putting her on a ladder moving her up the board, she was greeted with loud screams of "No! You can't do that!" from both Meredith and Hope.

"The reverse even rule only works when you roll with your left hand. You threw the dice with your right hand," Hope calmly explained. "You have to take your full number, which gets you on a chute back to here. Now, it's my turn." She rolled six, five, six, and four. "Oh good, I'm the first on the Monopoly board. I get a discount on all the properties I buy." She bought Baltic Avenue, Venture Avenue, and all the railroads. "And because I rolled more than a 20, I get to roll again." Three, five, one, and three. "Oh wow! All odds. You know what that means – another turn." two, three, five, and four. By now, Hope owned all of the properties on the board and was at the starting on the Candy Land board. "Your turn." She handed the dice to Sarah with a smug smile, and both girls broke out in uncontrollable laughter for what seemed like forever, especially to Meredith.

"What's so funny?" Meredith kept asking. "I don't get it? Are we still playing or not?"

Finally, Sarah composed herself, grabbed the dice, looked at the boards in front of her, and blew on the dice. "OK, OK." She rolled six, six, three, and two. She landed on the railroad on the Monopoly board.

"That will be $1,000 – please and thank you," Hope said with her hand extended.

"Wait a minute. I get to finish my turn. I rolled two sixes, so I get to roll again." Sarah grabbed the dice firmly in mock defiance. Four, three, six, and one. "Yes! I claim the special Odd Only Rule."

"What is that?" Hope asked.

"Only the even dice count after you roll two sixes if you roll with two hands."

Hope and Meredith looked at each other and shook their heads – dumbfounded.

"I swear." Sarah was saying. "Everyone knows that rule. It is a classic. Well, that gives me a 10, and I'm in jail. That makes me a criminal, and I get to steal your railroad properties. So, I don't owe you anything. Your turn, Meredith."

Meredith took a long time looking at her friends and at the board before she threw the dice. One, three, five, and three. She was still at the start of the Chutes and Ladders and she moved her piece backward across the starting point up to the finishing line on the Candy Land Board. "I get to move backwards because of the all-odd reverse rule." Then, she picked up the cards for the Candy Land game and shuffled through them until she found the right color to cross the finish line. "That's the standard rule that if two of the dice added together equal the other two dice – in this case 1 + 5 = 3 + 3. You get to choose the card you get in the Candy Land deck. I cross the finish line first. I guess that means I win."

Hope and Meredith looked at each other stunned for a few seconds. Meredith had outwitted them, beating them at their own game, so to speak. Silence was the only response Sarah or Hope could muster and then all three fell on the floor and rolled around in laughter so loud and long that Mrs. Wheeler came in to check on them to see if they were all right, which only made them laugh even longer and harder. She hustled them into the kitchen to help with the lunch.

They ate in the kitchen. Grilled cheese sandwiches, chips, and milk. Mrs. Wheeler supervised, but they all helped cook and serve them. The famous Wheeler fresh-baked brownies followed. They were homemade, so the girls helped by watching and handing ingredients to Mrs. Wheeler. The brownies did not last a half hour as the girls ate them while they were still hot. The cold milk helped. Then, it was back to the living room for a lazy afternoon of girl talk.

Sarah lay on the couch while Hope picked up the board games and put the pieces away. Meredith helped Hope. When she put the boxes away, Meredith sat on the floor looking out the window, Sarah turned onto her side. Hope returned to the room and sat down at the piano randomly hitting notes, occasionally hinting at a melody and even playing scales. The three sat like that for several minutes staring at the window watching the rain comes down in the yard and on the porch.

"I don't know about the rest of you, but junior high kinda scares me," Meredith broke the silence.

"Why?" Hope asked. She turned away from the piano to face Meredith.

"I've heard the kids are meaner, and we'll be the youngest. I really liked being the oldest kids in grade school, but next year … it's like we are starting all over again."

"But, it's the same kids who were in sixth grade when we were in third and fourth grade." Hope pointed out. 'I doubt that they have transformed into serial murderers in the past two years."

Sarah just shook her head, "They have become *teenagers.*"

"So?"

"Well," Sarah didn't know how to respond to Hope's lack of awareness on the subject. "Everyone knows that when kids become teenagers, they change. They become unruly and drink and do all sorts of bad things. They become mean."

"My dad doesn't think so. He likes the kids he teaches." Hope contradicted Sarah gently. She didn't want to hurt her feelings. "I guess we'll wait and see. I'm not afraid of the kids."

"My dad says that kids are the same in junior high and high school and elementary school, and he has worked at each level, so he should know," Meredith had a way of waiting until an argument was settled before she spoke up. "I am more afraid of the classes and the teachers. I've heard that they are really mean, not like in grade school, and they give homework every night in every class. If the kids seem mean, it's because the teachers don't protect you from bad kids. You know, bullies, and the teachers don't care about you at all. They won't even know your name and the counselors won't help you except to change classes if they think you are in the wrong class, and the lunchroom is really scary and huge, and you have to change clothes in the girls locker room, and take a shower in gym class, and you have to go to your locker between classes, but sometimes your locker is down the hallway, and it makes you late for class and … and … and …"

Meredith was often quiet and did not offer an opinion, but when she did, she sounded like a sewing machine, speaking mostly in run-on sentences.

Sarah and Hope were silent. Finally, Hope spoke to her gently, "Meredith, it will be all right. Every year, thousands of kids across America go to junior high. They all survive. No one has ever died from enrollment in junior high. We will adjust and survive and flourish. We are all good students."

Meredith caught her breath. "I know." She took a deeper breath. "Besides, there are some things I am really looking forward to ... like dances."

Sarah nodded. "There is a seventh grade dance the first Friday of school. I cannot wait!"

"Why?" asked Hope. "We had dances in sixth grade, and I doubt that any of our male classmates can discern their right foot from their left foot with any more accuracy than they could at the end of the school year."

"Yeah, but there are two other elementary schools joining us in seventh grade, and there just might be some other guys worth meeting, if you know what I mean."

"Eye candy," Hope said.

"Hunks," Sarah added.

"Seventh grade hunks," Hope corrected.

"I don't get it," Meredith added.

"Sarah is thinking that the crop of eligible boys ..." Hope began.

"Desirable boys," Sarah interrupted.

"The stock of desirable boys will increase because of the size of the population of junior high school." Hope shook her head. "Does that about sum it up?"

"Well, I happen to know this guy from across town – I met him at a softball tournament – let's say I am looking forward to slow dancing with him, if you catch my meaning."

"Everyone catches your meaning. You are about as subtle as a hand grenade."

"I don't get it," Meredith said.

Sarah sat up excitedly on the couch, "You all have seen this guy – at the swimming pool. He rode over on his bike one day. His name is ... uh, Ricky."

"Oh, yeah," Meredith squealed. "I remember him. He was really cute. He has curly blonde hair."

"Yeah, but he was with two other guys who looked like ..." Hope looked for the right words. "Let's just say I was surprised that their bikes didn't have training wheels."

"What do you mean?" Meredith asked. "They were older. In fact, they both smoked. I saw cigarette packs in their sleeves."

"That doesn't mean they were older, just stupider. But, you are right, Sarah, Ricky is cute, and if he is any indication of the seventh grade boys, we will be in for an interesting year."

Sarah nodded, "Ricky plays football. I'm gonna try out for cheerleading. Are you?" She turned to look at both girls. "Everyone who tries out gets to be a cheerleader in seventh grade; they don't cut anyone until eighth grade."

"No. No way," Meredith shook her head. "I'm going to be in the band. I've always wanted to be in the marching band in high school. Besides, I don't want to be out in front of everyone like that."

"I've thought about it," Hope said. "I haven't made up my mind, but I could see myself whipping the crowd into a frenzy." She jumped up and did the type of splits a cheerleader does then she hopped from foot to foot as she clapped in front of her and shouted, "Go team! Win team!"

It was all so sudden and so serious that Sarah and Meredith did not know how to respond. "That's ... that's really good," Meredith said.

"Yeah," Sarah whistled and then shook her head. "I didn't know you had been practicing. But you are really good."

"Thanks. I think I might be a natural."

"That would be so cool being a cheerleader with you," Sarah said with so much enthusiasm that she sat up on the sofa and almost fell off.

"Well, I haven't decided if I am going to or not." Hope did not want to leave Meredith out of the conversation. "I didn't know you wanted to be the band. It's been like a lifelong dream of yours?"

"Yeah."

Meredith diverted her eyes but kept talking, "I've always thought the uniforms were cool, and if you ever go to a high school game, the band seems to be the only ones having any fun, I mean in the stands. I'm sure the marching isn't any fun."

"I never thought about it, but you're right," Hope said.

"Cheerleading is a lot of work." Sarah added. "But, everyone looks up to the cheerleaders."

"What do you want to do when you grow up?" Hope asked. "I mean will cheerleading help?"

"I don't know if cheerleading will help, but it won't hurt." When Sarah talked, her voice became stern and her jaw tightened. "I want to run a business. You know, be a successful businesswoman. Rich, with the emphasis on 'rich.'"

"What kind of a business?" Hope thought it was an important question.

"I don't care. It doesn't matter. As long as I am successful and get to wear a ritzy wardrobe."

"I just want to marry and raise children of my own." Meredith spoke out, but realized that she seemed so old fashioned, she tried to sound apologetic about her wishes. "I'm gonna be a teacher, too."

"But, basically, you just want to marry and have kids?" Sarah asked in a way that sounded condescending.

Meredith just nodded and didn't say anything. Hope spoke for her. "There is nothing wrong with that."

"Well what do you want to do when you grow up?" Sarah turned toward Hope.

Hope looked surprised or more accurately, unprepared. "I ... I don't know. A lot of things interest me – science, history, literature. The piano is very important to me. I like music – classical music. I don't know ... maybe I'll go into medicine or be a teacher like my dad. He seems to like his job. I don't know yet. I'll figure it out."

Nobody said anything. They turned and stared at the rain.

After a long period of silence, Sarah finally spoke, "I hate rain."

"I like the way it looks," Hope responded, but another silence followed.

Sarah spoke out with something that was obviously bothering her, "There is nothing wrong with wanting to be a wife and mother, but I just don't … buy it. I don't believe in marriage. I just don't think it ever works out."

"I do," Meredith said. "My parents have been married 14 years. They are happy."

"My father left us when I was a baby," Sarah almost spit the words out. "Everyone Mom has dated since has refused to marry her – probably because of me."

"That's why you don't believe in marriage and I do," Meredith said triumphantly yet quietly. "It is more about you than about marriage."

Hope expressed sympathy for Sarah living through her parent's divorce.

"Yeah, well, I guess we all live our parent's legacy. I guess that's why you don't have any future plans." Sarah said as she gestured back over her shoulder.

"What does that mean?" Hope asked.

"You know," Sarah continued to point over her shoulder. In the back of the room was the fireplace and, on the mantel between two photographs, was the urn.

Finally, Hope grasped what Sarah was pointing at. "You mean my Mom's ashes? I never think about them. They are just … there."

"That has got to be creepy. I mean, you know, with the way she died, and all."

"What do you mean?" Hope asked.

"Suicide," Sarah whispered. "I guess that would affect how you see the future, you know, making plans and all."

Hope didn't say anything. No one did. No one had much to say after that. The silence was broken when Meredith's mother arrived to drive her and Sarah home. Hope was left alone in the front room, alone with the urn of her mother's ashes. She sat down at the piano and began playing scales staring at the urn.

She sat staring at it for more than an hour. The sun went down and the room was filled with darkness. Still she sat. Barely audible, she muttered, under her breath. "Suicide?"

Dinner that night was unusual. Attempts by her father and Granny to engage Hope in conversation were futile, but they accepted the moods of a pre-adolescent girl, and they were not particularly concerned by her distance. For her part, she felt an unreal disconnection from her environment as if she were observing the scene rather than being there. She sat quietly eating supper but, inside, her head were flashing images of her mother's death. However, the images were brief and disconnected. She could remember blood on the bathroom floor, a limp forearm hanging out of the tub, more blood dripping from the side of the tub, the white and black patterns on the linoleum floor disturbed by spots of blood, drips of blood from the long black hair hanging out of the tub. There was some sort of audio memory, too; some sort of guttural noise coming from her father that she could not make out and, even now, she could not recall except to recognize the sense of alarm directed, she thought, at her. Looking back, it seemed only to be a generalized bedlam. It had been a long time since she had recalled these images and, now, as they invaded her consciousness, she sat quietly eating supper. Her father and grandmother carried on a normal conversation. Through the years, at no time did anyone ever suggest to her that her mother's death was a suicide. The thought had never entered her mind; yet, it made perfect sense. Suicide seemed to connect all the dots of her mental images of that day. Never once had her father told her, nor had her grandmother. Hope sat there watching them eat their supper and talking about the new grocery store and housing subdivision. Hope felt herself leaving the room and floating away, never sure if she would ever return.

She left the dinner table and went to bed early, but she didn't go to sleep for a long time. She had too many questions and memories, and she had some new way of seeing everything. For the first time in her life, she had questions that she had no idea how to answer. For the first time, she did not know what she felt – anger, hurt, fear. For the first time, there was no one she could talk to. In the past, there had always been her father or Granny Wheels, but no longer. They had become part of the questions rather than a source for answers. For the first time, she felt alone – deeply, profoundly alone. She was going to begin junior high school by viewing everything through the prism of her mother's suicide.

Paradoxes Never Lie

November 18, 1979

Red River High School, Nettie High School

"Mr. Bradley! Mr. Bradley! I don't understand this at all. It makes no sense to me. It's just stupid."

"Oh, Kara, you know better than that. Just because you don't understand, it doesn't mean that it is stupid. You'll figure it out. I promise. Let me see what you are doing."

Clark stepped out from behind his desk and walked over to Kara's desk. He looked at the paper on her desk. "Kara, you know better than this. You know exactly what you are doing wrong. Each side of the equal sign is ... what?"

She wrinkled her forehead. Each side of the equal sign is equal ... is the same thing ... is ... I don't know what you want."

"It isn't what I want. That is not the point. If you do something to one side, what do you have to do the other side?"

"Huh. What? If you do something to one side ... you have to do the same thing to the other side. I mean if you want to keep both sides equal."

"OK. OK." He lifted up his two hands in the form in front of her. "This hand equals this hand, the left equals the right. Now if I take three fingers from the left hand," he folded down three fingers. "What do I have to do to the right hand to keep the two hands equal?"

"Fold three fingers down. Duh. What does that have to do with this stupid problem?"

"Well, Kara, you have 5X and you want it to be just X on this side. What do you have to do to make it just X?"

She just stared at him. "If I knew that I wouldn't need you, would I?"

Clark smiled. "You have a valid point there. Believe me, I don't think you really need me. Just think this out and you can get this on your own. What does 5X mean?"

"That there are five Xs, that X is five times, that five times X ... in this equation."

"So, how would you get rid of a five times?"

"Divide."

"Remember, you have to do it on both sides to keep it equal."

"So 5X divided by 5 is X and 20 divided by 5 is 4? X is 4?"

"How does that sound to you?"

"Is that all there is? That's easy."

"Well, that is only part of the problem, but it seems to be the part you are having trouble with."

"Hey. Bradley. Little help here. What do you do if it ain't even?" Max asked.

"Oh, Max. You're such a charmer."

"Mr. Bradley, my Dad said you were a Hippie," Tony from the back of the room spoke up. Clark ignored him, but Tony insisted, "Well, were you? Were you a Hippie?"

"I don't know, Tony. I guess it depends on how you define the term. What exactly is a hippie." As he spoke he moved to the front of the room and gestured to have the papers passed forward.

"Oh you know what a Hippie is: long hair, drugs, bell-bottom pants, protests marches, the whole thing," Tony said.

Clark collected papers and looked at the class, "I wore bell-bottoms and tie-dyed shirts, I had long hair and even a beard, drugs were never a part of my resume but I marched—a lot: ergo, I was a Hippie."

The class looked at each other and a general uneasiness seemed to fill the room. Clark spoke out, "I participated in quite a few anti-war meetings and marches, but I was in close contact with the FBI. You could say I was a Hippie for the FBI."

"You're kidding me," Tony said.

"No, not at all. Many of the people in the movement, the Hippies, were working for the FBI. At a meeting sometimes half the people would be FBI."

"I don't believe you," it was Max who spoke out.

"OK, don't believe me; I do not feel a need to convince you of anything. But I'm telling you, we, the FBI guys, we invented the peace sign, you know the two fingers. We would use it at a meeting to signal to each other."

The rest of the class was beginning to pay attention.

109

"When everyone started using the two fingers, you know it became cool, we had to switch to just one finger in a defiant manner. Hence the invention of what you call, the bird."

Patricia spoke out, "Now you are just putting us on."

"Really? You think so? Could be," he said.

Calvin, the class cynic, spoke out, "Even he doesn't believe half of what he says."

"Well, Calvin, you are wrong. I mean everything I say, I just don't always say everything I mean."

"What does that mean?" Max practically shouted.

"He is just screwing with our minds. It is like a riddle," Patricia said.

"I prefer to think of it as a paradox," Clark responded. I like paradoxes. Paradoxes never lie. Keep that in mind when we study imaginary numbers."

Suddenly, the bell rang and class was over. Clark moved to the front of the room.

"Try your best on the homework. I think you will be able to figure out the answers with the textbook and a little bit of effort on your part. Max, I think you need to look over the problem more carefully. If you need help, I'll be here after school and before school, and we will go over this in class tomorrow before we have a test."

Everyone left class and Clark was left alone. He smiled. That was his remedial class. He thought he would hate teaching them but, instead, he found them delightful, much to his surprise. Sometimes, they seemed really dense, but usually they just resisted thinking mathematically. It was as if they had a mental block against it. One particular student, Jack, was so burned out on math that he had trouble understanding even the simplest concept. Clark relaxed and let Jack slowly come around, and he hoped by the end of the year that he would have Jack solving word problems in the textbook. Right now, he would settle if Jack would do even one homework assignment. Still, he found Jack to be personable and kind of charming in his ignorance. No, Clark did not mind teaching this class at all.

Right now, he had to go down to the office and pick up the work sheets for his calculus class that the aide had run off for him. He noticed a police car parked in front of the school as he entered the office, and he noticed the police officer walking into Ralph's office.

"What's up?" he asked the secretary.

She just shrugged her shoulders.

Clark took his worksheets from the workroom and headed to his room when Ralph and the policeman passed him by walking briskly in the same direction.

"You can stay in your office, and I can get the boy if you want," the officer said.

Ralph just shook his head, "No. I'll do it."

"Well, we could have him sent to your office and meet him there."

"You don't understand, this is my responsibility, my job. I've known that boy for at least the three years that he has been in my high school, under my ... supervision. There is no one else that I would allow ... I don't care how hard it is. I should be the one to tell him."

Ralph spoke as he bounded the stairs to the second floor, and Clark couldn't hear anything else that was said. He saw Ralph enter A210, the room two doors down from his own classroom, and he saw Ralph put his arm around Sam Barnett as he escorted him into the hallway away from the door. Sam was a senior on the football team and a good head taller than Ralph. Suddenly, Sam faced Ralph and let out an audible groan that echoed through the hall and could be heard in the classrooms of A hall. Then, Sam started to collapse like a human accordion, sobbing hysterically. He would have fallen to the floor, but Ralph held him up. Ralph whispered into Sam's ear. Sam nodded his head. Gradually, he regained control and his strength returned enough for him to walk down the hall and down the stairs. Clark watched them walk by and could see Sam's tears and the obvious pain on his face. He wanted to reach out to Sam, but had no idea what to say or how to comfort such anguish nor had he any idea the source of the pain. Clark was shaken and as he returned to his desk to organize his papers, he couldn't lose the image of Sam collapsing in Ralph's arms. He wondered what could have caused Sam's reaction.

By the end of the period, nearly all of the students knew the answer to Clark's question. There were students in the office, there were students in the downstairs hallway, and there were students in the classroom. All of them heard enough to develop their version of what had happened. One student who was a neighbor of Sam's had the presence of mind to call home to talk to his mother for the true story.

As the students shuttled into calculus class, all of them were chattering about the events of the previous period. Clark picked up from the noise that Sam's father had committed suicide. Rumors were circulating that the father had used a shotgun in the living room, hung himself in the garage, used a pistol in the kitchen, and sliced his wrists in the bathtub. Some were sure that the suicide was a complete surprise while others felt that it was expected because the father was so depressed. Still others felt that the police thought it might be murder and that's why the police were there. It was due to the mother wanting a divorce; it was due to the father's gambling debts; it was due to business failures; it was due to the father's mental illness; it was due to the father being an alcoholic while others said drug addict.

Clark tried to get the class quiet and tried to teach, but they were having none of that. Today, they were too wound up, too busy grinding out rumors for him to get control.

Then, the intercom clicked on and Ralph spoke to the entire school:

"Students, may I have your attention? Something has happened today, something has happened to one of your classmates, something terrible and tragic. I know many of you have heard all sorts of rumors about what has happened to Sam Barnett. There will be time next week to separate the rumors from the truth. Today and for the rest of the week, there is only one thing you … we need to know. One of your classmates, one of your teammates, one of your fellow students is … hurting … and that person needs all the support we can give him. I trust that you will keep that in mind with all that you do in the next 24 hours. Sam needs our support … and prayers. I propose that we now have one moment of silence in Sam's honor." There was a long, silent moment. The student's looked around the room at each other, but none of them spoke, and after the silence when Ralph ended his announcement and returned the students to class, they listened to Clark's instruction.

The rest of the day, students were subdued and polite. A collection for Sam was started during lunch although no one was sure what was going to be done with the money. At the end of the day, Clark stuffed his papers into his briefcase and headed home. He pulled into the driveway of the elementary school to pick up Maggie. He helped her out of the wheelchair and into the car.

"I heard you had a traumatic day," Maggie said.

"You heard," Clark said. "I don't know how a kid can handle something like that. It was really something I'll never forget – watching this big macho kid crying like a baby. But, I'll tell you something, I have a new respect for Ralph. He handled Sam with grace and gentleness and said the right things. Then, he came on the intercom and established the right attitude in the school. He was brilliant. I don't know anyone else who could have done what he did today. He really met the needs of the student body as well as the faculty."

"I've known that family for years," Maggie said.

"I guess we should go over and see them, especially you," Clark said.

"Actually, you need to see Sam more than I do, but we both need to go over for the family, but not now. Right now, they have plenty of support. But, next week or the week after that, they will need help then. After the shock wears off ... when the reality hits and no one else is around. Then, we will go see them."

An Existential Love Song

November 1968

San Francisco, California

About 1,760 miles from the Red River

He went about his usual schedule of classes. She sat around the apartment all day. He cooked a meal or two, brought in a pizza and Chinese, she cooked a meal or two. They took turns washing the dishes. Conversation was minimal – polite yet unobtrusive. Two weeks passed like that when he came back from class and found her sitting at the table with a pile of crumbled sheets of paper in front of her. Her head was on the table. When he walked in, she bolted up and he could tell from her eyes that she had been crying.

He said nothing as was his policy. She stared at him. He looked back and sat across the table. "Would you like a neck rub?" he asked. She shook her head. "Are you sure? I am a champion neck rubber. I've won blue ribbons." Before she could reply, he was behind her rubbing her neck. He kept rubbing her neck gently while her eyes closed and she leaned back. The simple gesture, without any words, the gentle touch of his hands broke some barrier and melted her reserve.

"This feels really good," she almost purred. After a long period of silent reverie, she spoke, "I'm pregnant. I have been trying to write my mother and tell her. How do you disappoint someone you love? How do you destroy her dreams?"

Clark didn't say anything, but he gently moved his hands down and expanded the massage to her shoulders and the base of her neck. She let her head roll in his hands and her breaths came deeply as she spoke quietly. "I need to write her, but the words won't come to me. You see, my mother and I have a very special ... a very different kind of relationship. My mother is in a wheelchair. She is paralyzed from the waist down; a terrible accident when she was pregnant with me, early in the pregnancy. All she has lived for is me. She raised me to be free and independent. All the things she had lost. My going away to college meant victory ... for both of us. Now this. I don't know what I'm going to do. I don't know how she will take it. I just don't know. I feel like I've just stomped on her dreams."

Clark stopped rubbing her neck and walked around to sit across from her at the table. "I know that it is none of my business, and if you want me to shut up I will. I think you know I will, but I think I can help."

"I have to admit," she looked at him, perhaps for the first time today. "The neck rub was a good idea. Yeah, a really great idea."

"I am a math major, and I find most people make a common mistake in math and I find that people often make the same mistake in life. They become overwhelmed by the variables."

She looked at him without blinking. He continued, "What you need to do is breathe and focus on each variable, each problem, one at a time."

She didn't move, but continued to listen intently. He leaned forward, "It appears that you have already dealt with the first problem, the really big problem, you have decided to have the child rather than have an abortion. Do I understand you correctly?"

She nodded. "I thought about it. I even had an appointment. But, I just couldn't. I just walked away. That's when I ran into you at the coffee shop."

"How do you feel about the decision?"

"Good. If that's the right word. It is the right decision."

"Well," he pulled out a piece of paper from the desktop. "I guess the next question is ... adoption. Have you considered adoption?"

"No. Maybe. I doubt it." She took a deep breath. "I can't imagine going through with the pregnancy and giving the baby away, but ... I guess, I don't want to rule it out."

"I don't guess you have to decide that right now. So, what do you need to decide right now? What are the real issues facing you?"

"I have to tell my mother. I'll have to drop out. And I just hate the idea of going home pregnant. I'd feel like such a failure."

"Do you need to drop out? When are you due?"

"Late April. I guess I could finish this semester. I've only missed a couple of classes so far."

"Why can't you enroll next semester? Seems to me that in the worst-case scenario, you might have to take incompletes and finish the classes in the summer. And you might not have to do that, depending on the class."

"It all sounds good, too good." She was obviously thinking it over, but was troubled. "But, there are too many obstacles, too many problems."

"I'm sure there will be problems. Some you can't anticipate, but I know you well enough to believe that you can overcome each of them as they come up. It is worth a try, and you don't seem to be the kind of person who quits without trying."

She just shook her head.

"Well, it is certainly up to you. You don't have to do it alone. You have all your friends, all the people in the movement."

"I'm pretty much a loner – even in the movement, I stick to myself. Besides, I wouldn't feel right using people."

"You have me. You'll have me. And it is just not a sin to let friends help. The movement is about people if it is about anything."

"There are just too many issues."

He nodded. "Like what? Let's take each issue, one issue at a time. What is the first issue?"

She swallowed and rubbed her hands nervously. "I don't know … I'll have to leave the dorm. Where will I stay?"

"You can stay here."

She looked around the apartment. She stared at him. "I barely know you … no, I couldn't."

"OK," he nodded. "It's up to you. But you could."

November 12, 1968

He was sitting on the couch with a stack of folded laundry besides him and a basket full of fresh laundry in front of him on the floor. She entered with textbooks in her arms and a notebook full of papers. She shoved them onto her shelf on the bookcase.

She watched him. "I hate when you do the laundry and fold my underwear."

He nodded. "What a coincidence."

"To tell the truth," she shivered. "I feel kinda creepy."

"Me too."

"Next week, I do it," she insisted.

"Absolutely. That's the agreement," he nodded vigorously. "I wouldn't have it any other way. I need to spend some time in the library next week. You'll be done with your research by then, right?"

"Right."

"Look," Clark turned toward her. "You don't have to feel that you aren't doing your share. In fact, if anything, I'm getting the better part of the deal."

"OK ... I know. It's just I'm a little sensitive on this issue. It's important to me."

"The hard part for me is that I don't want you to feel that I'm taking advantage while I still give you ... respect, you know, dignity. Let you carry your share of the load fairly."

She nodded, "Just treat me like a guy roommate."

"Well, I wouldn't have any problem taking advantage of a guy."

She laughed. "I doubt that." She walked to the refrigerator and got an apple, took a big bite, and asked him if he wanted one. He nodded yes, and she tossed him one. He took a bite and continued folding clothes between bites. She took another bite and leaned against the refrigerator, staring at him before she spoke. "How would you treat me if we were lovers?"

"What do you mean?" he did not look up from the laundry.

"Would you still try to be fair or would you try to take advantage?"

"Oh, I would try to take advantage. Definitely."

"I mean about the chores and stuff." She stopped chewing.

"Hmmm," he stared at his apple. "That is a good question."

"It deserves a good answer."

He looked at her. He took a last bite of the apple and stood up. He walked over to her and took her apple core and put both of them into the garbage. He went back to the couch and sat down. "It does deserve a good answer, but not from me. Any answer I would give would just be words. You will have to provide the answer based on how you know me, how I act, how I am, not on anything I say."

She was stunned, but nodded reluctantly.

"You got some free time tonight?" he asked.

"What've you got in mind?"

"The Third Eye has a talent contest tonight. I thought I'd sponsor you — it's like five bucks — and we could split any winnings. Could be a hundred."

"I'd never win."'

"I've heard you. You're very good."

"I'm too political."

"So, don't sing anything political."

"You are asking me to sell out." She waved her arms in a dramatic gesture. "Compromise my artistic vision."

"Well," Clark thought about how to state his case. "You could use the money."

"Seriously, then my music would be something it isn't. It comes from a place inside of me — for me. I wouldn't want to adjust to an *audience*."

"Look at it this way: I am willing to spend five dollars to hear you play. Any song you want to sing. I like it that much."

"OK, I'll get my guitar," she said. "We probably have time to get a slice of pizza on the way. My treat, or I don't go."

He nodded.

She was the fifth contestant that night, and three followed her. The others all sang versions of popular songs – Dylan and Baez knockoffs with a Beatles mixed in and some traditional folk songs. She sang an intense version of "The Patriot Game." During round two, she sang a rousing version of "Union Maid" and she was invited back for the final round. The first finalist sang an almost rock version of "So Long, It's Been Good to Know You" with incredible guitar riffs between each verse and audience participation on each chorus. The rafters were still ringing when Grace took her place before the mike. She gently strummed her guitar, barely audible, and launched into her song with a voice like a crystal bell, each note piercing the silence:

"The water is wide, I cannot cross o'er.

And neither have I wings to fly.

Give me a boat that can carry two.

And both shall row, my love and I."

She stared out over the audience:

"There is a ship and she sails the sea.

She's loaded deep, as deep can be.

But not as deep as the love I'm in.

I know not if I sink or swim."

She closed her eyes, and raised her voice, leaning back away from the mike:

"I lean'd my back up against an oak.

Thinking it was a trusty tree.

But first it bended and then it broke.

Thus did my love prove false to me."

She reopened her eyes and lifted the guitar up to the mike and played an instrumental bridge before looking at Clark as she finished the song in full voice:

"The water is wide, I cannot cross o'er.

And neither have I wings to fly.

Give me a boat that can carry two.

And both shall row, my love and I."

She sat down to loud, enthusiastic applause. "That was … great," he said.

"Thanks," she nodded. "It was as good as I could do."

"Every note was perfect. I mean, it was pure. You know?"

"I knew I wasn't going to win. 'Rambling Woody' was great. He deserves to win. I just wanted to do something … I don't know – honest. You know?"

The owner of the club announced the winner and Grace did come in second place; she won ten dollars. On the walk home, she let Clark carry the guitar.

"That last song ..." Clark started to say something but he didn't know how to finish his sentence.

"Yes?" she asked.

"It was really ... good."

"You've never heard it before?"

"No. No, I've heard it before, but I've never listened to it before. You know? It is an existential love song." He pushed up against her so that his shoulder brushed hers.

"Yeah, I know what you mean," she nodded and took a few steps. "Actually, I have no idea what you meant. In fact I don't think I have ever used existential in a sentence before, at least not in reference to a folk song."

"When then?"

"Just to impress someone...you know, vocabulary. You are the only person I know who would actually use it in a sentence."

She laughed and put her head on his shoulder as they walked.

He put his arm around her. "I told you I had moves."

"So you did. But, this evening, my dear, has been my move."

The Newest Level of Dante's Inferno: Junior High School

September 5, 1982

Bowie Junior High School, Nettie, Texas

Still about 50 miles from the Red River

At 2 a.m., no one was awake on a school night. Hope knew this and counted on it. She woke and slowly adjusted to the low light level. Soon, she got out of bed and stepped quietly to the door. She walked into the living room and began a nightly ritual that had been going on since July 12th. First, she took her mother's ashes down from the mantle. She sat on the couch with the urn between her legs and stared. She moved the urn around slowly and rubbed it very slowly, but mostly she just kept her eyes focused on it. There had been some nights when tears would form and roll down her cheeks and, on other nights, a solitary tear would mark the end of her solemn ritual. However, tonight, she did not cry; instead, she just sat in some sort of stupefied state. Did a half hour pass or was it only 15 minutes or maybe it was even an hour? Hope was never sure. She finally put the morose yet sacred vessel back in place and went back to bed.

The next morning, Clark was pouring freshly brewed coffee he had made as Granny Wheeler served some scrambled eggs and toast. Hope appeared at the doorway to the kitchen. Granny noticed her first, and silently tapped Clark as he put the coffee pot on the table. He looked at Granny but didn't speak, grabbing a magazine, a journal article he was reading. "You want the usual cereal and fruit?" he asked.

"Yes," Hope said.

She was dressed in black Converse tennis shoes, black leggings, black T-shirt, black vest, black nail polish, and her hair was newly dyed black instead of her usual light brunette. Perhaps most blatant in her appearance was the fact that her hair was combed down, covering her face completely.

"I better peel the banana for you," Clark offered, "because I'm not sure you can see it today."

"I can see just fine," Hope said defensively. "Just fine."

"OK."

Unlike Clark, a simple OK was not enough for Granny. "Don't you think we could have a little explanation?"

"Excuse me. Explanation for what?"

"Your ... how you look. You have to admit you look a little different today."

"What is the big deal? I just felt like dressing this way. Let's not make a federal case out of it."

Granny was clearly stunned and wasn't sure what to say next, "It's just that ... I'm pretty sure you are breaking some sort of school dress code."

Clark stepped in. "Are you breaking any school rules?"

"No. What rule? I can't wear black? I don't think so. I can't color my hair? Tell that to all the blondes at school. Please. What rule am I breaking?"

"Sounds like you have thought this out, and you've made your decision. You figure the possible consequences?" Clark asked.

"What can they do?"

"Hope," Granny's tone was one of tenderness. "I just want you … to be sure. It's not just about the school, you know … the teachers and principal. In fact, it's not about them hardly at all. It's mostly about the other kids. How are the other kids going to react? The bus ride is going to be really long if you get on looking like you … haunt houses on the weekend."

"Granny, this is who I am. I can't change because other people don't like me," she said but there was a lump in her throat as she hugged her grandmother.

Granny responded, "This may be who you are today, but it might not be who you are tomorrow."

"I guess I could comb my hair back, but I'm keeping it black and I won't change my clothes."

"It's up to you," Clark replied.

"Good. Your eyes are too pretty to hide," Granny said, which only produced a groan from Hope.

She grabbed her lunchbox and books and left for the school bus. Clark got his briefcase and helped Granny get into the passenger side of the car. He would drive her to the elementary school before he would go to the high school. Then, he would pick her up on his way home. She would have to stay later than the rest of the staff, but that inconvenience was more than compensated by the fact she always finished the mountain of paperwork of a school nurse and the fact that Clark could always help her get in and out of the car while managing the wheelchair not that she couldn't do it herself. She had for years before Clark and Hope had moved in with her, but it was becoming more difficult as she became older, and it was nice having help. On the ride to school, Granny spoke first about the events of the morning, "You know you will be getting a call from Mrs. Martin this morning."

"Hope's counselor?"

"Oh yes."

"Hope really isn't breaking any rules, is she?"

"Probably not. Maybe. Sort of. She is being different. That is always against some rule. There is a general rule – dress code always fits under it – anything that interferes with the learning environment. They'll try to get her on that."

"That's nonsense."

"Nonetheless. You will be getting the call. Mark my word. And Clark ..."

"Yes." He was not at all sure he wanted to hear what she was going to tell him.

"It is probably not in Hope's best interest to communicate that you think they are all complete idiots."

"Even if they are."

"Especially if they are."

"As I go through life, a truism I have discovered is that all important decisions are made by people whose ability to make wise decisions are suspect, to say the least."

During the summer, Hope had requested that she ride the bus with her friends. Now, as she got on the bus, she did not sit on the left rear with the popular seventh grade girls across the aisle from the popular boys nor did she sit in the middle left with the other less popular girls who were still socially active in the school. Hope chose to sit in the front, right behind the driver – away from everyone else. Sarah looked up as Hope got on the bus; she was laughing at Ricky and another guy across the aisle. She tried to get Hope's attention, but gave up as soon as it was clear that Hope wasn't looking in her direction. Meredith did not give up so quickly. She asked – out loud – for Hope to sit with her. She pointed out that she was holding a seat, but Hope put her head down and slunk into her seat. No one sat around her as the bus made its rounds to school. The closest anyone came was Jeremy Dowd, an overweight, eighth grade social reject with greasy hair and perpetually dirty clothes. He sat in the row behind her, but he never talked to her. He knew better.

When the bus arrived, the students shuffled into the school. Some went to the band hall and some to the choir room, a few went to tutoring, but most went straight to their locker or the cafeteria. Few of the eighth and ninth graders stayed in the hallway. They felt more comfortable in the cafeteria where there was an eighth grade table and a ninth grade table. The seventh graders had an arrangement much more complex. They split along gender. The girls always wanted to be where the boys were and the boys always wanted to be where the girls were although neither group was conscious of their choice and certainly did not want the other group to be aware of their choice. They would both deny this arrangement if it were to be pointed out. Hope, on the other hand, would get off the bus and head straight for her first period class.

The teacher was not there. He never was. Hope sat in the last seat in the last row right next to the window. The teacher was a coach, and when he finally showed up, he was accompanied by a bevy of football players and a girl or two. No one noticed Hope. Hope spent most of first period looking out the window or reading her textbook. The teacher was slightly intimidated by Hope. She never raised her hand, but when he did call on her, she would answer the question as briefly and completely as possible. She had never missed a question on a test. She had the highest grade possible without any extra credit, and she wasn't going to do any extra work. He was pretty sure she knew more history than he did.

Second period was science and she didn't need to stop by her locker most days because all the materials she needed were in the class. She was the first one in the room and took her place at her table pulling out the materials she needed for the lab for the day, an experiment on electrical circuits and batteries. By the time her partners arrived, everything was set. First, Ben showed up. He was quiet and merely stupid.

"Thanks," he said. "You always have everything ready when we get here. We never have to do anything."

"That's the general idea," she replied with little acknowledgement of Ben's attempt at politeness. Ben did not know what to say to Hope and had no idea how to react to her.

By then, Michael, the third partner, made his presence felt. He threw a kiss at a girl in the back row and a mock punch at the guy behind him. He turned to his partners, "Hiya, Ben. Hope, when you gonna let me make you smile?" He laughed. Hope ignored him. "Jesus," he went on, "I hate this class. At these tables, you can't sleep and ol' man Hinds – what an ass!"

"I like Mr. Hinds," Hope responded to Michael and immediately wished she hadn't. "He isn't too bad. He actually makes me think sometimes. He asks questions that require something other than memorization, at least, in class. The tests are still pretty easy if you read the textbook, do the homework, or actually pay attention in class."

"Sure, if you do any of those things, but in science class ... who's gonna do any of those things?" Michael looked up and down at Hope like she was some sort of specimen in a lab. "No one except some like you. I mean, not any real people that I know."

Hope guessed that he wanted to hurt her feelings, but she didn't want to acknowledge that possibility. Beside she knew that over half the class felt the same way as Michael. She shrugged her shoulders, and turned back to her work

"I never understand any of this crap ... if it wasn't for you Hope, I don't know what I'd do."

"Fail, I would imagine," she replied.

"Come here let me give you a big bear hug as a thank you." Michael said as he tried to hug her. She gave him the type of glance that even he knew better than to test, as if he were a rotten specimen in some sort of a jar. "OK, OK," He turned away. ""Geez, never knew anybody so touchy."

She continued with the assignment, connecting a wire to a battery and then to a bell and a switch. At one point, she asked Ben to help by holding the wire down as she pinned the other end to the board. She never again acknowledged Michael.

Mr. Hinds made his way around the room checking on each group's project. Hope's was flawless as usual. Mr. Hinds asked, "Did Michael contribute anything to this project?"

"Yes sir, I sure did," Michael was quick to answer for fear that Hope would tell the truth. "I mean, Hope did all the actual work – the soldering and connecting – but I, we, Ben and me, we did a lot of the research."

"Is that right?" Mr. Hinds asked Hope.

There was a long silence and every eye in the room was on Hope. She looked at Mr. Hinds and she looked at Ben and Michael. She stared for a long time before she spoke, "They did their part; they provided … inspiration." Everyone broke out laughing and the tension in the room was lifted.

Mr. Hinds shook his head and went onto the other groups until the end of the class and it was time to clean up. He detained Hope as she was leaving the class, "Why did you cover for Michael?"

Hope didn't give a response. She just sort of looked towards the rest of the class as they walked out. Mr. Hinds nodded.

In the hallway, at her locker, Michael waited for Hope. "Thanks for covering for me … I wasn't sure if you would … I'm …" Between depositing papers and extracting notebooks, Hope gave him another withering glance, but he wouldn't give up, "If I can do something for you …"

"Do not … do not even begin to think that … I did that for you." She slammed her locker shut. "If I could get you in trouble and get you dropped from school, I'd do it in a minute."

"I don't get you, just when I think there ... that you might be capable of being a real ..."

"Oh, shut up and go away. I do not ever want to talk to you. It is painful to acknowledge your existence." She turned briskly into her third period class: Math.

Math was her last sanctuary for the day. The teacher, Mrs. Bryles, had been teaching for about thirty years and did everything the old-fashioned way. Seating was done alphabetically, so Hope sat in the front row two seats from the end. She was denied a view out the window, but at least she did not have to deal with the consequences of choosing not to sit next to Sarah or Meredith, who were both in the same class. No one sitting next to her asked to copy her homework, and she felt the freedom that academic anonymity brought. Every day in math class was the same and, although it was boring, she felt comfortable in the isolation and insulation of routine.

Today was different. She was handed a call slip requiring her presence in the counselor's office immediately. At first, she put it aside thinking she would take care of it later in language arts class where nothing ever happens of value, but Mrs. Bryles pointed out that the call slip said immediately and she would have to go. Hope stood up to leave.

"Better take your books and papers, just in case," Mrs. Bryles said.

Hope picked them up wondering if there really was an emergency if something happened to Granny Wheels or maybe even her father. Did Mrs. Bryles know something that she didn't know? She began to feel a little panicky as she walked through the halls a little faster than she normally would to get to the counselor's office.

Mrs. Martin, the school counselor, had her office on the end of the hallway on the second floor. Hope had seen her two or three times since school started – every time Mrs. Martin had initiated the contact to check on Hope's schedule. There had been some confusion because Hope had changed her mind about cheerleading and band, dropping out of both before classes really began.

"Every schedule change in junior high has a ripple effect," Mrs. Martin said.

Hope liked Mrs. Martin but in a polite, distant way. She did not feel that Mrs. Martin was a good counselor, but she was certainly a competent schedule changer. But, then, she wasn't sure what a good counselor would look like.

When Hope got to Mrs. Martin's office, she was shocked at what she found. Mrs. Martin's chair was facing an empty chair, obviously meant for Hope, and on one side, the left, was Sarah sitting in a chair and Meredith on the right side sitting in another chair.

Mrs. Martin gestured toward the empty chair, and spoke, "Your friends and I have been very worried about you, and we wanted to share our concerns with you. We thought this would be the best place to talk to you."

Hope moved behind the empty chair and stood still. She glared at Sarah, Meredith, and Mrs. Martin with equal intensity.

"I do not like this. I do not want this." She stood stiff like a cat about to pounce, gripping the back of the chair. "I don't have to put up with this. You have no right to …"

Meredith began to cry, and Hope pivoted toward her, and a flicker of sympathy prevented her from lurching at Meredith.

Mrs. Martin spoke with an even modulated voice, as softly as possible in an attempt to calm Hope and lower the emotional temperature. "You are right, of course. You do not have to participate. We cannot force you in any way." She shook her head and hands back and forth.

"We do not want to make you to do or say anything you do not want to do, but we hope you will listen … and let us listen if you wish to speak. We are here because we care. There is simply no other reason than to show you that we care."

As Mrs. Martin spoke, Hope studied the faces of Sarah and Meredith. She relaxed the muscles in her back, and moved to the front of the chair and sat down. "All right," she sighed. "What do you want?"

Sarah and Meredith were going to take turns but ended up speaking almost at once.

"We used to be the best of friends," Sarah started.

"We did everything together," Meredith picked up.

"Went swimming. Played games."

"Talked. Shared dreams. Planned our future."

"Had sleepovers. Ate your grandmother's brownies."

"Horseback rides."

"Movies downtown."

"Picking up guys at the theater," Sarah added.

"More like trying to pick up guys," Meredith corrected her.

"Sarah's first pizza."

"Meredith's first kiss."

By now, Hope's head had been turning back and forth so fast that everyone had to giggle, even Hope.

"But, now," Meredith began to sob between words. "You won't have anything to do with us. You won't sit on the bus with either of us."

"You won't talk to me in any of our classes. You won't even talk to us in the hallway," Sarah said.

"You won't sit next to us in any class," Meredith looked to Sarah for confirmation with a head nod. "You won't even sit with us at lunch."

"I know you will deny this, but I think you dropped cheerleaders because you didn't want to be around me," Sarah dropped her eyes and exposed a glimpse of vulnerability she usually denied.

A silence followed after the deluge of complaints.

Hope hung her head and slowly raised it, "That's not true … about the cheerleader thing," She spoke so softly that it seemed less like a denial than a confession to the other accusations.

No one moved. No one said anything. Hope stared at the floor.

A loud, anguished sob came from Meredith. "What did we do?"

Hope squirmed in her chair and started to speak but didn't know what to say. "You didn't ... It's not you ..." She tried, but she couldn't look Sarah or Meredith in the eye.

Another uncomfortable silence was gently interrupted by Mrs. Martin, "Hope. Can you help us understand?"

Hope took a deep breath and focused on Mrs. Martin. She stiffened her back and raised herself into the chair until she was sitting upright. She braced herself. "Friends are supposed to trust each other, and I can't trust them anymore."

"What?" Sarah reacted harshly. She was not expecting this.

Meredith, true to form, sobbed, "What did we do? How did we ..."

"Mrs. Martin, I found out this summer that my mother committed suicide, and I found out this summer that my friends, my so-called best friends knew," she looked at Sarah and then at Meredith.

"I bet you talked about it and talked about it behind by back countless times. Did you say my mother was crazy? Did you wonder if I was crazy?"

Meredith just sobbed and sobbed louder, while Sarah spoke out, "Honest to God, I thought you knew. Everyone knew. I mean, it wasn't anything we ever talked about behind your back … nothing like that. But, I thought you knew."

"So did I," Meredith finally managed to speak. "I would never … I didn't talk to you about it because … I mean, I didn't think you wanted to talk about it."

"It's not like a subject we would bring up. You know, if you wanted to talk about it … but we wouldn't bring it up," Sarah's voice sounded pleading, but sincere even to Hope.

"Mrs. Martin, my mother committed suicide." she gestured at both Sarah and Meredith. "They have both known for years; I just found out this summer. Mrs. Martin. My mother committed suicide, and they knew. I have difficulty looking at them or talking to them. I wonder about every time we talked and stuff.… I mean, how often did they think about my mother's suicide? Was it a cloud always hanging over our heads?"

"Of course not," Sarah said with disdain.

"Well, it is now," Hope responded. "I can't think of anything else."

Mrs. Martin nodded her head. "Hope, it doesn't sound like there is anything Sarah or Meredith can do."

Hope looked at Mrs. Martin and furrowed her brow.

"I mean," Mrs. Martin spoke very deliberately. "Your mother's suicide does not seem to be an issue to Sarah or Meredith, but you believe that it is. How can they prove to you that it isn't?"

Hope sat motionless. She was stunned at the quiet logic of Mrs. Martin's statement.

"Do you think ... maybe ... you could give them a chance?" Mrs. Martin almost whispered. A long silence followed before she spoke again, "Maybe you could take a chance and learn to trust them again?"

Hope waited before she slowly nodded yes.

"Will you eat at our lunch table today?" Meredith asked.

Hope nodded yes. Meredith took two steps and hugged Hope. "I have missed you so much," she cried.

Sarah joined in with a hug and the three hugged in the middle of the room around Hope's chair.

"Why don't the two of you go back to class? I want to talk to Hope a little longer before I send her back to class." Mrs. Martin said.

Meredith and Sarah picked up their backpacks and said goodbye, but with promises of talking to Hope later in the hallway and at lunch. Hope nodded yes and smiled weakly.

After they left, Mrs. Martin turned toward Hope, smiling, but Hope stared at the floor at first, then she looked up at Mrs. Martin. She was never quite sure which started first, but tears slowly began to flow from Hope's eyes and she began to tremble. Soon, the trembling escalated into shaking and, when the shaking reached the maximum intensity, a very guttural, primal gasping, grunting sound emitted from Hope's throat – a scream of pain rather than fear. Hope sat there gasping for air, crying, and shaking, and nothing Mrs. Martin could do would comfort her or end her convulsions of agony. Finally, after holding her and hugging her, Hope collapsed into simple tears. Mrs. Martin put her back into the chair and let her breathe. Hope looked at her with horrible eyes of pain, but no words of explanation. Mrs. Martin knew better than to ask for any. Hope pulled her legs up to her chest and turned sideways in the chair. She sat in a fetal position, still breathing in gasp of air between sobs.

Mrs. Martin walked into the outer office, picked up her secretary's phone, and called the high school. "Let me talk to Mr. Bradley right now. It is an emergency. I'll wait. Get him out of class. Now!" Several minutes passed during which time Mrs. Martin checked on Hope several times. She moved to the sofa at the back of the office and was asleep with her back toward the door. Finally, Clark was brought to the phone, "This is Clark Bradley. What is going on?"

"This is Mrs. Martin, Hope's counselor. You need to come and get her, right now. She is having – well, I guess had is more accurate – a nervous breakdown. She is asleep in my office right now."

"What? What are you talking about?"

"Meredith and Sarah confronted Hope with their concerns today in my office and when they left, Hope started crying and shaking. She had a nervous breakdown."

Clark was skeptical. "Meredith and Sarah are her best friends. She has been friends with Meredith since she was five years old. Nerves don't really break down." He was sure that Mrs. Martin was reacting to the type of junior high drama innate to adolescent girls.

"Nervous breakdown may not be an accurate diagnosis clinically, but I am telling you she has spent the last ten minutes shaking and violently crying. And now she is essentially sleeping it off. You need to take her home."

"I'll be right there." He made arrangements in the office including calling Granny Wheeler and leaving a message. Then, he drove to the junior high to pick up Hope.

When he walked into Mrs. Martin's office, she nodded in the direction of Hope. Clark walked over and picked her up off the couch. She hung in his arms for a few tearful silent moments before he whispered, "Let's go home." She nodded, he put her on her feet, they walked to the car, and not a word was spoken. When they got home, she wanted to go to her room and sleep. He nodded. She collapsed on her bed. He checked on her and put a cover over her.

Wine, Willie and God

May 14, 1986

26 Red River Lane, Nettie, Texas

Maggie was on the front porch after dinner watching the sunset in the west off to the left, as she was every night. It was indeed her favorite ritual. Clark joined her. "It is going to be a beautiful night, not too hot, but not chilly either," he said as he gestured toward the sunset. "Can I get you something?"

"Tonight would be a good night for wine. After Hope leaves, why don't we drink a toast and have a nice red wine," she nodded as if she was affirming her proposal. "The prom is a special night for a girl in these parts."

"I know. Believe me, I know. It seems every year the second semester is divided into two unequal parts – before prom and after prom. First, there is all the drama about who is going with who, and then there is all the hoopla about who can outdo who."

"What do you mean … outdo each other?"

He raised his voice and became more physically animated. "There is this crazy competition on who can come up with the best way to ask their date to the prom. All sorts of creative shocking ways of asking for a date dominate consciousness even though it is seldom a surprise."

"Oh, those zany kids!"

"It is really a pain in the ass for teachers. The competition becomes more and more … ludicrous every year … I guess it's what passes for romance these days."

143

"I think it's kinda cute," Maggie spun her chair to face directly into the sun. "I like it when the cheerleaders do something at a basketball game, or when a guy comes from the audience at an assembly and ask a girl to the prom. Wait, haven't you put questions on a test that the answer was matching two people for the prom?"

"Guilty," he said with a sigh. "And I once hid a slide in a PowerPoint presentation that asked a girl to the prom. I'm not above such … *hijinks*. But as a faculty member, after so many years, it just gets old. You know what I mean?"

"I guess so," she spoke softly. "But, you know it is their only prom. I mean you have one every year for your entire career, but they are only seniors once."

"I guess you are right. I didn't even go to my prom."

"Why am I not surprised?" She laughed, "I bet you stayed home and played chess with your dad or worked on solving quadratic equations."

"You're not far from wrong. I was pretty much a nerd in high school. I just didn't see any of that as relevant. Everybody gets all dressed up, looks pretty, and looks grown-up," Clark reflected. "I guess that is the whole point. It is some sort of rite of passage to maturity."

"Especially for girls," Maggie added. "Especially for girls."

Clark was not prepared for Hope when she walked through the door onto the porch. Her dress was light blue chiffon that shimmered in the light, with a darker blue ribbon for a belt. Unlike most of the girls at Nettie High School, Hope wore straps although she certainly had the physical attributes to

144

support a strapless gown. Her cleavage was apparent. Her hair was luminous and hung down her neck and shoulders, but it was not straight. Rather, it was curled and had white ribbons and some subtle flowers intertwined in her locks. Any makeup was very subtle and highlighted her features, such as a hint of eye shadow.

Clark found himself breathless and had he been her date, he would not have been able to speak. He might not have even recognized her except she handed him the camera and began directing him to take pictures. So, he dumbly nodded and responded to the orders of the day to take pictures of Hope and her date, Justin who showed up shortly after she appeared on the porch.

Justin drove up in his pickup truck. When he walked up to the house, his hair was slicked down and he was wearing a white jacket with tails over his black vest and black tuxedo pants, and his black cowboy boots were so shiny as to look like patent leather. He was somewhat in a hurry because he had reservations for The Olive Garden and didn't want to be late. Justin was a senior and not the kind of guy who had many dates in high school. The idea that the Olive Garden was not the appropriate place for the prom meal or that a pickup truck was not the appropriate vehicle never occurred to Justin. Clark took several pictures, and helped Justin put the corsage on Hope's wrist. Justin helped Hope climb into his truck, and they took off for the Olive Garden and the prom – a night of awkward romance ahead.

Clark watched them drive off and disappeared into the house to return with a bottle of wine and two glasses. He poured a glass for Mrs. Wheeler and one for himself before he talked, "My God, she has become beautiful. And so grown up. How did that happen?"

"You blinked," Maggie took a long drink, "It happens. In case you haven't noticed, she has become, er, ah, a woman. And her beauty is not skin deep. She has become quite the musician – piano, violin, and now the guitar. She is very accomplished." Maggie took a long drink of her wine. "You know she is going off to the prom carrying on a hefty family tradition."

"Oh?"

"Grace and I both lost our virginity on our proms. I venture to say more than two thirds of the girls in this town lose their virginity on the prom, and the other third have already lost it. I told you the prom is really important to girls."

"Right," he took a long drink and swirled the wine around in his mouth. "And according to you, no one ever graduates a virgin."

"I exaggerate," she took another drink. "Besides what do I know? I'm just the school nurse."

He took a long drink of his wine. "You knew about Grace and Ralph?"

"Sure," she said. "She came to me for advice, but she had made up her mind long before the actual night. In fact, how do you think she got protection? You don't think Ralph would have thought of that, do you? He was too overwhelmed with gratitude to think straight."

"You bought your daughter condoms for her prom date?"

"Yah, the mattress in the back of the pickup was my idea, too. Those pickup beds are hard. They can really hurt the back. I speak with some experience."

Clark looked at his wine, took another drink, and pondered the whole situation. He knew Grace had lost her virginity to Ralph the night of her junior prom, but the idea that Maggie was somehow … a co-conspirator was hard for him to comprehend. Suddenly, a new concern jumped into his head, "Justin was in a pickup truck."

"Yeah, but there was no mattress … that I could see."

"I'm being silly, I don't think I have anything to worry about. Not with Justin."

"You're probably right. Justin is kind of rural, not really Hope's style." She lifted her glass as if to propose a toast. He poured her some more.

"I guess you haven't heard the Ballad of Justin and His Prom Date, Hope." He took another long drink. "All during the month … started maybe a month ago … Justin kept putting up signs around the school about a countdown until he asks his date to the prom … 15 days until Justin asks his date to the prom, 12 days … etc. At first, they were posters on the hallways that kept getting bigger and bigger.

"The last few days...maybe four or five, he rented one of those electric billboard signs and put it outside the school parking lot. Justin has money if not good taste. He tried to put it on the school roof, but Ralph would not let him. Finally, the sign

147

said: TODAY IS THE DAY. Find out who Justin is asking to the prom at lunch. No one knows who he is going to ask.

"The whole school is abuzz – a wave of anticipation flows through the school. During fourth period, right before lunch, Justin shows up with a mariachi band following him down the hallway. Ralph allowed it because he is going along with the pre-prom mood in the school. He is dressed in a full tuxedo with tails and top hat carrying a dozen roses, he marches into art class with the band playing full force. The music swells and he falls to his knees in front of Flora Deminski. "Will you do me the honor of going to the prom with me?" he says. Only Flora has someone else she wants to go to prom with and is pretty sure he will ask her soon, and Flora hardly knows Justin. She looks at him, she looks around the room at everybody staring at him, tears come to her eyes, and she is obviously in some pain. She does not want to make Justin look like a fool or hurt his feelings. Justin realizes that he has made the dumbest mistake of his life and, in that brief ... we are talking milliseconds, both Flora and Justin both want to crawl away and die and neither knows what to do.

"Up hops our Hope who is sitting next to Flora at the same table. She stands up and acts like he was talking to her. No one else can really see. "Why, yes Justin, I would love to go to the prom with you.' She saves Justin and Flora, and both of them are deeply grateful. As an explanation, she tells Justin, everyone deserves to go to their prom, and she tells Flora, everyone deserves to go to the prom with who they want. Justin knows that the chances of a romantic encounter are nil. Hope said yes to him out of pity, but he is still grateful, and they will have a good time. But I don't think Hope will be losing her virginity tonight."

"But, it is her junior year. Her senior prom is next year."

He nodded. "You could have gone all night without saying that."

She lifted her glass, and he brought his glass over until they clinked, "To proms past and proms future," she said.

"May the regrets never exceed the debauchery," he added.

"What does *that* mean?"

"I don't know. It just sounded good." They both laughed loud enough to reveal the effects of the wine.

The awkward silence after a laugh lingered as they both stared into the recent darkness that was the horizon Hope had ridden into. Maggie spoke first, "Hope really is ... exceptional. You have done a great job as a father."

"Thank you, but you've been a little bit more than just a typical grandmother."

The silence lasted for several minutes before Clark finally spoke, "So, you knew that, as Grace put it, 'Ralph took me – even though I picked the spot – to the banks of the Red River, which really wasn't the Red River as we both knew, to make love even though there wasn't any love made that night – we just had sex.'"

She laughed. "That sounds like my daughter."

"What about your prom?"

"Not much to it, let's just say it involved a convertible and my high school sweetheart who died in the war."

"I'm sorry."

She drank some more wine and nodded. "How did you meet my daughter, I mean how did you get together with Grace?"

"Well … we saw each other at some anti-war meetings and rallies, you know across a crowded room. I thought she was … very … quite attractive."

"You thought she was pretty and sexy."

"Not really. It wasn't that simple. I thought she looked really interesting. I just felt that she was someone who was worth talking to and … I'm not going to lie, sexy on top of that. I was older. Shallowness, even sexy shallowness, just did not appeal to me. I could not get excited about … I wanted someone I could wake up with and still want to talk to. I mean it would be a lie to say I wasn't sexually attracted to Grace, but it would be too simple. Jesus, what am I saying? I haven't said these things out loud … ever. Not even to myself. This is good wine."

He took another drink. "I mean I never talked to her. We never said anything to each other until that day, that rainy day in the coffee shop. You've heard that story a few times."

"About a hundred."

"Well," he washed another drink around in his mouth. "It's all true."

"What about drugs?" Maggie asked.

"What about drugs? What do you mean?"

"I feel really uncomfortable asking this, but it is something that has bugged me for a long time. Did drugs play a role in your relationship? I mean, everyone around here thinks you got Grace hooked on drugs and … "

"Oh, Maggie. You know better." He shook his head. "First of all, I don't think anyone every got Grace to do anything against her will. She truly was immune to peer pressure. I won't lie to you – I respect you too much for that and too much water has passed under the bridge. We used drugs, but very little. It was the '60s, and we were in college, you know? All of her involvement with acid was before I met her; she told me she took it a couple of trips. We smoked a little pot, but not much compared to everyone else we knew. We never kept a stash. I couldn't afford to be casual about drugs. The FBI used to keep tabs on me. Because of my history with the civil rights marches, they watched me. Whenever I participated in any anti-war demonstrations, they made their presence felt and I knew if I did too many drugs, they would swoop in. Ergo, I never did acid or anything beyond pot. The pregnancy and Hope's birth pretty much stopped any drug use for both of us. It wasn't a hard decision; we didn't miss it. People around here might think we were drugged out hippies just because we had long hair, but we weren't. You should know better."

"I did, basically, but I needed to ask, for my peace of mind. Lots of times, drugs can change people. What you are saying is the same thing Grace told me, except about the FBI. I don't think she knew about them."

"I told her … eventually. But, you can rest assured; our relationship was never about drugs. I'm not sure what it was about, at least, initially. I never figured out why she approached me at that coffee house, you know, what the allure was."

"Grace had seen you across the crowded room; you know, at the protest meetings. She noticed you, and she found you interesting. But, mostly, she was intrigued by you; you were a mystery – a romantic mystery."

"I know, I know." He put his fingers together and made quotation marks in the air, "I was 'the Legend.'"

"The rumor was that you had marched with King and gone to prison in Alabama. Was any of that true?"

"Yeah. But, it wasn't much."

"Really? You don't seem like the going to prison type."

"Oh? What type is that?"

When Maggie didn't respond, Clark continued, "I was arrested and went to prison three different times, at three different marches. About an hour or two each time, along with about 50 to 100 other people. I don't like to brag, but I am proud of what I did, mostly. I think we accomplished something, especially in Alabama in '65."

"So, it was true," she looked at him with admiration. "You did go to prison. You're a damn jailbird."

"I learned a lot from those marches and those arrests ... a lot." He shook his head as a reaction to returning memories.

"What did you learn?' she probed. "I hope you don't mind me asking, but this is a side of you I've never seen. Seriously, what did you learn?"

"What did I learn? I learned about people and how decent some people can be and how inhumane other people can be, and both can be acting from the same source of motivation – hope for their children and fear for their future. I learned that kindness and gentleness is the only thing that ever wins in the long run and, in the short run, it gets ground up and crushed most of the time. One of the true paradoxes of living, I guess. I learned that people do not make sense the way math makes sense, but they act from some sort of tragic, flawed rationality when viewed from their own limited perspective. I learned that there is nothing more powerful than vulnerability, and vulnerability is the greatest source of fear. And I learned that everyone is afraid; fear is the great motivator. Fear makes us mean, and fear can cause us to transcend our worst instincts. Fear can change us." He drank the last of his glass of wine.

She reached over and poured him another glass. "Sounds like you have a story to tell." She waited for a response and when none came, "And I want to hear it."

He took a drink and shook his head, "I don't want to talk about it; it is too hard, too difficult."

"OK," she said. "You don't have to tell me anything, but it has been my experience that when people tell their stories, their deepest stories, the stories they don't want anyone to know, it usually produces a good results. It brings people together. Our dark secrets that we are afraid for anyone to find out, usually involve things we most have in common."

"I'd tell you about the time I faced fear – the most frightened I have ever been, one of those gut checking moments in life – there aren't many – and I failed. I'd tell you that story, but I'm afraid you would never look at me the same

153

way. You would lose all respect. It is not worth it – not worth the risk." He took another long drink.

Maggie took a smaller drink and twirled the wine in her glass. Then, she readjusted herself in her wheelchair. "I don't want you to feel uncomfortable. If you don't want to talk, then don't, but I can tell that you have been carrying this story around a long time, and I think it is time you let go of it. The stories that are the hardest ones to tell are the ones we most need to let go of. I doubt that it will affect my view of you. You didn't kill anyone, did you?"

He shook his head no.

"You didn't rape anyone?"

Another negative head shake.

"What did you do that was so bad?"

He drained the bottom of his glass, "Only a few people know this story and fewer have heard it from me. I didn't even tell Grace the whole story, but I'm gonna tell you everything and finally set the record straight – get it off my chest."

She twisted her wheelchair around so that she faced him. "Tell me. Tell me what happened."

He poured another glass of wine. "All right." He took a drink and put the glass down on the table. "I think I've drunk enough wine to tell you the story. I've not told many people. I told Grace, some of the story and my supervisor at CORE knew the true story, but that's about it. I didn't even tell the FBI when they interviewed me. It was a long time ago, but only you could get me thinking about this ... and only the wine would get me talking about it." He turned toward the darkest part of the horizon and started talking.

"1964 … summer. You have to understand the person I was at that time. I was the quintessential nerd. I really had no friends, certainly no girlfriends. I never had a date in high school. Numbers made sense to me. I loved math and that was about all I thought about. I could philosophize for hours about the Fibonacci sequence. I could rhapsodize about the aesthetics of algebra and geometry. The balance and logic of math pleased me and gave comfort to me. I enjoyed the predictability and balance of it all. My life was one of order and exquisite logic. But, I was beginning to feel empty. There is only so much loneliness that calculus fulfills. I was just beginning to question my approach to life. I had graduated in December, and my parents had died in January. Suddenly, I was adrift in some sort of primal way. My insecurity was profound. I had no mooring – no anchor. My world no longer made sense. My parents weren't supposed to die. My reality lacked logic. I had no home – no family. I was adrift. I had managed to make it through the first semester of graduate school, but my heart wasn't in it. I was lost and looking for something … a direction … a purpose … I don't really know how to explain it. One of my professors called the Civil Rights movement the great moral movement of my generation, and that was all the justification I needed. I just wanted to have a reason to get up in the morning, something to join. The movement offered me a sense of belonging and a sense of purpose, of value.

"I volunteered to go to Mississippi and tutor math and do some voter registration. The thought that it might be dangerous did not really enter my consciousness even during the training in June. We did all these scenarios with threats and people shouting and waving sticks and guns, but it was just role playing. At that point, all life was role playing for me, and everything had an unreal, disjointed, disassociated aura about it. I was sleepwalking through life. I just wanted to get down there and wake up, hopefully to feel alive. I saw it as a way to become more human. I was more focused about the math and saw the voter thing as ancillary. I was naïve and just not at all aware of the tone and seriousness of the movement. When the speakers would talk about voter registration, I would think in terms of a simple form, but I would get ... excited thinking of teaching math to rural, uneducated kids, like I was going to be some sort of educational Pied Piper stamping out ignorance and eliminating poverty with the power of my own brilliance. Danger seemed irrelevant. Who would want to hurt a math tutor?

"The reality was quite at odds with my romantic vision. There were several different programs with varying degrees of coordination. Tutoring was sort of a front for the voter registration, except I clung to the math tutor identity and would teach math as often as possible as long as possible. I didn't seem to be accomplishing much as a math tutor, and I was skeptical about the value of voter registration. Still, voter registration was the real reason for our efforts yet I would naively cling to the math tutoring as my real purpose. We would work all day, sometimes late into the night trying to convince blacks that they needed to register to vote and teaching them how to register and where to go to register. There were a lot of us in Mississippi that summer and we were pretty high profile, some counties more than others. We worked in teams two, three, four – usually at least one of the team was black; colored as they were called then.

156

"In June, Goodman, Schwerner, and Chaney disappeared, and everyone knew they were dead, killed by the Klan. Some of us pulled out. When their bodies were found in August, the leadership sent word that we should all leave because of the imminent danger. New plans and organization would be made to insure safety. They planned to return in the fall. My particular program got the word late. We were always a little more academic oriented than the other programs or appeared to be, and I decided to do one more swing through my county. I hadn't really been harassed very much by any whites and we were close to a hundred miles from the part of Mississippi where the bodies had been found. I felt safe. Sunday afternoon, we – me and William J. Mason, my colored companion – delivered some pamphlets and a few math textbooks to a small church in the countryside and were driving back to our main office; we were scheduled to leave the next day. We stopped to get gas in some small town halfway to a little bigger town that was on the road to Jackson. For the life of me, I could not tell you the name of the town. I was really tired as I remember. So, I asked William to drive. I went into the store to pay for the gas and get a couple of drinks. I remember I got a Pepsi for me and a grape soda for William. I took a large gulp of my Pepsi and stepped outside when everything in my life changed.

"William was being held by two policemen while a third policeman – the biggest man I had ever seen – he must have been 6-foot-5-inches tall" and weighted more than 300 pounds – he was standing behind William with a baseball bat. He was winding up and hitting him as hard as he could, lifting him off the ground right between the ribs and the hips. Dust flew off William's body, and I could hear the air leave his lungs, but William never screamed. He uttered a near silent moan of low decibel, but extreme intensity. One look at his eyes and I could see the incredible pain he was enduring."

"They were trying to inflict maximum amount of pain and damage with minimum amount of visual record. There would be a little bruising, but terrible internal injury. They were aiming at his spleen and kidneys," Maggie said. "They probably learned it in the military. A body cannot take too many of those kinds of blows. What did you do?"

"I peed my pants."

Maggie did not respond.

Clark turned back toward her. "Literally. That's all I did. I just stood there pissing all over myself. I think I dropped the sodas and I think I must have dribbled the mouthful of Pepsi I had because I couldn't swallow and I couldn't talk. I wanted to say something, but words wouldn't form. So, I just stood there urinating all over myself.

"The policemen, especially the big one with the baseball bat, thought I was funny and they started laughing at me. I don't know, looking back, maybe it was good. It stopped the beating. The big guy walked over to me and poked me with the bat in my balls. I doubled over. He said, 'We got a nigger breaking curfew, and we got a Yankee pissing on our street. I don't see we have any choice but to lock 'em up."

"'Officer?' I said with as much respect I could muster though I wasn't sure my voice could speak without cracking, 'Is there something wrong?' I did not want to sound frightened nor did I want to sound antagonistic. 'We will be glad to leave immediately and obey any law that we may have broken.'

"With that, he hit me with the side of his hand drawing blood from my nose and knocking me to the ground. 'You're one of those Yankee smartasses Freedom Riders, ain't you?'

I tried to stand up but he pushed my face into the gravel. 'Ain't you?'

'Not exactly.' I didn't want to lie, but I didn't want to be affiliated with the Freedom Riders. I knew how much they were hated. 'I'm not with the Freedom Riders, but I have been tutoring math and doing voter registration with some of the niggers down here.'

There was no use trying to deny it, the pamphlets were in the car. I knew that using the word 'nigger' was better in this situation than any other word I could have used. I managed to sit up. 'We ... I have not been in this county before.' I heard a very loud thump and looked toward William. I saw him slump to his knees, his face contorted in terrible pain. Then, his eyes rolled back in his head, and he fell forward flat on his face."

Maggie shook her head back and forth.

"Maximum damage without leaving any marks."

He nodded. "I just knew that he was hurt, and hurt badly. They threw us into the back of a squad car. They drove us down the street to the jail, literally carrying us and throwing us in a cell. The jail was an old grocery store. The cell must have been where the refrigerator had been. Everything was small and cramped. They gathered together on the other side of the jail and began talking in a tight circle. I figured they were planning how to get rid of us. William woke up long enough to vomit a mixture of blood and bile. He looked at me and whispered, 'I am hurt, bad hurt ... not going to last long.' I put his head in my lap

159

and tried to comfort him. I took my shirt off and wiped his mouth and face.

"I could barely hear them, but somehow I pieced together that they were waiting for sundown to do anything, and I wasn't sure William could make it to sundown. I made a pillow for William's head with my shirt and some rags on the cot in the cell.

"I shouted to the guys across the room. 'Look, we have to send an itinerary; you know, a kinda flight plan when we leave on one of these here trips with an estimated returning time. If we don't show up ... hell, half the FBI are already in Mississippi because of those dead white boys, you know those Jews and the colored boy over in ... Money. I don't show up, the other half are gonna be all over this place looking for me. Now, you might be able to get away with beating up a colored boy here, but if he's dead and I'm missing, you are gonna have a shitload of trouble. You might be able to get out of it, but I'm just thinking you could save yourself a whole lot of trouble if you just let us go. Hell, you made your point. We ain't coming back here! Hell, I know I ain't!'

"The big guy just laughed at me. 'You think we are afraid you are gonna come back, pissboy?' He walked over toward me, and towered over me.

"'And you think calling them boys Jews and Willie here a nigger is going to fool us? Or that the FBI is going be looking for you.' He turned to all the other guys in the jail. 'What do y'all think? The FBI is gonna get us.'

"They all laughed. He turned back towards me. 'Look, you pathetic piss-soaked turd. You just want to save your own ass. You'd say anything – you're so scared.'

"'You're damn right, but you also know that there is some truth in what I'm saying.' They started to think about it, William beat up or dead wasn't a problem, but a dead white boy with the FBI all over, might be a problem."

Clark looked directly into Maggie's eyes. "They huddled together, and I tried to calm myself and use the mental discipline of math to solve the problem facing me. I came up with a solution. I told them I saw Willie when he fell against the desk as he came into the jail. That mop and bucket over there was in the way – and if I have anything bad to say about y'all, it's that you didn't put the damn mop away. Willie slipped on it. You know he wasn't used to wearing shoes, and he took the god-awfullest flop I have ever seen. His feet must have gone 5 feet in the air and when he landed, he came down on the corner of the desk. I am willing to sign a report to swear that was how Willie received his injury. This would relieve them of any responsibility for Willie's injury, and it would give them a way of letting me go without worrying about me bearing witness against them. What could I say if I had signed the report?

"They looked at each other. I figured they needed a little more convincing, but that I needed to be real careful what I said next. 'Look, I want to be not dead. I'm not really loving Mississippi right now, I plan on being gone from this place from here on, but I want to leave with a long life ahead of me, and I think this provides the best chance.' They nodded and talked together. They wrote a report. I copied it onto an official form and I signed it. They opened the cell and said I could leave, but

Willie had to stay. Willie had to stay. They would take him to the colored hospital down in Jackson.

"I knew William was not going to make it to Jackson, and I knew they weren't planning on taking him there anyway. There were a lot of things that ran through my mind. If Willie stayed, he would be dead before morning. 'I think it would be better if Willie went with me. It would raise less concern than if he was missing.' They insisted that it was me alone or no deal. I nodded. 'I care more about living than I care about this colored boy.' They handed me the car keys and I walked to the door. I could see the car outside – 15 feet from where I was standing. I wondered if I would have time to get somewhere and call for help. But, I doubted it."

Clark stared into the night, transfixed and silent. He became aware of Maggie's wheelchair squeaking as she rolled an inch closer to him. "What did you do, Clark? What did you do?" she asked.

"I made a decision. I could not leave William alone. I could not let him die like that. It was not right, I could not do it, but if I didn't, I was going to die, too. I was sure."

He stared for a few seconds before he shuddered and Maggie broke the silence, "And?" He didn't speak, too deep in thought. "You can't stop there. What happened next?" Maggie pleaded.

Clark found his voice and began again, "I stopped at the door, 10 feet from the car, and turned around and said to them, 'I am not leaving without Willie. I really think you should reconsider. I just think the FBI and my supervisors are going to be suspicious if I show up without Willie. You have the paper;

162

there is nothing they can do to harm you. If anything, you'll make them all look pretty foolish with that paper. But, whatever, I am not leaving without Willie. I guess you will have to kill me, too.'

"Actually, that is what I wanted to say, but I didn't get any of those words out. Once again, I just froze. I turned toward them and cried. I mean, I cried. I wanted so hard to speak, but no words came out of my mouth, I just sobbed. Inside my head were two thoughts fighting for escape: One, plead with them, beg them, appeal to their logic, and two, I'm going to die! I was not able to articulate either thought. I just stood there crying.

"Somehow, William staggered across the room and fell into my arms. We walked to the car together, me crying the whole time. He collapsed in the passenger's seat and I got behind the wheel. We took off. I don't know if they felt sorry for us, or if they just wanted to shut me up, or if they saw some truth in what I had been saying about the FBI. We drove for about an hour. William knew a doctor with a clinic on the highway. There were some FBI agents there. I left William with the doctor and took off; I didn't stop until Dallas"

"That is an impressive story," Maggie said as she drained her glass of wine. "Do you think they really would have killed the two of you? I mean killing is awfully ... extreme."

"I have no doubt." He shook his whole body as if shivering. "I think they wanted any excuse when they stopped us and dragged us into the police station. I remember they said things that hinted at stopping the boys in the other county and pulling something off under the FBI's nose. They were talking to each other; they weren't trying to scare us. I have not figured out what exactly stopped them. But, I know this:" He looked at her and dropped his voice to emphasize the seriousness of what he was about to say, "When I turned away from the car and said I wasn't leaving without Willie, I accepted the fact that I was going to die. I knew it was over, and they were going to kill us."

"Why did you go back? Why didn't you jump in the car and take off?"

"I don't know," he shook his head and rubbed his forehead. "I've thought a lot about it. I wish I could give you some sort of heroic answer, but even as I turned around, I wanted to jump in the car. Time suddenly stopped and I had this moment of ... clarity – a terrible epiphany. I understood life's essence. Life is about choice. And I was facing a choice. I didn't like the choice. You know what I mean? Am I making any sense? Even as I was standing there, I wanted to choose to get in the car and drive off, but I couldn't. I hated that I couldn't." He looked at her and shook his head.

She nodded, "I know. I know."

"I just couldn't let William die alone. He didn't deserve that. I really wanted to jump in the car and drive away, but I couldn't. It might have had something to do with my parent's death. They had died six months earlier. If I had been in this situation a year earlier, maybe I might have taken the car and ran. But, now I knew. Everyone dies, and I just didn't want to let William die alone, and I wasn't willing to die knowing I was the kind of person who would run away. I couldn't live being that kind of person. I wasn't happy with it, but I made my choice and I have never been the same person."

"Clark," Maggie was nodding her head. "You know what you did? You grew up. You became who you are. You were how old - 21?"

"Just turned 22, but, I can't use my age as an excuse. There were soldiers in World War II who were my age and younger. They won medals for valor and fought courageously, and all I could do was cry … and piss in my pants. I found out I was a lousy coward."

He walked over to the wine bottle and poured another glass. "I went on one more march, the next year in Selma, but everything was different after Mississippi. I felt like such a fraud. In Selma, I didn't even feel real. I was just a shell, and empty body marching—I dissociated the whole time. I returned, retreated actually, to graduate school. I took more classes, declared a new major – a couple of times. I had several half master's degrees – all in some sort of theoretical math field, if you can imagine anything more removed from life. I'd take several classes toward a degree and then lose … interest. In the meantime, the anti-war movement invaded the campus. I went to a few rallies, mostly out of curiosity. The FBI had a file on me from Mississippi, and when it looked like I was going to participate in the anti-war movement, they began checking in on me. An agent from the FBI came and visited me. He told me that William died after I left Mississippi; he lasted less than a week. The report I signed made any conviction impossible."

Clark took another drink." You know what I remember the most from the jail? There was a big picture over the desk of the high school championship football team of 1957." He shook his head. "All white kids, of course, and it looked like several of the deputies were on the team."

165

She nodded her head up and down and sat silent for a long time before she spoke. "I was about the same age – 22 – about to turn 23 when my ... I reached my turning point ... when I had my, what did you call it, 'my terrible epiphany' ... when I too first met Grace." She cocked her head to the side. "I guess you could interpret that sentence in more than one way, and all of them would be accurate."

"Sounds like you, too, have a story."

"You have heard it before ... the accident, and the pregnancy."

"There is more to the story; I told mine. Now, it is your turn."

She shook her head, "There is not enough wine in Texas."

"You got me drunk enough to tell my secrets, but you won't share? There is something wrong here," he walked over and grabbed a new bottle of wine opened it and poured more in her glass to top it off, then he poured more in his own glass. He clinked his glass to hers, "To intimacy, true intimacy. The kind with no secrets, the only kind that really matters."

"OK," she drank and looked into his eyes. "You better be prepared. I was raised in a small town in eastern Kentucky – coal-mining country. I couldn't wait to get out of there. As soon as I could, I joined the army and trained to be a nurse in the war. I ended up stationed in a hospital in the Pacific theater. I was a good nurse, I never lacked intelligence. One of my patients was a wounded Marine – Corporal James Wheeler – handsome, dashing, and heading back to the front as soon as his wounds healed. We fell in love; he proposed. He promised a life on a ranch in Texas, which sounded romantic and exotic to these 19-year-old ears. When the war was over, and I reconnected with Jimmy, we moved to Nettie and I found it anything but romantic and exotic. The ranch was hot and dirty, and the town was stifling with its lack of intellectual stimulus. I, of course, would not have put it that way. I just said it was boring – boring and full of ignorant people, as ignorant as any I had left behind in Kentucky. Nettie was not the paradise I had been led to believe it was. In the meantime, Jimmy lost the cattle from disease and lack of maintenance during the war. His father had died, and there was no one else to manage the ranch. We were left with a lot of land, but little income. But, we had each other and we did have this beautiful house. I became a school nurse and was the main source of income, which bothered Jimmy immensely. What bothered him more was my notoriety, my fame. When I saved little Richie Talbert, I became a local hero and that drove Jimmy crazy. Well, you know that story. We were both miserable, and we both blamed each other. The honeymoon was over, as they say. At that point, we had the accident involving my horse, and a motorcycle out on the road leading to the old highway. What no one knows – and you will never tell anyone … " She hesitated for a long time in complete silence.

"What?" He said, "What am I sworn to secrecy to never tell anyone?"

She regained her focus and shook her head, "You can't tell anyone is that the accident was my fault. My horse ran into the motorcycle. Jimmy and I were riding – we did that quite often in the evening – and we were down the riding path where it joined the road and the motorcycle came by at the same time. My horse was frightened and bolted into the side of the motorcycle. I flew off the horse and fell on the pavement. I was knocked out, and the horse fell on me before she died.

"When I woke up in the hospital, I knew immediately ... my background as a nurse in the war. I knew what had happened. I knew my spine was broken. I spent the day thinking about my situation – acclimating myself to being paralyzed. I thought about life in a wheelchair. I thought about life with Jimmy. I thought about life in Nettie. Before the accident, I wanted out – out of Nettie, out of my marriage to Jimmy, out of my limited Texas life – the narrow horizons, out, in every sense of the word. And, now, I was never getting out. In fact, my life was even more restrained. I was going to be imprisoned to a wheelchair with paralyzed legs. Free spirits seldom have handicaps, I thought. I was doomed.

"I could not stand the idea. I just wanted to die. Every time I would close my eyes I would hope that I would not wake up, and when I woke, my first feeling was enormous disappointment. Immediately, I wanted to die and committing suicide was my only option. I started planning to kill myself. When you are paralyzed in a hospital bed, there are not many opportunities for suicide. I tried to hide a plastic knife from the dinner plates, but the staff was too conscientious to leave anything behind when they cleaned up. Finally, I noticed that one nurse disposed of a syringe in a trashcan on the other side of the room. I could not reach it, but I started plotting. I could pull all the tubes out and drop myself to the floor and crawl over to the can, get the needle and inject air into a vein and be dead before anyone could find me, but I soon realized that I probably would make too much noise and would be caught long before I accomplished my mission. Besides, I wasn't really sure if I had the strength to crawl across the room. I had to improvise.

If I used my blanket to knock the trashcan over, I could pull the needle over toward me so that I wouldn't have to have to crawl – just drop to the floor and insert the needle. It took me nearly an hour before I knocked over the can, and the needle did not fall out on the floor like I had planned. But, between the blanket hitting the top of the can, tipping it over, and the sheet hitting inside the can like a towel in a shower, the needle slowly emerged, and I pulled it closer to the bed. I was about to drop down out of the bed and use it when I noticed the time on the clock. It was time for rounds. I rolled the needle under the bed and pulled the sheet and blanket back on the bed. I hoped the nurse would just pick up the trashcan and not look under the bed."

Clark sighed, "I am exhausted just listening to you. It must have taken you a couple of hours."

"It was more like four hours. I started around two and rounds were just before six in the morning," she lifted her glass for another drink of wine.

"You were very dedicated to the task," he said.

"I was committed. When the nurse finally left the room – she had not discovered the syringe – I was exhausted. I took a few breathes to gather my strength and was about to lower myself onto the floor when Jimmy and the doctor showed up. The doctor brought me all the results of the lab tests. They confirmed everything I had guessed: Spinal cord fractured and permanent paralysis from the hips down. I turned to look at Jimmy. His eyes were red as the doctor said – I'll never forget his exact words – "As near as we can tell, there is no damage to the baby." Jimmy and I both said "Baby?" at the same time. That was how we found out I was pregnant.

"Suddenly, everything was different. Now, if I killed myself, I would be killing a baby, an innocent baby. My baby. Oh, I still wanted to die, but I felt like I had one more chance to do something ... to leave something behind ... to have mattered.

"When everyone left and I was alone again, I reassessed things. I really looked at myself, and I didn't like what I saw. I did not like the idea of being a lifelong resident of a wheelchair. And I did not want to burden my baby with a handicapped mother. I was going to produce a life while I was busy dying – hoping to die. There would be time and opportunity after the birth to commit suicide. I would have the baby and then kill myself."

"What made you change your mind?" he asked.

She looked at him. "I don't know if I could explain it in words that you would understand."

"I will try to understand," his voice sounded soft yet intense.

She nodded knowing that he would not take no for an answer, "The short answer would have to be God. I found God."

He seemed stunned. He was not prepared for her answer. He realized that she went to church every Sunday, but it always seemed more like a social event than something with spiritual significance. She never tried to get him to go to church, and she never spoke to him about religion. She took Hope to church, but he did not place any significance upon it. They attended church, and he did not except for the rare occasion of a special event like when Hope would play the organ or something. He stammered, "I didn't know ... I didn't think ... religion was that important to you."

She shrugged her shoulders, "I said I found God – didn't say anything about religion. Religion, if anything, came later. I mean the pastor from the church came to see me every day that I was in the hospital."

"Pastor John?"

"Pastor John was probably two years old when this all happen if that, maybe he wasn't even born yet. No, I'm talking about Pastor James. He was three or four pastors ago. Pastor James kept praying, telling me that God never gives you more than you can handle, and I keep thinking: I wish God had less confidence in me. He would say everything is a part of God's plan, and our job is to fulfill our part without questioning, and all I could think was what kind of sick deity has such a sadistic plan? No, I wasn't finding any comfort coming from the church. The women in the church brought me flowers, blankets, and baskets of stuff, and I liked all of it, but it didn't help me feel any better. The agony, the desire to die, was just as intense as the first day.

"When I came home from the hospital, I adjusted to the wheelchair and acted like I was living as normal a life as possible. I would cook, wash dishes, and do the laundry. At first, the women from church came over and helped, but I learned to adjust and they came less often. I would get up and fix coffee ... watch the sunrise ... on the porch as always. Jimmy moped around as much as I did. He felt guilty, and the more I would forgive him, the more he would feel guilty. We talked less and less. He couldn't handle the guilt, and he could handle forgiveness even less. I was putting in my time. I knew it would be over soon. I had made some investigations into adoptions and even began the process.

"Then about the sixth month, things started to change. I felt the baby kick. Slowly, this abstraction became a reality. I had a life growing inside of me. The more I thought about that, the more miraculous it seemed. And the more I developed a relationship with this life inside of me. I began to wonder how this baby would look, how it would act, who it would grow up to be. Would it grow up to learn the important lessons of life? Would its view of life be limited to the horizons of Nettie? Who would teach it the important lessons of life? Slowly, I began to dread saying goodbye to it and, slowly, I began to think maybe I could teach it the important things in life – how to love, who to love – and slowly I stopped calling it an it, and I began seeing my baby as a human who deserved a mother who loved her more than anyone else could love her. Slowly, I began to see myself as that mother. Maybe I could be more than just a vessel.

"I began to consider that maybe, just maybe, I was up to the challenge of raising my baby, and the more I thought about that the more excited I became. I started planning things like cradles and cribs. I had Jimmy make accommodations around the house, and I readied myself for the birth. Lying in bed, I would think of all the things I would do with my baby, all the things I would teach her, all the games we would play. I realized I had a reason to live, a purpose. I talked the board into giving me my job back as school nurse certainly with the help of Mr. Talbert. I was alive again; in fact, I was more alive than I had ever been.

"One night, lying in bed feeling the baby kicking, I realized all of my joy, all of my new contentment, my new peace of mind was a gift of God ... not in some superficial, trite, cliché that my pastors had given me, but in some profound, sobering way. I mean, if God is love … this love I was experiencing was enriching me. Do you have any idea what I mean?"

"I think I can relate to what you are saying," he nodded. "With childbirth came love. Real love."

"Exactly! I didn't name her Grace by accident."

"But, because of her …" he searched for the right words. "The more you love, the more you are able to love, right? And that love is grace? And, for you, the source of that grace is God?"

"Where does God end and grace begin? I don't know," She said.

He looked at her and then turned to look into the night. He stood there motionless, pondering her words. Several minutes passed before he spoke, "I like your theology. I like it better than any I've heard from a pulpit. It makes sense to me."

She nodded, "Thanks. I don't think it is original. You don't believe in religion, do you?"

"No. Not much. I saw too many people using religion to justify segregation and all sorts of violence during my time in the South."

"You can't blame all the churches for the sins of a few. You know, Martin Luther King was religious."

He nodded. "I know. That was the part I never could … reconcile. You know, my father use to say that all the really great evils in the world were done in the name of righteousness. In my experience, I think he was probably right. More people have been hurt by religion. You know, trying to convince someone that their religion is the one true religion to the point of torture or murder. It just seems to me that tolerance and religion are the antithesis of each other."

She kind of smiled at him, "Well, you just managed to denigrate all charities and ministries not to mention moral campaigns like the civil rights movement. You can't tell me that they don't do some good."

"I don't want to disrespect your beliefs or insult your church. Mostly, I just view the church with apathy, especially when I'm too drunk to care."

"Would you call yourself an atheist?" she looked at him quizzically.

He was silent for several seconds as he thought about his answer. "Would I call myself an atheist? That would depend on who was asking, why they were asking, and how safe I felt in answering. For example, I would have a different answer to the PTA than to ... you."

"I am doing the asking. Would you call yourself an atheist?"

"Well, I won't lie, but I have to start by saying something like 'I don't like labels for spiritual belief systems' and then I would explain my evolution on the subject, my faith journey – whatever that means."

She sat back in her wheelchair and folded her hands together in front of her face, "What would you tell your daughter?"

"With Hope, I would be up front – and I have had this conversation with her – and I would say that I do not know what God is. I mean, I sure do not believe in the god I hear most people describe. It just seems to me most people believe in a God that is a watered-down Santa Claus or some sort of megalomaniac, sadistic, micromanager. I think I told her that I could never believe in a religion where God is a noun instead of a verb."

"What does that mean?"

"I don't remember, but it sure sounds profound, doesn't it?"

"Well, for someone who has no religion, you sure act religious," she spoke as she wheeled herself across the porch to get another bottle of wine. She poured another glass and offered him one.

He shook his head no, "How can you drink so much? If I have another glass, I will go spinning off of this porch."

"Practice … I used to drink a lot … alone … most nights … until you and Hope showed up."

He stood up quickly and almost lost his bearings. "What do you mean I act religious? I resemble that remark … er, resent it."

"I just meant, if you don't believe in anything, why do you teach? You could make more money in private industry. And why do you teach the way that you teach? I mean, you are the champion of the kids. You could get a lot further by teaching more traditionally, and avoid a lot of hassles. And if you don't believe in anything, why did you go back for William? And you didn't have to marry Grace. And you didn't have to stay here with me and raise your daughter here in this hick town. Let's face it, you and Nettie are not exactly a match made in heaven. No, I think if you don't believe in anything, you have some explaining to do."

He sat back down. "I've never thought of it that way. But, even though I'm drunk, I still think it is a pretty big leap to think … just because I try to do the right thing … I have some sort of unconscious faith in God."

"And maybe you just need to redefine God."

"What do you mean?"

"Stop viewing God as the author of a series of short stories called the Bible and look at God as the mortar between the bricks of the narrative of your life – the melody, if you will, that is you. I mean, God is not limited to the Bible. There is more to him than one book. To me, God is always greater than man's ability to understand God. Use that as a starting place, and you will realize that everything everyone says about God falls short of … knowing God, or experiencing God."

They sat in silence as he pondered what she had said.

"Like water," he said.

"What?" she shook her head?

"I was just thinking how everything is made up of water – blood, plasma, cells, you know like the old song. "There is only one river. There is only one sea. And it flows through you. And it flows through me. Maybe God is … water; I mean like water. All through us and all about us. I mean … it's like a fish is made of mostly water and he lives in water, but does a fish know what water is? Are we like fish?"

She nodded, "Is there anything that is not God? Where does God end? Where is the edge? Tillich used the term 'The Ground of Being' to define God."

He looked at her and rubbed his eyes. "Good for him. Who is Tillich?"

"Someone I read. I read a lot on religion, different theologies."

He nodded, "I remember reading somewhere, someone who said...Christ points the way, and most people stare at his finger."

She laughed. "I think that was in Parade magazine. Don't get me wrong. I like church and I find a lot of ...spirituality in church, a lot that is holy, but it's not always in the pulpit."

"You know, tomorrow when I wake, I hope I remember the best parts of this conversation, but I doubt that my hangover will let me, he said."

"You gonna stay awake and wait for Hope?"

"I will be doing well to stay awake long enough to finish this sentence ... or crawl all the way to bed." With that, he left the porch and headed toward his bedroom.

"Goodnight," she said to him as staggered into his room and she turned to face the dark horizon to watch for Hope. "It was good talking to you. We don't do this often enough."

A Moral Dilemma: Principal, Principle and Daughter

August 26, 1985

1124 Canyon Drive, Nettie, Texas

The week before school actually started was always a frustrating experience for Mr. Bradley. On Tuesday, there would be a district-wide convocation meeting that he hated to attend and usually did not. The purpose of the meeting was to inspire and put people in a good mood for the upcoming year. Clark just found it depressing and crowded. He didn't really need to be inspired; if anything, he needed to be hosed down. He was a romantic and an idealist, and he looked forward to being with his students with a passion.

The convocation felt like a Hitler youth camp with everyone screaming and shouting *en masse* via cues from the podium. The rest of the week was spent in faculty meetings going over any changes in rules for the next year – modifications in the dress code, how late could a student be before he or she was classified as a truant, how many points could be subtracted for late work – policies that Clark found trivial and frankly silly. He tended to ignore them, but then his students tended to dress appropriately, come to class on time, and turn in their work on time. One day would be spent in a district staff development based on subject matter.

In these meetings, people who were no longer classroom teachers would instruct classroom teachers on how to be better classroom teachers by demonstrating the worst possible classroom instruction technique ever devised by man: the overhead projector, complete with handouts. A seemingly endless supply of handouts would be passed out, and the same endless supply of transparencies would be displayed on the overhead while the expert would read what was on the transparency, a copy of which was on the overhead, and a room full of teachers could sit and nod and say, "Yes, that is exactly what it says on my handout, too."

If there was anything more worthless than staff development, Clark had not discovered it. During the entire week, his whole being wanted to scream, "Leave me alone and let me teach! Let me get in my room and get ready for my students."

Finally, on Friday, he had the whole day in his room, alone, to get ready. He used his time productively and relished every moment.

First, he went over his classroom rolls and recognized some names in every class. This gave him a feeling of joyful anticipation especially because in his fifth-period class there was enrolled one Hope Bradley. He was glad that she choose to take the challenging pathway through high school and enrolled in pre-calculus her sophomore year, even though he was the only pre-cal teacher. The fact that she was going to be in his class thrilled him. How often does one get to show off in front of one's daughter and do the thing one does best? He was confident that it would be a meaningful experience for both of them.

Having finished looking at his rolls, Clark aligned the desks, neatened the bookcase, and made the room presentable. He was sitting down to work on lesson plans and worksheets for the first day when Mickey walked into the room and asked to talk. Mickey had taken an Algebra II class from Clark his junior year and made decent, but not outstanding grades.

"Sure," was Clark's answer as he sat behind his desk and motioned toward the desk in front of him.

Mickey moved around to face Mr. Bradley, sat down, looked up at him, put his chin on his hands, tried to say something, took a deep breath, tried again, looked straight at Mr. Bradley, and burst out crying. Clark was completely off guard. He did not know what to say or how to respond.

"There, there. What's wrong? It will be all right," Clark heard himself saying not believing anything that was coming out of his mouth and not believing that it was coming out of his own mouth.

Mickey composed himself as best he could although he was still obviously distressed. "You were the only person I could think of that might help me, Mr. Bradley. They ... I've been kicked off the football team and I can't be a student council officer or in the Honor Society. It's not fair. It's just not right."

"You're telling me that you have been kicked off the football team and all these other things. Why?"

"I got an MIP early in the summer."

"What's an MIP?"

"Minor in Possession. It's like a ticket. It's not like a DWI; it's a misdemeanor. It happened early in June when school was out. I wasn't drunk. It wasn't a serious, you know, public intoxication. They handle that really different. I was just ... in the wrong place at the wrong time."

"So, you weren't drunk. Were you drinking?"

Mickey shook his head no, but Clark was skeptical, "If you weren't drinking, why did the police …"

Mickey interrupted him, "Let me tell you the whole story. It was the first Saturday of the summer – the first party of the summer. Now, I usually don't go to many parties, but this was special. I knew Ashley was going to be there and I really wanted to get to know her. We met as ushers at graduation, and I really thought she was something special. We were going to meet at the party. She isn't much of a party person, either. In fact, this was her first party. We sat together at the party most of the night just talking to each other, getting to know each other, hanging out. Sometime in the evening, I'm gonna guess about 10 o'clock, a guy who graduated the year before – I don't want to say who – but he was really drunk, started causing trouble for this girl. She had a new boyfriend and this guy wanted things to be like they were last year before he left for college. It looked like there was going to be a big fight, but I stepped in between the two guys and stopped the fight but, as he was leaving, the guy sprayed me with a beer. I smelled like a brewery. A half an hour later the police busted the party, and they charged me because of the way I smelled. I mean I tried to explain what happened, and the cop could see I wasn't drunk, but he charged me anyway. I think he felt he had to because of the way I smelled. I told my dad about it and had to pay the ticket myself. Frankly, I had forgotten about it until today."

"Mickey, let me see if I understand. You were at this party, but you did not have anything to drink. The police gave you an MIP because you smelled like the beer that was on your shirt when you broke up a fight." Bradley cocked his head and then shook his head slowly, "Something doesn't sound right. Ashley? Was she drinking?"

Mickey lowered his eyes more than his head, "Yeah, sort of. She had a wine cooler. One. Honest to God. I was with her the whole time. She nursed that thing all night. She just wanted to look like she was drinking. She wanted to fit in. She got an MIP also. In fact, if she hadn't had the wine cooler in her hand, neither one of us would have been ticketed." He just shook his. "None of this would have happened. She paid her own fine the next week. We didn't think anything about it. Hey, we were sorry it happened. We didn't go to another party all summer. If there was something to be learned, we learned it. But, Ashley is a cheerleader and she has a sister in ninth grade who is also a cheerleader. Ashley's father found the receipt for the ticket last week – I don't know how – but, he hit the ceiling. He wouldn't listen to her side of the story, or he didn't believe it. He didn't want her to set a bad example for her little sister, he didn't want her to get away with a rule violation, so he made her quit the cheerleading squad. Actually, he made the sponsor kick her off because she broke the no-drinking rule. Coach Davis couldn't let the cheerleader sponsor out-discipline him. He can't ignore a football player for breaking the same rule. So, now we are both setting examples. And the whole thing stinks.

"You know who called the police to complain? Doug, that's who. I wasn't going to tell you his name. Doug was the guy who threw the beer on me. After he left the party, he staggered home – he lives a couple of doors down the street, and he called the police. All the really drunk people were inside the house and the cops only looked in the yard by the pool where Doug told them to look. There was a half-dozen ticketed, but if the police had gone in the house, half the football team and half the cheerleading squad would have been arrested for being drunk out of their minds."

Bradley stared at Mickey for several minutes in silence before he spoke. "All things considered, it doesn't seem like the punishment fits the crime. Something is really out of balance here. Have your parents talked to the coach?"

"My mom and dad have been with the coach and Mr. Plymale all morning. They even went to the superintendent. Mr. Plymale and the superintendent fully support the coach, and the coach wants to set a precedent and use me as an example. That's why I came to you. I thought maybe you could talk to the coach or Mr. Plymale. Maybe they would listen to you."

"I don't know if it will do any good, but I'll try talking to Mr. Plymale. I don't think a conversation with the coach has much chance of being productive. I'll call you tonight and let you know what I find out."

Mickey nodded and stood to leave. "Mr. Bradley, this is wrong."

"I've known Ralph Plymale for 11 years, and he has always been a fair and decent principal. I can't believe that he would allow this type of injustice to happen on his watch."

Mickey shook his head and walked off.

Clark and Hope had lived in the same house, Mrs. Wheeler's home, since they moved to Nettie. It was located on the corner of Red River Lane and Canyon Drive on the north part of town. When they first moved in, there was no other house around nor any other street for that matter, but several newer housing developments had been built up in the last three or four years.

On the western side of the house was a large field, which used to be a cotton field a long time ago before it was part of the large pasture, but now it was used as a small pasture for a few horses and a cow or two. The field kept shrinking as houses were built closer and closer to their house. On the other side of the field, maybe 50 yards and two houses south on Canyon Drive was the Plymale's new house. Clark could see it as he pulled into the driveway and he noticed that Ralph was out mowing the yard. He would be done shortly, Clark could see.

First, Clark wanted to talk to Hope about Mickey. He knocked on her bedroom door and asked to come in. Hope was sitting on the bed with Mrs. Wheeler sitting in front of her. Hope was holding a guitar. The guitar – her mother's guitar. Clark was stunned and the shock must have shown on his face. Hope explained, "Guitar lessons, Mom's guitar. I … didn't think you'd mind. Was I wrong?"

"No, no. That's fine. I was just surprised. I haven't seen that guitar out of the case in years. I'm glad you are using it. But, I thought someone was going to teach me?"

"I am, whenever you have the time," Mrs. Wheeler said. "You want a lesson right now?"

"Not tonight."

"You have been saying that for 11 years."

"Soon. Soon. Hope, listen. I need to ask you about a couple of kids at school."

"Dad, remember, we had an agreement. You said you wouldn't ask me about anybody or anything at school. Remember? Confidentiality? Privacy?"

"This is different."

"If there is one exception, there will be others and soon."

"OK, OK. Never mind. I don't want to violate your civil rights." He turned toward Mrs. Wheeler, "How is she doing?"

"On the guitar? She has the touch. She'll be a picker."

"I get it from my mother," Hope smiled.

He looked at her and then he looked at her again. It was one of those moments when he realized just how long it had been since he had really looked at her as she is, and not as she had been. He suddenly knew how quickly 11 years had passed. He nodded. "Look, I'm sorry I asked you. You're right. It was unfair; it won't happen again."

"Want to hear me play?"

"Not now. Later."

He knew that he wasn't ready to hear her play that guitar – he wasn't sure he would ever be. He walked into the kitchen telling himself that he needed to do something, he needed to do something now for more than one reason. "Whatever I need to do, it starts with Ralph," he said to himself.

He grabbed a six pack of beer from the refrigerator and headed for Ralph's place. The sun was setting at Clark's back and in Ralph's face as Clark approached the Plymale homestead. Ralph was hosing the grass off his feet. He threw Ralph a beer and Ralph broke into a big grin, "Nothing beats a cold *brewski* after mowing a lawn in the summer heat. The missus doesn't like me keeping any around on account of Meredith. She says I'll just drink them. She has a point." He popped the top of the can and took a very long drink, let loose a deep sigh, and rolled the can across his brow.

"I came to talk to you about something … something kind of important," Clark said.

"I figured as much." Another long sigh. "Mickey or Ashley?"

Clark took a swallow of his beer. "Near as I can figure Mickey did not do anything wrong."

Ralph was nodding his head.

"His only crime was being in the wrong place at the wrong time." Ralph continued nodding as Clark continued talking. "More accurately, he was in the wrong place at the right time to prevent a big brawl. Mickey is a good kid, the type of kid we want every kid to be like. Even if you think he did something wrong, I'm not sure what it was. But, his punishment is way out of proportion to his crime. Why the hell do you keep nodding?"

Ralph took another long drink, emptied his can, and grabbed another. "I agree with everything you say."

"Then what are you going to do?"

"Nothing."

"Nothing? I don't understand."

"No, you don't understand. I agree with everything you say, but it doesn't change anything. The coach has made his decision, and I am not going to undermine his discipline and reverse him. Neither will the board. Or the superintendent. Or the people in this town, for that matter."

"But the coach is wrong. His decision is wrong."

Ralph shook his head. "It doesn't matter. There is a bigger picture. The authority of the coach must be maintained at all cost. No matter what. You can't run a football team by committee."

Clark cocked his head. "Even if the coach is wrong?"

Ralph nodded. "Some would argue, especially if the coach is wrong, but I won't go there."

"That is idiotic."

"No, it isn't. How do you expect the coach to control the team, make them have productive practices, and all that stuff if his power isn't absolute?"

"In this enlightened age, you think coaches should be dictators? Like World War II was fought for nothing. Might as well let Hitler rule a country if he can have a winning record."

"That's quite a leap, don't you think?"

Clark just kept shaking his head. "Power corrupts; absolute power corrupts absolutely. I just don't think anybody should make decisions like this without some sort of checks and balances. The power to destroy lives is too great. Somebody has to look out for kids."

"Coaches are evaluated every year, just like all personnel."

"Yeah, but the only thing anyone looks at is the winning record. No one seems to care if the kids on the team are … hurt."

"Winning records indicate character development," Ralph said as he chuckled and took another long drink of his beer.

Clark couldn't believe his ears. "Even you don't believe that."

"Football – sports – develops many long-lasting values that the board thinks are really important to the development of our youth."

"I won't argue with you about that, but injustice? Is that really one of the things we want to teach? Because, in this case, that is the main lesson."

"No, it isn't. Look, the coach really didn't have a choice. Once the cheerleader sponsor kicked Ashley off the team – and she had to because Ashley's father went ape-shit and had a hissy-fit – the coach really couldn't look the other way."

"This is so wrong."

"No. No it isn't. You are taking too narrow a view. If Mickey is let back on the team, everyone will say you can drink in Nettie if you play football. It's all OK if you play football well enough to be on the starting team. No one will understand the nuances of the situation."

"So, we sacrifice Mickey for public relations?"

Ralph nodded. "It is the best alternative. It is the only alternative."

Clark while shaking his head spoke through clinched teeth, "I thought we were supposed to operate in our student's best interests."

"We are."

"How is this in Mickey's best interest?'

"We have to think of all of the students, not just one."

"What are we accomplishing if we sacrifice even one student when it is wrong?"

"It is a choice you sometimes have to make."

Clark nodded. "Sacrifice a few for the good of the many."

"Something like that." Ralph shook his head. "Clark, there are no Bad Guys here...not the coach, not me. We all want what is best for the students."

"No Bad Guys. Just the system. I really don't like football." Clark dropped the beers on the floor of the garage. "It is a choice you have to make. I won't make that choice, and I won't put up with this, at least, not without a fight. I'm not going to ... just roll over."

"What are you going to do?"

"I don't know. Something. I know a thing or two about civil disobedience and how to mount a protest movement."

"I hate to hear that, Clark. I truly do. This is not a battle you can win."

"I have to try."

Ralph shook his head. "Clark, you cannot defeat the system, and I can't protect you, even if I wanted to – I would hate to lose you, but this is greater than even football. I know it seems like nothing is greater than football, but this is."

Clark cocked his head.

Ralph lowered is voice emphatically, "This is about rules and those who make rules. You cannot fight them. They will not lose. They cannot afford to lose."

"What kind of a person would I be, what kind of a lesson would I be teaching, if I didn't try?"

Clark turned briskly and marched back home. His trip back was much shorter than his journey to Ralph's house. Almost running by the time he reached the back door and burst into the kitchen, he had a look on his face that Granny and Hope had never seen before. Hope looked up from her dinner at Granny with a helpless, silent plea for an explanation. Both women instinctively knew not to speak.

Clark picked up his dinner and moved towards his room. He stopped at the doorway. "I'll eat in my room tonight. Can you make me a pot of coffee? And Hope, can you bring me your school directory?" Abruptly, he exited. Granny and Hope moved simultaneously to complete his orders, but they stopped and looked at each other. *What is going on?* They seemed to say to each other, although neither spoke.

Hope brought him the directory, but he was on the phone and did not acknowledge her presence as she left it in front of him. He sat at his desk with his hand rubbing his forehead. Somehow, he managed to eat about half his dinner, and Granny took the plate out when she brought the coffee in.

At that point, he was still on the phone, first standing, and then pacing while he talked.

They talked in the kitchen while they cleaned the dishes.

"Have you ever seen him like this?" Hope asked.

"No."

"He seems so agitated. It's kind of scary or creepy."

Granny shook her head, "I wouldn't use the word agitated. He seems energized."

"It still seems weird."

"You got any idea what it is about?"

"Yeah, I think so. Everyone is talking about it. A football player at school was kicked off the team. It wasn't fair."

"That explains it."

"Since when does Dad care about football so much?"

"He doesn't. He cares about injustice."

Hope nodded, and she turned toward his door.

Clark spent the next four hours on the phone. Sometimes, Hope could hear him because he would be talking loudly and, sometimes, he would be talking in whispers and she could not hear him, but she could still tell he was busy on the phone. It was nearly eleven o'clock when he finally came out of his room looking tired, but still very agitated. Mrs. Wheeler had gone to bed, but Hope was still sitting in the kitchen waiting to see if she could help. They stared at each other.

"Look," he started, "this is about school, but it doesn't involve you, and I don't want to put you in the middle of this."

"This is about Mickey, isn't it?"

He nodded.

"I was at the party, Dad, and he wasn't drinking. Believe me, he was probably the only football player who wasn't drinking, but he wasn't. He doesn't deserve this."

He continued to nod, but spoke up, "I believe you. But, you were right. It wasn't fair for me to ask you. I believed Mickey when I spoke to him."

"What are we going to do?"

"Well, I spent the last … what time is it?"

"You've been on the phone four hours."

"Really? Wow. OK, four hours talking to almost all of the members of the football team. I talked to Mickey, the captains, the starters, the remaining seniors, and then I started on what's left on the team. There is no practice since tomorrow is Saturday. They are all going to meet tomorrow in our backyard at 10:30."

"Our backyard?"

"Yeah, it will be big enough because they don't have to sit down. If we met anywhere else, they could use the police or something to break up the meeting, but there is no law that we could possibly be breaking in our backyard. And Mr. Plymale will be able to see them from across the field. He will know what we are doing. The meeting itself might be all we will need to do."

Hope nodded because she didn't know what else to do.

"Don't you see? The only power the team has is the team itself. Mickey has talked to the coach and the principal, and nobody is willing to listen. But, if the whole team speaks with one voice, they will have to listen."

She continued to nod.

"The football team is going to go on strike."

August 27, 1985

Mickey showed up at 10 o'clock. By 10:30 a.m., Mickey was pacing back and forth in the backyard with Mr. Bradley. By 11 o'clock, no one else was there. Mr. Bradley was no longer pacing. Clark took Mickey into the house and put him in front of the telephone with the directory to the side.

First, he called Johnny, the starting quarterback who was a senior and captain of the team. "Johnny, this is Mickey. I'm here at Mr. Bradley's. I thought you were coming. What happened? Uh huh, yeah. Well, I understand. Sure. Thanks, anyway."

Mickey turned to Mr. Bradley, "Johnny's parents wouldn't let him come to this meeting. Let me try Otto. He's more independent than Johnny." He punched the numbers on the phone, and waited for the ring tone.

"Hey, Otto. This is Mickey. Yeah, well ... oh, that's bull! Thanks." Once again, he turned to Mr. Bradley. "Otto doesn't want to risk his last chance to play football. You think there is any point in calling any of these others?"

"Probably not. I am so sorry, Mickey. I thought we could win this. If they had stuck together …"

"If my teammates had been teammates."

"Nobody came by. Nobody called. I don't believe it."

"I saw a truck drive by, but it didn't pull in. It just drove by," Hope offered. "At least that one truck came by."

"Well, Mr. Bradley, you tried. It's not your fault. Thanks."

Clark walked Mickey to the door and shook his hand. He nodded goodbye. Then, he walked back into the house. Clark filled a glass with water from the sink, drank it down with one long gulp, walked slowly into his room, slipped into the chair in front of his desk, and pulled out a sheet of paper. Hope followed him slowly. She was afraid to talk, but her curiosity was stronger than her fear. "What … are you … doing?"

"Writing a letter of resignation."

He looked up her, "Hope, I just cannot teach anymore at a school that … allows, that perpetuates such blatant injustice. This thing with Mickey is just the latest example. The whole system is corrupt. It's all about power. Nobody really cares about the students. The football team is more important than the student body. I can't – I won't support that system anymore.

"And the students. I am so disappointed in his teammates, but not surprised. In many ways, they are typical, I just don't think I can teach students that are so self-centered. Their values are so warped! What the hell! They go to Red River High School that is nowhere near the Red River. The whole thing is an illusion, a twisted illusion. I just don't believe in the process ... the institution ... the participants ... I can't control much, but the only part I can control is me. I do not have to participate in the insanity.

"This just isn't me. I have never been a part of the establishment. I have always more comfortable protesting the establishment. I need to use all of my energy and mental focus in opposition to such a repressive environment."

He turned to the paper on the desk. "In fact, I have a moral obligation to oppose the school, the institution, the whole system. Evil flourishes when good men do nothing."

Hope turned and ran into her room, leaving Mrs. Wheeler to face Clark. She rolled to the doorway. She stared at him a long time before she spoke, "Sometimes, you have to rise above your principles."

Clark looked at her. "What do you mean?"

"You sit there spewing forth your self-righteous platitudes – you sound like bumper stickers from the '60s. But, you aren't on a college campus anymore. You are in the real world with real people, and compromise sometimes is necessary. What about Hope? Your resignation puts you on the moral high ground, but where does it leave her? Won't you be abandoning her? I think you will have to decide what is more important: your principles or your daughter, not to mention all the other students in the years after her."

Waking Together Again for the First Time

December 5, 1968

San Francisco, California

Clark was lying on his right side but on the left side of the double bed when he woke. Grace was facing away from him on the right side. The first thing he was aware of was the chill in the air – the window was slightly open. It seemed like a good idea when they went to bed last night, but the lack of a good heater and the early morning weather made him reassess that decision. He rolled over and put his arm around her pulling the cover up over her shoulder and arms – a very protective move. She was asleep as far as he could tell, and he did not want to risk waking her. Actually, her eyes were opened focused far way, and when he put his arm around her and covered her, she accepted the gesture silently and gratefully. She closed her eyes and fell back asleep; she felt safe. Whatever demons she had been wrestling with, she had vanquished, or perhaps, he had vanquished. Later, he got up and went to the bathroom. When he returned to the bed, she rolled over and laid her head on his chest. She breathed deeply as if asleep.

"You are not really asleep?" he asked.

"Yes, I am."

"OK."

They stayed like that for a while before he spoke, "I'm glad you are asleep because my arm is growing quite numb."

"Do I have to move?"

"No, not if you don't want to, but …" he moved his left arm to move her lower on his chest so that his arm became less of a pillow and more of a fence.

"I feel kind of perverse … twisted," she spoke in deeper, more husky voice than usual.

"How so?"

"Well," her voice returned to its usual tone. "I've never really slept with anybody with whom I've had sex, and now I find myself sleeping with someone with whom I have not had sex. Isn't that warped?"

"Maybe a little ironic," he shrugged his shoulders as much as he could under the circumstance. "I just thought it was a good idea last night … with the cold wave coming in … I mean thermodynamically, you know. Purely thermodynamically."

"I'll have to admit, I'm beginning to like this arrangement."

He smiled. "Me, too, but I'm glad you have come to the same conclusion."

"Right. Well, leaving the window open was not a good idea." She gestured toward the window across the room, which was a scant two inches open.

"I don't know. It kinda depends on how you define good."

"Well, I am freezing."

"That's funny," he smiled. "I'm feeling pretty cozy. I kinda like it."

"I think," she spoke in a mock serious voice, "that someone needs to get up and close the window."

He nodded, "Yeah, that's probably true."

Neither one moved. She still clung to his chest.

"Well?" she asked.

"Well, what?" he responded.

"Are you going to close the window?"

"Not me. I'm perfectly comfortable – cozy even."

"I can stay here all day."

"Me, too."

She hugged him tighter, "It's Saturday, and I don't have anywhere I have to be." Still, no one moved. "You know you are going to get hungry before too long."

"Yeah," he said as he stroked his chin and pretended to look thoughtful. "I'll probably get up when I get hungry."

"Me too." Still neither one moved.

"You hungry yet?" he asked.

"Nope."

"Me either," he said as he pulled her closer. She responded by hugging him tighter.

"Have you got any plans for Christmas?" she asked.

"What do you mean?"

"Are you going home for Christmas?"

"Grace, this is my home," he said in a tone that was uncharacteristically flat. "What about you? You going home?"

"No, I can't really afford it. Besides, I'm not really ready to face my family. I'm gonna tell them I have to finish some research." She was troubled by his remarks. "What do you mean this is your home? Don't you have a family?"

"No I don't." There was a flatness in his voice.

"OK." She did not want to probe.

"It is not a great secret or anything," he spoke after taking a deep breath. "I just don't like to talk about it. My parents died while I was an undergraduate. They left me some money. That's why I can afford this apartment and graduate school."

"I'm sorry," Grace wasn't sure what to say. "I didn't mean to ..."

"It's all right. I just don't like to talk about it."

"You can talk to me," she lifted her head up from his chest and looked up at him. "But you don't have to."

He stared at her before he spoke, "That song – the one you sang. It reminded me of them on so many levels. I'll tell you all about them someday, but not today. Today, we have to make Christmas plans. You know – decorate, make breakfast, and close the freakin' window before we freeze to death." He jumped up and shut the window.

The Truth Will Set You Free – Or So They Would Have You Believe

September 5, 1982

26 Red River Lane, Nettie, Texas

He went into the kitchen and made a sandwich while he called Granny. She said she would get a ride home and that it was a good idea to let Hope sleep, but that he should check on her often to make sure she was asleep. She would be home early to fix dinner and check on them both. He suggested that she get a pizza on her way home – he would call it in. Then, he sat back and waited for Hope to wake up wondering what was wrong and how he was going to make it right.

By the time Granny appeared and the pizza was unboxed and put on the table, three hours had passed. The aroma filled the house, and Clark thought it was time to wake Hope. He looked at Granny and said, "Wish me well." She nodded.

He walked into her room. He looked around the room for the first time in several years. He was not sure when the room transformed from a little girl's room into a teenager's room. Gone was the wallpaper with cute frogs and unicorns. The room was painted a dark blue with a collage of rock stars and movie celebrities – the Beatles, Waylon Jennings and Willie Nelson– all rather unconventional. Right in the middle, bigger than any of the others were two figures: Bob Dylan and Van Cliburn. Off to the right was the largest poster, an ad for "Catcher in the Rye." Another wall had a mirror and some minor decorations for hanging belts and jewelry. There was a record player and a record collection that took up most of one wall and a bookshelf dominated the last wall opposite the closet. Her bed was situated between the closet and the bookcase. A small desk was crammed into the space between record player and the corner. She really did not have much room. Clark sat down on the desk chair and turned it toward her bed. "This is really … cozy." Then, he nodded at the posters above her bed. "Still stuck in the '60s, I see."

"It is a good place to be stuck," she said.

"Bob Dylan? He was always my favorite. I didn't realize you were a fan. "

"Are you kidding? Nobody, I mean nobody has ever made songs better than Dylan. He is the greatest."

"Is? I didn't even know that he is still making albums."

"He got religion and most people don't like his last couple of albums."

"I use to have a friend back in San Francisco who resented Dylan. He hated the way Dylan seemed to know what changes he was going through before he knew it himself. Seemed like every time Dylan would put out an album, it would be some radical direction that he would love and he hated that Dylan could figure out what he was going to love before he could.

"Notice I've chosen to ignore Van Cliburn. I never could get into classical music, but I envy people who do."

"Well, a lot of people ignore classical music, but it sure says as much as any of these other guys … just a different language," she said.

There was a silence, a strained silence, and both realized that the time for chitchat was over.

"You didn't come in here to talk about Dylan, did you?" Hope stated with a certainty that carried an air of dignity more advanced than her years. Clark looked at her lying in the bed looking so vulnerable.

"We have some pizza in there." He gestured toward the kitchen. "You must be very hungry – no lunch and all."

"With pepperoni?" she asked in what amounted to a little game they played.

"Is there any other kind?"

"I am hungry," she responded as she stood to go to the kitchen, but first she stopped and hugged her father. "Thanks for coming and getting me today, and thanks for not asking any questions, I mean, right away on the ride home. I couldn't have handled talking."

They walked to the kitchen with his arm around her. "You know. You are going to have to talk to us and tell us what's going on."

"I know," she nodded. "I know, but I talk better after pizza."

"Everyone talks better after pizza." They sat down at the table, and began to eat.

They ate in silence. No one was going to push Hope to talk before she was ready. When she finished, she stood up and said, "Now, I want to practice my piano. Then, I will talk."

Hope went into the living room and sat at the piano. First, she played scales and then she practiced two classical pieces she was working on. Her tone was strident and harsh but also, at times, gentle and quiet. She hit very few false notes. Clark and Maggie listened more intently than usual because the music sounded more intense than usual. After playing for an hour and a half, she walked into the kitchen and announced that she was ready to talk.

The three of them gathered around the table, Maggie poured some milk and served some cookies. And Hope began, quietly. "I really don't know very much about my mother. I mean, I know she was smart and that she lived here with Granny Wheels, but the only thing I really know ... the only thing you ever say is that I am just like her." Tears began to form in her eyes.

Maggie spoke, "You are not just like her; your hair is different and you are taller. You are more coordinated than she was. You are more talented than she was. She could never play the piano like what I just heard – that was beautiful, by the way. But, you have many traits in common."

"Every time you smile, I see your mother," Clark spoke so quietly even Hope had to strain to hear him. "And there is a twinkle in your eyes that she had. You share the same sense of humor, or more accurately, the same laugh." He waited to continue to catch his breath and swallow the lump in his throat. "When you are focused, your vision penetrates like no one else I have ever known except your mother. There are gestures you make ... " He shook his head. "You are not her, but I see so much of her in you." He could not speak any more, and just shook his head.

Hope sat in silence before bursting forth in a torrent of tears and uncontrollable sobs. "Will I go crazy too?'

"What?" Both Maggie and Clark said simultaneously. "Your mother was not crazy," Granny said, and Clark added, "Your mother was the most mentally healthy person I've ever known. Who told you she was crazy?"

By now, Hope was sobbing hysterically and Granny was trying to wheel herself over to hug her and comfort her. Hope screamed out, "Did she hate me?"

"No. Of course not," Maggie was grabbing arms and legs as Hope flailed about uncontrollable.

Clark darted across the table, lifted Hope off her chair, picked her up, and held her tight until she caught her breath. "Shhh," he kept saying as he patted her on the back and rubbed her head. "Breathe. Just breathe."

Finally, Hope got a breath, leaned back, and spit at him, "Why did she kill herself? And why didn't you tell me? How can I believe anything you say?" She wrestled herself free of his grip and started to run into her room.

Clark, for his part, grabbed her arm and stood stunned in the middle of the room. He turned toward Maggie. He began to understand her pain.

"That's why you've been getting up at night and touching the urn!" Maggie offered. "Suddenly, it makes sense."

"You knew?" Hope asked.

"Knew what?" Clark more dazed than anything.

"She's been getting up at night and touching the urn with Grace's ashes." Granny spoke. "I haven't said anything because … I don't know. I figured it was something she needed to work out on her own, but Hope, you have got it all wrong. Your mother did not kill herself."

"Your mother was full of life more than anyone I have ever known," Clark said. "She did not want to die. Suicide? Out of the question. She did not commit suicide. What made you think she did?"

"The kids at school … they all know … they said everyone knows. And what I remember, too."

"The kids at school?" Granny spoke out. "What would they know? How would they know anything?"

"What do you remember, Hope?" Clark spoke sternly but gently.

"Well, I remember seeing all this blood … and it was dripping down her arm … and it was in the bathtub … and there was all this water. She cut her wrist, didn't she?"

"Oh, God. Oh, God," Clark sat down and had to cradle his head in his hands. "That is exactly what you saw. We came back from a walk in the park. But, no, Hope, she did not cut her wrist. The blood was from her head. When we opened the door, there was water from the tub all over the floor. You started to jump and splash, but I could see Grace in the tub. I jumped in front of you, slamming the door, grabbing, pivoting back toward our neighbor. First, I slipped and you started to cry, but I got you downstairs. I told Isabella, our neighbor, to call the police and the ambulance while I ran upstairs holding my mouth trying not to vomit. My first thought was to save you from seeing your mother. Somehow, I knew she was … dead. I guess mostly I did … save you. The police did show up although I had to call them. Isabella was illegal and would have nothing to do with calling the police.

"She had simply slipped in the tub, broke her neck, and cracked her skull. There was a tremendous amount of blood loss and it flowed down her arm to the floor, but her death was due to the broken neck. It was the most horrible thing I have ever seen. I felt like all of the air in my lungs had been sucked out of me. I feel that way to this day if I picture it. I'm not sure my lungs have ever filled completely since that day …" Clark had to put his hand over his mouth. Ten years later and his stomach still leapt to his throat when he thought about the experience. Clark put his head down on his arms on the table and wept silently.

A silence hung in the room before Hope walked over and put her arms around her father.

"She fell? She fell in the bathtub?" Hope was shocked. "My mother died from a simple fall in the bathtub. No. No, that can't be true."

"I don't know how these rumors get started. You say Meredith believed it. She should know better. Ralph knew what happened from the beginning," Maggie was beginning to refocus on the present. "I'm going to go call him right now and get to the bottom of this." She wheeled herself off into the living room.

Clark lifted his head up off the table and looked at Hope. "You have been carrying that around for how long? I'm so sorry."

"Since July. I'm sorry that I didn't trust you ... Oh, Dad! I think the truth hurts worse. How horrible! A fall in the bathtub." She burst into another wave of tears, and collapsed into his arms.

He held her in his arms and rocked her back and forth gently.

"Your mother loved you so much! She never experienced any post-partum depression, or if she did, it didn't last 30 seconds before she left the hospital. Her eyes would light up whenever she would look at you, whenever you would burp or giggle or smile. She would beam. Often at night, she would wake me up so we could watch you sleep. She loved being your mother, and she loved you with all her being. All of her ambitions, all of her plans to save the world – and there were many of both, believe me – all were put on hold the first time she saw you. Just being your mother suddenly became her top propriety. She wanted to earn the right to be called your mother."

Hope listened to his words and a different kind of tear began flowing down her cheek, cleansing tears, and her eyes began to shine in a way he hadn't seen in a very long time. For the first time in awhile, she felt a pride in her mother. But her joy, if that is the right word, was short lived, replaced by an authentic sorrow. She shook her head. "I miss my mother."

"So do I."

"But, somehow, I feel closer to her now ... more than ever."

"I know. I know." They hugged silently. "You know when I feel close to her?" He asked to break the silence. She shook her head, but didn't say anything.

"I feel close to her every morning when I wake you up and see you on the other side of the breakfast table, and every night when I tuck you in. In countless moments during the day — when you laugh a certain way and when you scrunch up your forehead — little gestures."

"I want to know more about her. I want to know everything about her."

"Well, I think that would be a good goal — a good thing. Your grandma can tell you all about her growing up and …"

"I want to know all about her. Like, how did you meet?"

She pressed against his shoulder. He began, "We met at a protest march, sort of. To be clear, the first time I saw her was at an anti-war demonstration. She was giving a speech between marching. I was just in the crowd, but I took one look at her and I thought she was …" His eyes looked unfocused and he stared at the wall across the room.

Hope tried to regain his attention and finish his thought. She leaned back in the chair. "You thought she was the most beautiful girl you had ever seen. You were smitten — love at first sight."

"You making fun of me?"

"No, Dad. But, come on. You don't strike me as a cliché. Did you really think she was *bee-you-tee-full* — love at first sight?"

"No, I didn't," he said. "Well, yes, too. It wasn't that she was pretty although, God knows, she was that. But, what caught my eye was that she was so full of confidence … passion … authentic energy … a sense of self. I do not know how to describe it or explain it. I've never seen anyone before or since with such an essence of … life. Her eyes … sparkled? Radiated? Glowed? She emitted a force that was so … I don't know … She made you feel glad you were alive. She was so …"

Here, he clutched his hands into a fist and shook it, "Yes! I felt immediately inspired by her, and I knew, I knew somehow she was always going to be a big part of my world, but I doubted that I would ever even be a sliver of her world. I don't know if you can even understand what I mean."

"I do. It's like Bob Dylan and me. His music, even the songs written long before I was born, are really important to me – central to my life. But, he will never even know who I am."

"Yeah, I mean, I was a nerdy math major about to complete my class work on my master's degree with no idea of what I was going to do. I had participated in a few marches in the South – civil rights marches. I even managed to get arrested a few times. Actually had a bigger reputation than I deserved on campus, but I was nothing – small potatoes – compared to her. She was this life force about to change the world. I lived in a world of tangents and cosines, and she lived in a world of cultural upheaval – the Age of Aquarius.

"I began to attend more and more of the protest movements and free speeches. I even began to participate, just a little. It would be wrong to say I did it because of her. She wasn't at all of the same places. I just began to listen and the movements all made sense to me. Fortunately, my studies were almost complete, so I could afford the time. Occasionally, our paths would cross at these events. She would always take my breath away, but I never learned her name and never talked to her.

"One day – one rainy day, I slipped into a coffee house to dry out and get some much needed coffee. I was sitting shivering, literally, when your mother slipped into the booth and said, "I think you really want to buy me a cup of coffee." I was stunned. I must have stared at her for like a minute, and she was getting ready to leave thinking I was brain dead or something when I finally got it together enough to say, 'I'm thinking a cup of clam chowder. I really want to get you a cup of chowder. I think I'll even join you.' 'Do you think we'll fit?' she said, and that, as they say, was the beginning of a beautiful friendship."

Granny came into the room and exclaimed, "I just got off the phone with Ralph. It was an interesting conversation."

Hope and Clark looked at each other, and turned to Granny expectantly. "Well?" they said in unison.

"Ralph was aware of the rumor, but he had not addressed it directly with Meredith. He told her that Grace died in an accident, but he never was specific. He never felt that he needed to, or that Meredith needed anything more specific. He had heard some teachers talking in the teacher's lounge and he corrected them, but they insisted that the accident sounded phony. He knew many people believed the rumor, but he didn't know what to do about it and he wasn't sure it was a problem. He was really surprised to hear about what happened today. He didn't know that Hope was so affected. He is going to speak to

Meredith, but he still isn't sure what can be done to get everyone else to believe that the rumors are false."

Clark sighed, "I can't believe that the teachers think that Grace committed suicide."

"You know," Hope sounded more optimistic and full of energy than she had sounded in months. "It doesn't matter. I don't care what they think. I am so relieved to find out the truth, and I just don't care what anyone else thinks."

"Or," Maggie held up a piece of yellow paper and waved it. "We could show people the article from the San Francisco newspaper that tells of the Grace's death. If you want to, Clark, you could copy the article with the date and everything and put it in all the teacher's mailboxes. And Hope, you could show it to your friends and some of your teachers could read it to class, and we could put an end to this rumor."

Hope grabbed the paper away from Granny and started to read the article.

Clark shook his head. "I don't think I want to do that. I'm like Hope. I can live with their disbelief. I don't really care what they think."

Maggie stiffened. She did the equivalent of sitting up in her chair. She spook firmly and decisively. "I do! It hurts me too much to think that people believe that Grace committed suicide … But, it's not about me; it is about Grace. I do not want the people in this town to misunderstand her – to misjudge her."

"Dad!" Hope suddenly shrieked. "It says here that Mom was two months pregnant and that the baby died." She looked up at her father with a stunned silence.

"Yes. You lost a mother and a brother at the same time."

She looked at him with a new sense of empathy. "And you lost a son as well as your wife."

He nodded.

"Oh, Dad." She gasped, reflexively drawing her hands to her mouth and then was silent, keeping her eyes on him.

He stood up, clinching his teeth and blinking his eyes. Slowly, she moved toward him, and they hugged in silence.

"It hurts too much to face another day"

April 21, 1989

1124 Canyon Drive Nettie, Texas

The alarm went off and Ralph awoke. He rose up on his stomach, turned off the alarm and rolled over on his back. He stared at the ceiling for a few minutes before he swung his feet over on the side of the bed and started the process of leaving the bed. Absentmindedly, he slapped the bed, but there was no dog to summon. He was alone, profoundly alone.

He stood up and made the bed. It was hardly wrinkled. He only slept on one side and he didn't really move much in his sleep. He selected his underwear and socks for the day, his slacks, shirt, tie, shoes. He laid them out on the bed neatly as he went into the bathroom to shave and shower.

He dressed slowly and deliberately. He stood and tied his tie while looking in the mirror over his chest of drawers. Lastly, he brushed his hair. There was less of it than there used to be, but he was still a ways from being bald. It still made a part. He stared at his reflection. "You send your daughter to college to get an education, maybe to get a husband. You don't send her to fall in love with some nut job and get murdered by him." He wasn't sure if he actually said the words out loud or if his thoughts were so loud as to interrupt the relentless silence. It had become his daily ritual. Spoken out loud, as a reminder or as a defense, the sentence became his way to start his day. Long ago, at another time in his life when he felt life had ended for him, Mrs. Wheeler convinced him that he should go on with his routine. He could hear her voice, "Take one step at a time; eventually, the bounce will return to your step. You don't think

213

it ever will but at some point, meaning will return to the routine."

So, he got up every day and went to school … in silence.

The phone rang. Ralph stared at it as if it was a foreign substance to him. He wasn't used to hearing anything in this context. He picked it up. The voice from the other end sounded familiar and strange at the same time, as if it were in a long tunnel.

"Ralph? Ralph? You there?"

"Yes."

"I need a ride to school – car trouble. Can you pick me up on the way?"

"Yes. All right."

"Ralph, you OK?"

"Yes."

"You sure. You sound … different."

"Clark, my wife left me two and half years ago, and she took the dog. I miss that dog. I'm already behind on teacher evaluations, and I have a hostile meeting with the PTA scheduled for this morning. Two students were suspended yesterday for fighting, and my daughter is dead. Other than that, I'm fine."

"And your neighbor needs a favor. Maybe I can treat you to a pizza and a six pack tonight. Sounds like you could use some old fashion 'va-sever-eraten.'"

"I'm all right. I'll see you in few minutes. Be on the porch."

When Ralph picked Clark up, he asked Clark about his classes. Like, how he thought they would do on the AP exams, the enrollment size for next year. Mostly, they rode to school in silence.

Later that day, Clark noticed that Ralph wasn't in his usual post supervising the cafeteria during lunch. The next period, when he collected some tests he had run off, he stepped into Ralph's office to check on him. Gayle, his secretary, told him that Ralph went home early. "He just didn't feel like being in school today, you know, with today being what it is and all."

Clark was confused. "I was counting on him for a ride. It's not like him. What are you talking about? What is today?"

"Today is the anniversary of ..."

"Meredith's death. Oh, my God. I forgot it was today."

Clark walked out into the hallway and stopped abruptly – stunned. The librarian, Mary Herkowitz, happened to be nearby and when Clark started to waver she asked, "Is anything wrong?"

"What? Mr. Plymale was supposed to give me a ride after school, but he left school early. I would have thought he would have told me."

"He probably just forgot."

"That's not like him." Clark shook his head. "Not normally like him at all." He pivoted and rushed back into the office. He told Gayle to cover his afternoon classes, and then he ran into the vice principal's office.

"Ron, I need you to take me home right now. Actually, I want you to drive me to Ralph's home after we stop at Pizza Palace and get a couple of pizzas and some beer. I don't want Ralph to be alone right now."

The vice principal looked up from his desk. He never knew Clark to make such a strange request in the middle of the day, but he had known Clark for several years, and he trusted his judgment. Without hesitation, he stood up and nodded OK as he headed for the door. Clark stopped at the desk to call Mrs. Wheeler to let her know where he was going.

It was just past 2 p.m. when they pulled into the Plymale driveway. Clark exited the car with two pizzas and two six packs of beer. Ron asked if he should come in or hang around. Clark shook his head. "You need to be back to the school. Someone needs to be there. I just wanted to ... I'm sure Ralph is ... will be back tomorrow."

Ron drove off and Clark turned toward the house not knowing exactly what to do. He went to the front door and knocked. No answer. He entered calling Ralph's name, but there was no answer. Just the silence. He went from room to room. He finally found him in the back room – the game room. He was facing the sliding glass door with the western exposure. There were no lights on, but the sun was bright enough to illuminate the room even with the overcast nature of the day. Ralph was sitting in an overstuffed chair pulled in front of the pingpong table facing the door. There was a generic folding chair to his left in front of the table.

216

"Ralph, I've been calling your name. Didn't you hear me? I brought you some pizza and beer like I promised."

"I heard you. I just wanted to be alone ... watching the sunset."

Clark pulled the folding chair over to be closer to Ralph. "I've never known you to turn down a pizza and beer." He put the pizza on the table and popped the top of a can and handed it to Ralph. Or, more accurately, he placed it in Ralph's hand. Ralph held it without any conviction. "Besides, the sun won't be down for several hours."

Clark looked around the room. Nothing was out of place. Nothing was disturbed. But, there was the silence — a relentless silence. There was still three or four hours ahead of them before darkness. He turned the chair toward Ralph, sat down, and leaned forward. "I'm scared," Clark said. "Ralph, are you thinking of killing yourself?"

Ralph turned his head toward Clark and then turned back toward the window. "This used to be Meredith's favorite room — her favorite view. She would come down here and do her homework ... watch the sun go down ... and more often than not, fall asleep in this chair."

Clark nodded, "She was a quite a girl. It is a terrible loss."

Ralph's eyes were the kind of red that comes from crying longer that tears last. "I don't think I'll ever stop hurting."

Clark could only nod, "The pain is just as great today as it was a year ago ... the wound just as fresh."

Ralph sighed, "And it has been every day. When my mother died, I thought I would never get over that. Mrs. Wheeler told me to just put one foot in front of the other – go about my routine, and one day the pain wouldn't be there. She was right. But, this time, it isn't working. Every day, every step, I feel … the loneliness … the emptiness … I hear the echo … of the silence … and it just keeps getting worse. Clark, I hurt … so … much."

"I know. The pain is just relentless … no letup." Clark moved in closer to Ralph. "I wish I had some magic words to ease your pain. I don't. All I can tell you is … I am here."

Ralph looked up at Clark and collapsed in his arms. He cried; an unrestrained screaming sob. His shoulders shook, and Clark had difficulty holding onto him, but he held on until his sobs became gasps, and Ralph's energy level reached the softer quiet level of breathing.

Clark finally spoke, whispering into Ralph's ear, "I don't want you to die."

"But, I don't want to live."

"I know. It hurts too much to face another day."

"No. No. That is not it. I can face another day. I just don't want to." Ralph pushed himself back into the chair, "I know I can go on. Effectively. I have for a whole year. But, what's the point? I mean, why do this to myself? What noble purpose do I serve by … bearing this much pain? I just don't have any … motivation."

"What about the people who love you?"

"Who would that be?"

"What about the kids at school? Mrs. Wheeler? Me?"

"The kids at school. Right. The next day, there will be a new principal, and soon no one will remember me. Mrs. Wheeler will understand. And you? "

"Yes, me. Don't discount that. I know we disagree on some things."

"Everything."

"Not everything. OK, almost everything. I respect the job you do as principal. You're a great principal, better than I could ever be. But, it's more than that. We have a lot in common – been through a lot together. I don't know where I'd be without you."

"What are you talking about?"

"Listen, Ralph. I've never told you this before, and I should have. I don't know what I'd do … who I would be if I weren't a teacher, and I wouldn't be a teacher if it weren't for you. And I'm not sure how Hope could have made it through junior high without Meredith and your support. When I told Hope how Grace died, Meredith was the only one who immediately stood by her. Meredith … and you."

"Well, I knew Grace."

"That's something else we have in common. We both loved the same woman."

There was an energy returning to Ralph's answers. "Let me see if I got your reasoning right. I don't really want to live anymore, but I should because some people don't want me to die. That about right?"

Clark nodded.

Ralph nodded, too. "I'm not sure that's enough, but it will have to do. If the pizza is pepperoni."

"Of course. Is there any other kind?"

Ralph shook his head. "You really are a hopeless hippie."

They opened the pizza boxes. After a slice or two, and a beer or two, discussions on upcoming tests, class officer elections, proms, and some other topics that the two could never see eye to eye on, Clark turned serious again. "Ralph, you need to promise me you will talk to someone ... someone professional. I mean I think this has been a real crisis, and I don't think you should take it for granted that everything is OK just because the emergency is over. You have to wake tomorrow and you are still ... hurting. We haven't solved anything."

"Clark, I am all right. It was just the anniversary thing. I don't need to talk to ... a shrink."

"There is a gun in the chair ... by your leg. Don't kid yourself. Today was a serious threat."

"I don't know who to talk to."

"It doesn't matter who. Talk to the pastor of your church. He is trained in these things. Call the hotline in Dallas. But, you need to talk to someone. I'm not leaving here tonight until you make an appointment."

Ralph stared at Clark long enough to know that Clark was serious. "All right. All right. I've been a Methodist most of my life; I'll call the pastor." Clark walked across the room and brought the phone to Ralph. He traded the phone for the gun and he listened as Ralph made an appointment for the next night.

Ralph turned and said, "Well, I guess you can go now."

"I am in no hurry. The sun hasn't set yet. We still have a lot of pizza and beer left. 'The time has come, the Walrus said. To talk of many things. Of shoes – and ships – and sealing wax – Of cabbages – and kings.' Unless you don't like the company."

"I feel like you are babysitting, and I don't like it."

"Well, let's pick a fight. How about the stupid Honor Society: The leaders of tomorrow today get to select the leaders of tomorrow, today."

"I don't feel up to any of your asinine arguments."

"Then just listen and nod and while I pontificate about all things educational." Clark and Ralph talked all night. Sometimes, they argued, although it was a while before Ralph became impassioned about the subjects Clark introduced. Sometimes, they talked about old times, even Grace, and sometimes they managed to laugh. It was early in the morning before Clark walked home across the vacant lot separating the two homes.

He walked out the sliding glass door as the sun was coming up and Ralph was sleeping in the big chair. He patted the pistol in his pocket as he walked home across the vacant lot.

Mrs. Wheeler was in the shadows on the porch out of view as he approached. "Is everything all right?" she asked.

"It will be. I think."

"Are you sure?"

"No." He turned back to face the Plymale house. "But, I think so."

They stared for a long time.

"Clark Bradley, you are a good friend."

"Ain't No Wrong Reason"

January 4, 1969

San Francisco, California

The fall semester had ended with all A's for both Grace and Clark. For him, the grades were not a surprise. Even though he had started a new major – psychology – in graduate school, he had made all A's. That one of his classes had been a statistics class certainly helped. For Grace, on the other hand, this was the first semester that was all A's. Usually, she made one or two B's. She never made below a B. The strain of the pregnancy might have been a good reason for a drop of grades, but the support and help from Clark compensated nicely, and she ended up doing quite well in all of her classes. She did drop a class, but she felt she could take it in summer school. She was only that one class behind her graduation plan. She knew she was running out of time to tell her mother about the baby, but she figured the longer she waited, the more hours accumulated, the closer to graduation, the more likely she would elicit something approaching a positive response. She hadn't even told them that she had moved out of the dorm to live with Clark. The due date was in April, and the spring semester would be over in mid-May. She wasn't sure she could pull it off, but she could get close and with Clark's help, she was feeling more confident.

She signed up for 15 hours for the spring semester. One class was accelerated and would meet on Saturday morning, but would end in March. One class met at night on Tuesday and Thursday, and the other classes were clumped together on Monday, Wednesday, and Friday. Clark worked his schedule around hers as much as possible. Graduate school seemed to afford more flexibility. She was looking forward to the classes and feeling optimistic even if her anxiety level about the pregnancy was still high. When she would think about the baby, unanswered questions would just agitate her so she tried not to think about the future. "Best to live in the now" became her mantra.

Then everything changed dramatically one afternoon. She came into the apartment carrying a bag of groceries. Clark had dragged a chair from the table to the wall and was sitting down while talking on the phone. He motioned to her to sit down and made a gesture for her to be quite and not speak. Grace could tell immediately something was wrong; he was frowning. She started to say something but caught herself before she spoke. "Of course," he said. "I understand." He looked over at Grace, put his hand over the mouthpiece on the phone, and mouthed the words "It's your mother."

The color left Grace's face and she felt like she was going to faint. Instead, she put her hand to her mouth to keep from vomiting. Clark continued to hold his hand over the phone as he mouthed the words, "It's about your father." He gestured as if to hand the phone to her. She shook her head. He cocked his head sideways and offered again. She nodded slowly as a tear rolled down her cheek. "Grace just walked in," he said. "Do you want to talk to her or do you want me … of course … I will be glad to … I understand … I appreciate …" he handed the phone to Grace.

She took a deep breath, changed places with Clark, bent over, elbows on knees, and began, "Mom, what's wrong?"

There was a long conversation. Clark knew the content of most of it having heard most of it before Grace arrived. Grace's father had died. Clark walked over behind her and rubbed her neck. She touched his hand. Mostly, she just listened. Once in awhile she would say a perfunctory "Yes" or "No" or sometimes she would make barely audible noises.

During the course of the conversation, it became clear that Grace's mother had become aware of Grace's situation. She knew Grace was pregnant, that she had moved in with Clark, and that she was going to keep the baby, but was still planning on finishing school. She had discovered all these things while she tried to reach Grace to tell her that her father had died. She expressed complete support for all of Grace's decisions, but nonetheless Grace had chosen not to share these things with her – she had discovered them by accident.

After talking for what seemed like endless hours but, in reality, was less than a half hour, Grace said, "Yes Mom, I promise. I'm really sorry ... I didn't know what to do ... I promise I won't. I will keep in touch. I'll call you. Next week, and I'll write ... every week from now on ... because I want to. I love you ... I just forgot how much ... and I lost touch with how much you love me ... I won't forget again. We'll talk again, soon. Bye, Mom." She put the phone down and turned toward Clark. She stretched her arms out, "Please hug me." They embraced.

She buried her head in his chest and cried silently for several minutes. "I didn't want her to find out this way. She was so hurt."

He nodded. "I'm sorry. She already knew everything by the time she talked to me."

"You didn't do anything wrong. She liked you. She said you sounded very responsible. She found out mostly from some of the girls at the dorm and some people in the movement. I just hate that she found out so third party. I should have told her. She didn't deserve this. I feel so bad." She sighed and more tears followed.

Clark moved her to the couch and position himself next to her. He tried to put his arm around her, but she was more in the mood to sit up. He responded by asking, "Was she angry at you?"

"No, she wasn't angry. She was totally understanding and supportive. She just wanted to know how she could help ... what I needed," Grace started to cry and the next words were hard to understand. "I could tell she was disappointed, but more than anything she was just so ... hurt that I hadn't ... confided in her, hadn't trusted her. That's why I feel so bad. Like I betrayed her. You know?"

"I'm sure you felt ..." Clark searched for the right words. "There was a reason you felt like you couldn't tell her."

"I just didn't want to disappoint her," Grace looked at Clark pleadingly. "She has lived with so much disappointment. I didn't want to be a source of another ... life has been one big disappointment after another for her. I just couldn't be another one."

Clark could only nod.

"She came from rural West Virginia," Grace went on with the narrative. "The war was her only escape from poverty – coal mining, share crop poverty. She became a nurse in the army; it was a way out. She met my father – a rancher, a cowboy from east Texas all handsome and dashing in his uniform. He seemed to promise a life of adventure and riches. They married and when the war was over, they moved to Nettie. It wasn't as dirt-grinding poor as West Virginia, but it was every bit as intellectually and emotionally suffocating. She had tasted Europe and wanted more. He wanted to get back to his normal life: drinking beer, riding horses, and drinking more beer. She settled down in Nettie. She learned to love the ranch, but she never could adjust to the 'small horizons,' as she put it. She was trying to figure a way out when he caused the accident that …

"The accident left her in a wheelchair the rest of her life. Her escape from Nettie was out of the question. But, she had me, and I became her hope for a future beyond the small horizon of Nettie. All my life, I saw it as a dream we shared: To grow beyond east Texas, to live out her dreams. I never saw it as a vicarious burden, more like a shared vision.

"I went away to college as far away as I could go– not just in terms of mileage, but more in terms of culture and values … and here I am; throwing it all away."

Clark nodded, "How does having a baby destroy the dream?"

"Doesn't it? I mean, having a baby means a certain amount of responsibility. It means making certain choices. It means no more freedom."

"Is this something your mother said?" Clark asked. "Or, is this something you realized on your own?"

"I … what are you asking me?" Grace was confused in a disturbing way.

"Well," Clark wasn't sure how to frame what he was about to say. "I just think you should ask your mother how she

227

views the idea of being a grandmother, and if she thinks your birth was an infringement on her freedom."

"I know what my mother would say because she just said it," Grace was regaining the energy that Clark was accustomed to seeing in her. "Mom was excited and supportive of the baby. I think she doesn't see the baby as destroying any dreams, but as adding a new dimension to our dreams."

Clark nodded and smiled.

Grace added, "I am beginning to see it that way, too. The baby gives me — us — a new purpose for our dreams, new dreams. Thanks to you."

"Me?" Clark was stunned. "We've never talked about the baby. What have I done?"

"You have been you. I have grown to trust you. As long as there is someone, someone person I can trust, then maybe, maybe I will not have to give up my dreams, but only expand them."

Clark stared at her, but he was speechless. He had no idea what to say or do.

"Clark," Grace lowered her eyes. "Now would be the time for you to take me in your arms and kiss me, you know, make your move."

"Oh … OK." He leaned forward and kissed her awkwardly, but she moved her hands to his face and caressed him. Soon any awkwardness was gone. They kissed for several minutes and neither could tell if it was one long kiss or several kisses, but they were interrupted by the phone.

"One of us should answer the phone," he said.

"I will," she said. "It might be my mother again."

She turned from Clark and went to pick up the phone. "Hello. Oh, Hi Mom ... I can't ... I will ... all right. That would be good. No, just me, I think ... that would be best. Thanks. Really, thanks. I love you, and I'm so sorry ... I was just so ... no, I won't let anything come between us again. I promise. Talk to you again next week? Of course ... 'til then."

She turned back to Clark who was putting the groceries away. "She called to tell me about my father's funeral arrangements. She offered to fly me home, but I didn't think I should in my condition. She's going to have some flowers sent in my name. She wanted to know if she should put your name on the flowers, but I told her not to."

"OK," Clark nodded. "How do you feel about your Dad's death?"

She looked blankly at him and shrugged her shoulders.

"I gather that you weren't very close to your father."

"I think I've seen him ... maybe a half dozen times in my entire life," she said with a sudden coldness in her voice. "I don't think I've spoken to him at all in the last five years. He was not much of a provider. I don't think he ever paid child support, at least not in the last half dozen years. Mom had to work her whole life in that wheelchair ... a school nurse. He provided the house and the land. He inherited both, but he lost the working part of the ranch soon after he returned from the war. He wasn't much good at managing things. About the only thing he was good at was drinking. He was very good at that, especially after the accident.

"I don't know exactly how the accident happened. I just know that he and Mom were riding their horses and he was drunk and somehow ran into a guy on a motorcycle. It killed the guy and Mom's horse and severed her spine. That is when he really started drinking. Mom forgave him, but he could never forgive himself. Actually, Mom always said that he began drinking so heavy because he could not accept her forgiveness.

"At any rate, when he would work, he would sometimes send money to us. But, most of the time he just drank his money away. Mom would try to help. I don't know how many times she bailed him out of jail. She even tried rehab hospitals a couple of times. Too much guilt, I guess.

"Too bad. Every one said he was really handsome and charming and when he went into the army. When he came home with his pretty bride, he was a well-to-do small rancher, but he lost his cattle to an anthrax epidemic in '48, and he really wasn't prepared for any other line of work. In a lot of ways, his life was all downhill after the war. He couldn't live up to the future the army seemed to promise him.

"Mom said they found him in a ditch outside of town. No one knows if he died from a heart attack or exposure or what. The last time I saw him was my senior year. He was passed out in the city square under a park bench. I tried to wake him up and take him home, but he didn't recognize me. He didn't know who I was. I take that back. He came to the house the last day before I left for college. He showed up and gave me $300."

Clark nodded. Then he walked off toward the bedroom. She followed him. He sat on the bed, his back toward the door where she stood. "What's wrong?" she asked.

"I don't know," he shook his head. "Your father just died. You seem more upset about your mother finding out about your situation, but your father died. It just seems like it is a time for him. You know, to acknowledge his tragedy."

She nodded. "I have cried more tears than you will ever know. Do not think that you can tell me how to mourn." She began to raise her voice until it became almost a shriek, "Missed birthday parties, empty Thanksgiving plates, broken Christmas promises – there was the father-daughter banquet in junior high that he showed up to drunk. That was probably the last straw. I gave up on my father years ago. If I do not conform to your idea of mourning it is because he has been dead to me for years." With these last words, she was shaking.

He put his arms around her, and she accepted his hug. "I'm sorry," he began. "I did not mean to judge your feelings ... I didn't know. I understand pain. Fathers can cast long shadows."

"I guess your reaction was more about your father than my reaction to my father. Am I right?"

"Maybe. Probably." He let go of her and turned back to the window, his hands on the frame, holding himself up.

"Do you want to talk about it?" she asked with as gentle a voice as she could muster.

"No, but I think I need to. But, not right now."

Several hours passed. They ate dinner in silence, and he did the dishes without talking to her. She went into the bedroom and sat on the bed reading. He came in and stood by the window, looking out into the darkness. He looked at the floor, then at her, and then back to the floor. "The hard part is where to start."

She moved onto the bed, but behind him and started rubbing his neck. She whispered into his ear, "I'm here."

"My parents were pretty old when they had me – in their 40s, and I was an only child. They spoiled me growing up, but we were really close. I didn't have many friends. We did everything together. Dad was a college professor – Physics – and Ma taught math in the high school; small-town intellectuals. That was my background. I had no choice but to be a genius. They taught me well. I was always the smartest guy in class, usually that included the teacher. When I graduated, Dad insisted that I go to college on the West Coast. Ma wanted me to go to Purdue less than fifty miles from home. But, Dad insisted, and he won. I was always confused about going away like that, but I figured he knew what was best. I did grow a lot being away from home. I was a math major but a Physics minor. Right after graduation, during my first semester of graduate school, my parents died. They fell asleep with the gas heater and no pilot light ... and they ... did not wake up."

Grace stopped rubbing his neck and gasped, "How horrible!"

"Horrible? They went to sleep and didn't wake up. Can you imagine a better, more peaceful way to die? I received a considerable amount of insurance money and a nice sum for the house, certainly enough to pay for all the graduate school I could ever want to pursue and start a life afterward."

Grace did not know what to say but she found herself reflectively covering her mouth.

Clark sighed deeply. "Are you religious? Did you go to church, I mean regularly, back in Nettie growing up?"

"Yeah," but her answer lacked sincerity. "We went every Sunday, but it was more a social thing than a spiritual thing; I never took it too seriously. I wouldn't call myself very religious. To tell you the truth, I haven't thought about religion in a long time. I've been too busy thinking about this world to think about the next. Why do you ask?"

"We were atheists … always were. If we talked about religion, it was to mock it, you know, laugh at the silliness of it. Then, they started going to church that last year. The last time I saw Dad was during Christmas break, and he wanted to talk about religion. I did not know how to relate to what he was saying, and frankly, for the life of me, I cannot remember what he said exactly. He talked about grace and tried to explain the concept to me. Grace and faith. But, he could have just as well been speaking a different language. To me, faith was a synonym for magical thinking, and grace, well I had no idea what he was talking about. To me, with my intellectual background, if you couldn't measure something, it did not exist."

"I guess that is one way we are different," she interrupted him. "I've always been the kind of person who is most interested in those things that you can't see. It has handicapped me in some of my classes, even my psychology

233

classes. I've sorta felt that anything that is observable and measureable isn't worth observing and measuring."

"I understand what you mean. I've come to appreciate your approach. That's why I'm taking the classes I'm enrolled in and transferring from math to psychology. I guess that's why I marched in Mississippi and joined the anti-war movement. I believe there is more to life   ... than can be counted. I'm trying to understand." He took a deep breath before he continued.

"But, you don't understand. My father was not the kind of person to leave the heater on without a pilot light. That just wasn't consistent with his personality. He was very cautious about things like that. It is not the kind of thing you can prove, but I'm convinced that my father killed my mother, and then committed suicide. When I finally sold the house and was going through some papers Dad had left, I found that Ma had been diagnosed with dementia, and Dad had a tumor on his lung. I think Dad just wanted to save Ma from having to bury him and living her last years in a mental hospital, and I think he wanted to provide for me the best he could, and save me from both things. He did everything out of love. He made the ultimate sacrifice for the love of his family – wife and son."

"Oh, Clark," Grace said because she could think of nothing else to say.

"I think he thought he was providing grace for me, and maybe for his wife. I think his faith brought him to that conclusion."

He took several deep breaths before he continued, "Do I wish he would have talked to me? Yes. Do I wish he would have made a different decision? Yes. Can I blame him? No. Can I forgive him? I am trying." Clark closed his eyes and lowered his head.

Grace put her hands on each side of his face. She bent into him and kissed his cheeks, wiping his tears away with her lips. Then she kissed him on the lips. At first, Clark accepted the kisses dispassionately. Grace became more animated with the kisses, and Clark returned with fervor. They kissed and hugged and rolled together on the bed, hands busy exploring faces and backs while their kisses continued and built in intensity.

Finally, Clark pushed her back and bolted upright, "No," he affirmed. "When we make love, I want it to be for the right reason, not because you feel sorry for me." He stood up and turned to face the window his back toward her. "That's why I didn't try anything that first night ... I didn't want ... gratitude would not have been the right reason. Pity is not the right reason, either."

She stood up and, unknown to him she slipped off her dress. She walked across the room, and pressed her nearly naked body against his backside. She whispered in his ear, "There are many wrong reasons to have sex, but ... " She turned him around and kissed him before she pulled back and stared in his eyes while she held his head, "I'm not sure there can ever be a wrong reason to make love."

He put his arms around her and hugged her tight enough that he could pick her up and carry her to the bed. They made love. They made love in all the meanings those words imply. When they finished, they both felt that they were no longer two separate entities, but had become one unit.

"You don't quit on love just because it hurts."

October 28, 1987

Downtown Nettie, Texas

Meredith showed up exactly on time at 5 p.m. for her shift at the pumpkin patch of the First Baptist Church of Nettie. She had worked at least one shift every season since she was a junior in high school, and she certainly wasn't going to let college get in the way of the tradition. She saw it as her duty, her obligation, her responsibility, besides she enjoyed it, usually. However, tonight did not offer much chance to be rewarding.

"Hi," she said to Mr. Sanders whose shift was finishing as she was starting. "I'm relieving you now. You been very busy?"

"Nah." Mr. Sanders sniffed his running nose. "Most everybody's got their pumpkins by now. There's an away football game in Celina. Half the town left an hour ago. It's been threatening to rain all afternoon. It's a little nippy, too."

She looked around the church yard from the doorway to the parking lot. There was maybe a dozen bunches of pumpkins with several pumpkins in each. "I don't guess anyone rotated the pumpkins. It really needs to be done if it's going to rain."

Mr. Sanders was handing her the apron with the change in it as he shook his head, "I sure didn't. My arthritis is just too bad. I'm doing well to sell these pumpkins and haul them off to the cars when I have to."

"That's OK.' She said. "I don't mind. It will give me something to do before it rains."

236

Mr. Sanders hurried away just as the rain started to fall. It was a gentle mist. At least Meredith was dressed for the weather. She was wearing cowboy boots, jeans, a sweater, and a jacket. She had on a scarf and a green wool cap with matching gloves. She worked for a half hour pushing and turning the pumpkins so that all of them would be in a new spot, less likely to rot. The pumpkins were spread around the yard in bunches. There must have been close to a hundred left on the ground that she rotated. There were also quite a few smaller pumpkins in the bleachers and boxes of gourds. At least they did not need to be rotated.

The rain was getting harder and as she ran to get under the tent. She sat down behind the table and waited for customers. She didn't wait long before she saw a car drive up into the parking lot and a lone figure get out and head for the tent carrying something. Meredith never could identify the person until she spoke and then she recognized the voice. "Nice that we're having weather. I thought you might like some hot chocolate."

"Hope! I can't believe that it is you. What are you doing here?"

"I heard that you were here tonight, and I thought you would like some company."

"Oh, Hope!" Meredith's squeals turned into tears. "It has been so long since I have seen you! I have wanted to talk to you and ..." She couldn't finish her thought because she was too busy hugging Hope.

Hope, for her part, was concentrating on balancing the hot chocolates and not spilling the contents. "Let's sit down and

237

we can talk. I don't think you will have too many customers to interrupt us," Hope said.

"It will be like old times," Meredith said.

"Only wetter."

Meredith laughed. "I missed your humor; I've needed your humor. I've missed you so much."

"How have you been?" Hope asked.

"I have been good." Meredith said, and then looked down at the cup of chocolate in a gesture that said the truth was somewhat short of her words.

"Really?" Hope turned her head. "I'm your best friend, remember? You can't fool me. You shouldn't try. I've heard you have been having a hard time."

"Where did you hear that? From Granny Wheels? From your father?"

"Mostly from your father … through my father. Rumor has it that you've had a rough time this semester. What's going on?"

"Oh, God! Did Dad put you up to this?" Meredith threw her hands in the air. "This is so … humiliating. I am fine. Believe me, I am fine."

"I do believe you." Hope said. "I'm not sure your father put me up to anything. I came in this weekend and stopped by school to see Dad. When I saw your dad, I asked him where you were this weekend. He told me you were going to be here at the pumpkin patch, and I should stop by. On the way home, my dad said your dad had been worried about you. That's all, nothing else. I gathered it was about the divorce, but it was just a guess."

Meredith was silent.

"Look, your parents were together a long time." Hope said. "For her to up and leave him right after graduation, must have been really hard on you."

"I got over it," Meredith smiled. "I'm getting over it. Actually, we got over it pretty quickly. I mean we were stunned at first. It didn't seem to make any sense. My mom always seemed to be the height of domesticity, you know, housewife supreme. But, I guess it was just an act. It was for many years. What was harder for Dad to get over was me leaving for college. When Mom first left, that summer, it was really ideal. Dad and I had the most fun. But, when he took me to my college dorm, man ..." She just shook her head.

"Well, my freshman year, I came home every weekend that first semester; it's only about an hour drive to Denton. We adjusted really well. You know, during the week, Dad was still principal and I was away at college. Weekends, we would go to football games, make dinner together, catch a movie, and go to church. Neither one of us really missed Mom."

The rain started to lighten up a little, and Hope found herself leaning back because she could hear Meredith more clearly.

"Oh, good. Maybe it will stop raining altogether, and we'll get some customers," Meredith said.

"What happened? Continue with your story. We're sophomores now. What happened the second semester of freshman year?" Hope asked.

"I started staying in Denton more … you know, studying for a test, researching a paper. Dad was OK with that. In fact, one time he came up and took me to lunch. By the end of the semester, two things changed. First, we, or actually I, discovered that Mom was living in Denton and working at a boutique on the town square. After that, Dad refused to come to Denton again. Secondly, I met a guy."

"Meredith Plymale! Shut up! You met a guy?" Hope displayed the proper amount of mock shock. "Tell me about this guy; I want the details – all the sordid details."

"There is nothing sordid; he is just a sweet guy: Travis Scanlon. I met him at a sorority rush party, but I didn't pledge. Travis didn't want me to."

A call pulled up into the parking lot and a woman got out and rushed to the table. "I need three pumpkins for a party tonight," she said.

"What size?" Meredith asked as she stood and stepped to the front of the tent.

"Doesn't really matter as long as they can be carved on." She looked around and picked up one big pumpkin close by. "This will do."

Meredith grabbed two more pumpkins the same size and helped her put them in the car as the rain increased slightly. She took the money, put it in the apron, returned to table, and sat next to Hope. "That might be our only customer. Doesn't look like the rain is going to stop anytime soon." She looked around the pumpkin patch trying to avoid eye contact with Hope.

"Meredith," Hope tried to get her attention. "Hey! You were telling me about Travis."

"Well, there is not much to say. We have been seeing each other for several months now – seven or eight."

"Are you exclusive?"

Meredith smiled smugly and nodded.

"Mere, this is a major development. How can you tell me there is not much to say? It seems to me that there is a lot to say."

"Oh, Hope, it is wonderful. I love him so much and he loves me."

"Well, tell me about him."

"Well, he's sort of cute," Meredith said. "But, you know, not too handsome – looks aren't his strong suit. He's kinda short. He's from around Fort Worth, a senior, a business major, finance, an only child, kinda insecure. He gets jealous easy. He doesn't like it when I see my mom, but then neither does my dad."

"You see your mom?" Hope was surprised.

"Yeah, well, once I knew she was in Denton, it seemed like the right thing to do. She is living with a friend of hers from college – the owner of the boutique. They have an apartment together. Her friend is going through a messy divorce, too."

"Sounds like you have spent some time with your mother."

"Actually, we have started going to dinner every Wednesday. It started out as lunch, at Dairy Queen, but now we're up to dinner at El Mariachi, a local Tex-Mex restaurant. But, I tell you, I'm getting to know my mom for the first time in my life."

"What do you mean?"

"Mom left because she felt smothered by Dad; she couldn't ... I don't know. She was always the high school principal's wife. She never felt that anyone knew her. She said Dad was the worst. He just locked her into a role and wouldn't let her out. You know how Dad always seemed henpecked, like Mom had rules for him. You know, he couldn't have beer at the house, couldn't eat too much pizza ... all sorts of stuff. Well, most of that stuff, Mom never said, but Dad wanted her to say it, so she never contradicted him. She became something she wasn't, but even he lost touch with who she really was, and when she tried to be the real her, he just wouldn't allow it ... he wouldn't acknowledge it. Does that make sense?"

"Maybe."

"Mom had this image of being a perfect housewife and mother. Dad wouldn't let her get a job, and volunteer work was awkward for the principal's wife. She felt like she couldn't really complain, but she felt lonely – deeply, deeply lonely. She put up with it until I graduated, and then she said she wanted out. She hasn't filed for divorce because I think she still loves Dad. But, those are my words. She says that she misses the person she married and courted, but she isn't sure he still exists. She says

242

she hasn't filed for divorce because she hasn't quit given up on him, but each week makes it harder to believe that he is going to come after her. I think if Dad wanted, he could talk her into coming back, but he is too bitter right now."

Hope shook her head, "I'm sorry to hear that."

"Oh, no," Meredith responded. "I have more hope for them than I ever did before I went to Denton and started seeing her. I think Dad will eventually come around. I don't think he likes being alone. You know as long as he has me, he doesn't need her. I think that was one of the big issues between them. Once I came along – especially the older I got, Dad spent all his time being my father and very little time being a husband. Maybe Mom was jealous, I don't know. You know I've only heard her side. Dad won't talk to me about it. It drives him crazy that I see her. He feels betrayed ... really angry. But, it does explain why he seems so ... bothered by Travis. He doesn't want to lose me." Meredith shook her head and shrugged her shoulders.

"All this talk about me. What about you? I haven't seen you in over a year. What is new with you? I need an update. Do you have a guy? I heard you do."

Hope was surprised by the question. "Of all the things that have happened to me the last year, my dating history seems to be the least significant. Where did you hear that I had a guy?"

"From Sarah."

"From Sarah? Oh that figures. Sarah ran into me on a date about six months ago – we were going to a movie. What did Sarah say? That I was engaged or something. I tell you Sarah is something else since she graduated."

"Yeah," Meredith nodded, "who would have thought. Remember when she swore she would never get married, didn't believe in it? Who would have thought she would be the first one married?"

"You know what gets me is that she dropped out of college to marry some guy and raise his kids. She has like three kids from his previous marriage."

"He is a widower. Did you know that?"

"No, I didn't know that." Hope was stunned. "That sort of makes a difference. I can see Sarah marrying a widower, but I still have difficulty seeing her as a mother ... of three. Where is she?"

"She is outside of Waxahachie in a humongous ranch house. I think she is planning on going to junior college when the youngest is school age."

"Is she happy?"

"I don't know that she would use the word happy. She is settled."

They sat in silence for a few minutes before Hope finally spoke, "We need to go see her. All three of us get together again like old times. Soon."

"Yeah. Soon."

There was a subtle yet unspoken realization that they would not get together; not soon, not later. It was a sobering realization that left both of them staring at the rain in silence for several minutes.

"If we don't get a customer pretty soon, I'm just gonna close down, and we can go home and visit in my den," Meredith said.

"Can you do that?"

"No. I have to wait for Mr. Williamson to show up, take the money from me, and turn all the lights off and so forth. Besides, I'm going back to Denton tonight as soon as I get off here. Should be 8 o'clock. Travis wants me back."

"Mere, you're driving back in this weather?"

"It's only an hour drive, and Travis doesn't like for me to spend a night away from him."

Hope leaned back in her chair and cocked her head sideways.

"Yeah," Meredith said. "Travis and I are sharing an apartment. I moved in this semester."

"Does your father know?"

Meredith's facial expression said everything. Of course, her father did not know and, of course, she trusted Hope not to tell. Nothing had to be said out loud.

"Mere, I can't believe you. Keeping secrets, living with a guy. What has happened to you?"

"Oh, Hope. Love has happened. Remember in high school? All the girls wanted boyfriends. I mean you didn't because you were so independent, but I really wanted one –

245

somebody to love me, and somebody I could love. Well, now I have one, and it is better than I could ever imagine."

"Sounds like someone has lost her virginity."

Meredith gave Hope a smug smile, made a flirtatious gesture with her face, and rolled her wrist suggestively, "Honey, I didn't lose anything. I know exactly where it is."

"Mere! Who are you? What did you do with the Meredith Plymale I've always known?"

"Hope, I'm still me. I've just grown up. I mean, haven't you changed since high school?" She turned her head sideways. "What about the guy Sarah saw you with? Is he the only guy you've dated? Are you telling me that you are still a virgin?"

Hope looked away from Meredith; she tried to avoid eye contact. "I only dated him two or three times."

"Hope. Hope, look at me. Are you a virgin?"

"I'm not at all sure that I want to give you that information. It really is none of your business."

"I think you just answered my question."

They stared at each other for a few seconds before Hope broke out in laughter. "His name was Robert; it seemed like the right thing to do."

"Are you still seeing each other?"

"No. No." Hope looked around. "It wasn't the right thing to do."

"What do you mean?"

"Well, you tell me how you felt the first time. What made you say 'yes?'"

"Well, Travis wanted me … he wouldn't take no for an answer and he wanted me as much as I wanted him, as much as I hoped he wouldn't take no for an answer." She closed her eyes and rocked back in her chair. "It was exciting. It was heartwarming. I felt so loving and loved and so … close. Well, you know."

"No, I don't. I didn't feel any of those things. It just seemed perfunctory … mechanical; like I was doing something that I was expected to do, but I didn't get anything emotional from it."

"But it hurt?"

"Yeah, it hurt."

"But, somehow, the pain didn't matter, at least for me," Meredith said.

"The embarrassment meant more to me than the pain. I just couldn't wait to get out of the bed and go home."

They sat in silence neither one knowing what to say. The rain let up, and a customer drove into the parking lot. Meredith helped the mother and her two children pick out two medium pumpkins and one small one. Then, she returned to the table.

"I think the rain is over." Meredith said. "But, I still don't think we'll have many more customers."

"Yeah," Hope responded. "Doesn't look like it."

"So, tell me about yourself." Meredith asked. "What are you up to? I heard you dropped out of college."

"I find the rumors about me are always greatly exaggerated."

Meredith nodded her head. "When you didn't get into Julliard, a couple of kids thought you were going to kill yourself."

"Because of my mother. I thought we put that rumor to rests in junior high. Christ, once a rumor ... I don't know how long it takes to squash it."

"Most people know. It's only a few who still think your mom killed herself."

"Yeah, but I'm still a marked girl. You know, the daughter of a woman who people use to think killed herself, but didn't. It's still a stigma."

"Really? You think so."

"Sometimes." Hope sat in silence. "Then again, sometimes I think the reality is worse. I mean, if she had committed suicide, I would try to make sense out of it, try to understand it. If she had died from a disease. But, how do you make sense out of slipping in the bathtub? How do you come to terms with that? How do you get closure? The randomness is almost unbearable."

Meredith looked out at the wet parking lot and said nothing.

"Texas Christian offers a music degree, and they have a connection with Van Cliburn. I thought I could major in piano and be almost as well off as at Julliard. But, I was turned down, I began to realize that I was never going to be anything but a second-rate pianist."

"Hope, you always played beautifully. You were ..."

"I was very good. I am very good. But, the truth is my hands, my fingers are too short to be the maestro of the piano. Second rate is still pretty good, and I was ready to except my fate. If I couldn't be a great concert pianist, I could still play and teach, and do a lot with music. So, I enrolled at TCU as a music major with a piano specialty. But, I was unhappy almost immediately."

"What was wrong? You didn't like Fort Worth? Or TCU?"

"No. I liked both of them. But my major – not so much."

"You didn't like your professors?"

"No, they were great."

"Your classmates?"

Hope shook her head and she could see that she was frustrating Meredith. "I just began to see my major as ... pointless. Pointless and indulgent."

Meredith didn't look any less confused. "Hope, what are you saying?"

"I don't know, Mere," Hope looked exasperated. "It's like – piano is a tool, music is a tool. I've lost touch with what they are tools for. I can't think of a reason to play music." She looked at Meredith as if for an answer.

Meredith tried to provide one. "For self-expression?"

Hope shook her head and shrugged.

"For beauty?"

"Why? What good is beauty and self-expression in themselves?"

Meredith cocked her head, and Hope said, "Those things – beauty and truth – seem to me only valuable if they serve some higher purpose, and I didn't have that-- I don't have that."

Meredith shook her head, "You use to say that life was just a symphony…"

"I know, and people were just the notes. Well… I've lost my… melody."

Meredith didn't respond.

"I changed majors, dropped out of the music program, and have been bouncing around trying to find something … anything. Currently, I'm majoring in undecided. I've taken classes in sociology, anthropology, psychology, biology, and economics. Still looking for something to major in."

"I'm sure you will find something, and if you are like me, maybe it will be someone."

"You know, Mere. I'm happy for you and Travis, but I don't think …"

"I never thought so, either. You know, when I went away to college, I pretty much accepted my fate as an old spinster schoolmarm. I was going to be a school teacher, never marry, and live my life through my students. My dad was more of a role model than I realized. I was too fat to attract anyone. But, Travis changed all that."

"Mere, you have lost a lot of weight."

"Travis has me on a diet."

"He has you on a diet? He doesn't like it when you see your mother? He doesn't like it when you see your father? He won't let you pledge a sorority? Am I starting to see a pattern? Are you his girlfriend or his project?"

"Hope, I know what you are getting at, and yes, Travis is … demanding. Yes, he is controlling. But, he is worth it. More importantly, I love him."

"Mere, as long as you are happy, you have my complete support."

Meredith lowered her head and started to cry. "Hope, we have issues; we have fights. Sometimes, when he gets mad, he …" She stopped and leaned forward and whispered more because she was ashamed than she didn't want to be heard. "Hope, he has hit me. Twice."

Hope's mouth dropped open and her hand reflectively rose to her jaw. "With a fist?" she asked.

"No. No. Open handed. The first time." Meredith dripped her eyes. "Look, he was sorry and he knows he has a problem. We have been working on it. We are seeing a counselor at the college, and I told him I would never marry him until I was sure he would never hit me again. He has promised, and so far, he has kept his promise, even when I make him mad like coming home tonight to work this pumpkin patch."

"Oh, Mere. I don't like the way this sounds."

"I don't either. I don't want to be an abused woman, but love doesn't stop when it gets difficult. I think that's the mistake my mother made. You don't quit on love just because it hurts. You don't quit on love. You work on it."

Hope looked skeptical.

"We are going to work on it." Meredith said. "Love is not always easy, but love is worth working on."

"I hope you know what you are doing."

"I do. We do."

"Yeah, I can do this."

September 4, 1974

Red River High School, Nettie, Texas

Clark turned on his right side. His eyes opened ... for the fourth time. He looked at the alarm clock. Fifteen more minutes. He rolled onto his back and stared at the ceiling. There was no point in trying to go back to sleep.

"What were you thinking?" he said out loud. He swung his feet over to the side of the bed and shuffled off to the shower. From the shower, freshly shaved, he dressed in his best new clothes – fit for a teacher on the first day of school: Dark gray socks, tan boat shoes, khaki pants, light blue button-down Oxford shirt, and a red and blue striped tie. "God help me," he sighed out loud as he adroitly made the loops for the tie. "Really? A red and blue striped tie?" He looked into the mirror as if he could not recognize the clean-shaven, short-haired teacher staring back at him. "You certainly look the part. How long do you think you can pull this off?"

Mrs. Wheeler was smiling as she served breakfast as he entered the kitchen. "I heard all your caterwauling. You'd think you were going to a Nazi death camp. What, do you think you are pretending to be what you aren't?"

"Mrs. Wheeler ... this ..." he gestured up and down his whole body from head to toe, "*this* just isn't me."

"Then who is it?" she asked.

He looked at her with a hint of a smile, but any reply was put on hold when Hope walked into the room, rubbing her eyes. "You a sleepy bug today?" he asked her.

"No. Just my eyes."

"I guess someone is ready for the first day of school," Mrs. Wheeler said as she put a plate of scrambled eggs in front of Hope.

"Oh, geez! I can't eat this much! If I eat this much, I'll pop and 'splode halfway through the day. Dad …"

"You need a good breakfast, and if your grandmother goes to this much trouble …"

Mrs. Wheeler chimed in, "You're just excited. Now, you have plenty of time before you have to leave for school. You and I can eat slowly while your Dad leaves. Tomorrow, I won't make so much."

"I want to get to school early," Clark said. "I am too nervous to digest a big breakfast. I'll just eat some toast and coffee. Then, I'm hitting the road."

"Clark, it is two hours before classes start. Sit down and eat."

"Yes ma'am. I'll sit and eat, but I won't swallow until noon."

She laughed, and he managed a hint of a smile.

Twenty minutes later, he found himself in the parking lot of the high school with his hands on his steering wheel. He sat there staring straight ahead. He thought of turning the car around and driving off – escaping.

"Is this really what I want?" he asked himself. He let Mrs. Wheeler and Ralph talk him into doing this because it sounded like a good idea at the time, a way to get Hope settled while he pondered alternatives for his future. He was doing this for Hope, he told himself. He said it out loud, "I'm doing this for Hope." That was enough to get him out of the car and into the school.

When he entered the building, the halls were not completely empty. There was the lone couple at the end of the hallway – too much in love to wait for the regular school bell. There was the forlorn sound of desks being rearranged in some distant classroom and bulletin boards being adjusted here and there. Mostly, there was the empty sound of a high school waiting for the influx of students.

Clark went to his room on the second floor – A214. He opened the door and turned the lights on. He walked to the windows and looked onto the parking lot. There were a few cars, but mostly, it was an empty place. His room looked to the south and he could see the sun was high in the sky to his left. It would be a brutally hot day. Beyond the parking lot in front of him was a large … what? Cow pasture. This was indeed a rural school. But, beyond the pasture were house rooftops of the creeping urbanization still far off but not for much longer. Already the western horizon was filling with houses and soon the east would, too.

He turned and surveyed his room. He had thirty-six desks arranged in six rows of six desks – all facing north. There was one long blackboard behind his desk.

He sat at his desk and arranged papers. Neat stacks of papers for first period: Algebra I; third period: Calculus; and fifth period and sixth period – Algebra II. The class rolls were placed on top of each stack. Lesson plans on top of each roll. He was prepared, but was he ready?

Clark sat at his desk in silent reverie, going over his lesson plans and concentrating on his first words with which he would start each class. He took his clues from his textbooks – algebra would explore the concept of sets and subsets, calculus would look at the history of math. He sort of knew where he would start, but the first words seemed to elude his mind. He set at his desk and polished various opening remarks, "Hello, class. Welcome to the wonderful world of algebra." He shook his head.

"Good morning. Together, we are going to explore the magic of algebra." Another shake of his head. He got up and walked around to the front of his desk. "Hello, you probably didn't know, but you've waited all your life to learn algebra." He saw his reflection in the windows at the back of the room. "Oh, Lord," he said out loud. "If I talk like that, I'd better sit behind the desk so they can't hit me with their books.

"I can't say any of those things. Ralph says I need to be positive, but ... do I have to be so ... phony? Someone else can say that. What do *I* say?"

Suddenly, a bell rang. Five minutes until first period. He opened the door and stood in the doorway. Students started coming in, first a girl, then two boys, another two girls, two more boys, and then the rest began streaming in. He nodded at them as they entered. They were kids – teenagers – and he felt comforted when he stood in front of real people instead of empty desks filled with imagined terrors. The late bell rang. He grabbed his roll and moved to the front of his desk. Two boys came rushing in and hurried to find empty desks. Another girl came in even later with a note from another teacher that Clark supposed was an excused tardy slip.

"Here I am, taking roll," he said as he preceded to call each name, changing a James to Jimmy, correcting mispronunciations when needed. Only one student was absent, there were only two students not on the roll, and they had the necessary papers to be in class. Roll was complete. Still, he did not know what to say.

"This is your algebra classroom. This," he pointed, "is the right side of the room. Actually, it is your left side. It has a blackboard on it. We may or may not be using it. This is the back of the room with the windows that look out onto the parking lot and the cow pastures beyond. On the right side of the room, my left, is a bulletin board. I suspect before the end of the semester, there will be something on the bulletin board as soon as I figure what one puts on the bulletin board of a math class – great algebra formulas from history, maybe?

"Here I am, standing in the front of the room. There is a blackboard behind me. I anticipate using it a lot in an activity I like to refer to as teaching.

"My name is Clark Bradley. You can call me Mr. Bradley, or … Mr. Bradley."

He finished and did not have anything else to say. Really, he could not think of anything else to say. He stared at the class. Silence. No one said anything. It was as if he had used up his entire supply of spontaneity and improvisations. He was paralyzed. But he had a vacuous grin on his face.

No one spoke. The entire class stared at him, and just as importantly, even more awkwardly, he just stared at them. Soon, the students began to look at each other while he continued to move his eyes around the room from student to student. Still, nothing was said. The silence could not have gotten more uncomfortable, more inappropriate. Finally, a girl in the front row spoke out, "Aren't you going to go over the rules?"

"Rules?" He asked.

"Yes," she elaborated. "You know ... class rules. All the other teachers start with the class rules."

"With the class rules?" he seemed confused.

"Yes."

"What's your name?"

"Carol."

"Well, Carol, Thank you. This is kind of a new gig for me ... all the teachers start with class rules then. That right?" He looked to the rest of the class for confirmation, and they all nodded yes.

"Why?" he asked.

"That's the way you're supposed to start." A boy in the back said although Clark was never quite sure who it was.

"Well, then, I guess that's the way we should start, then." He moved to the right side of the desk, put down his rolls, picked up a piece of paper and a pencil. "What kind of rules do we start with?"

Everyone started to talk at once, but nobody really said anything until Carol spoke up and tried to get order, "You know, rules about how we should act."

"Don't interrupt others." Someone from the back sort of yelled out – perhaps the same one who spoke out earlier.

"Raise your hand when you want to talk," a girl from the back and right of the class said.

"Be in class on time."

"Like when the bell stops ringing, in your desk young man." This was said by the student who was late.

"I noticed you were a little late by that definition. What's your name?"

"Me? My name is Andrew, Drew to my friends. Teachers call me Andrew."

"I wasn't trying to get on your case, Andrew," Clark kind of moved in Andrew's direction, who was sitting in the middle of the class. "I was just pointing out that the rules don't seem to be that effective."

"Everyone has the same rules."

"Well, Andrew, if everyone has the same rules, what's the point going over them?"

"There are special rules in every class, too."

"What kind of special rules?"

259

"I don't know."

"You have to explain the rules on the first day so we know when we break a rule," a girl on the left side of the room spoke out.

"Name?"

"Kerrie."

He nodded. "Let me see if I understand what you are saying, Kerrie. I need to explain any special rules so that you can be held accountable if you break any rule, any important rule. It's like you can't be expected to obey the rules, the important rules if you don't know what those rules are. Does that about sum it up, Kerrie?"

She nodded yes, but it was a slow, unconvincing yes.

He paced back and forth across the front of the room with his hand on his chin. "I'm confused," he spoke as he continued to pace up and down the rows. The eyes of the students followed him. "You are all ninth graders, and you are all intelligent – I mean you are enrolled in algebra class. Yet, you don't know how to behave without a list of rules? I would think you would have reached a level of sophistication in your education ...

"I'm not sure what special rule ..." By now he was at the back of the room. "I'm not really big on rules, but here is one I think I can live with." He walked briskly to the front of the room grabbed a piece of chalk and wrote in big letters across the blackboard:

Rule #1: Don't Do Anything Wrong.

The class sat in silence – stunned. A boy on the left side in the back of the room spoke in a soft voice, "What does that mean?"

"I'm sorry," Clark responded. "I didn't get your name."

"My name is Dwayne."

"Well, Dwayne, I didn't quite hear you. What did you say?"

"I said, what does that mean?"

"What does what mean?" Clark moved toward Dwayne, "I'm still having some difficulty hearing you. Your voice is rather soft."

"Don't do anything wrong? What does that mean?"

"What do you think it means, Dwayne?" A few students giggled. "No, I'm being serious, and I'm not trying to … make you feel silly or put you on the spot, but it seems to me an important point, what does wrong mean to you? And the rest of you?" He gestured to the rest of the class.

Dwayne looked flustered and stumbled for an answer. "I don't know. Joking around when you're teaching."

"Yeah, that sounds bad. What about the rest of you?"

"Talking over others.

"Sleeping in class."

So many students were speaking out, Clark was losing track of who was saying what. "These all sound like pretty bad things to do, but why?"

Dwayne answered, "I'm not the teacher. I just know these things are wrong – always have been – in every class. Always will be."

Clark smiled. "What I'm asking you is, why? What so wrong with those things?"

Kerrie spoke up, "Are you saying these things aren't wrong?"

Clark turned toward her, "What do you think?"

"I think that's crazy. I think it is wrong to interrupt the teacher …"

"Or other students," Clark added.

"Yeah, sure," Kerrie went on. "It is just impolite to interrupt, to sleep in class, or disrupt class – they are just wrong. Everyone knows that."

"Well, if everyone knows what's wrong, then you don't need me to tell you. You don't need me to spell it out for you." Clark took off walking briskly to the back of the room, stopping on the left side, "But, I have a deeper question for you to ponder: Why are these things wrong?"

When no one responded, he walked slowly to the right side of the room, turned to the class, and gestured as if to say … well … what is the answer? Finally, Carol spoke out, "It is just a matter of … courtesy or decency. Common respect."

Clark nodded. "Everyone deserves to be treated with respect … and dignity."

He let his words sink in before he continued. "What else?" When no response was forthcoming, he asked the class, "What would class be like if this one rule was constantly broken? Everyone was always joking, no one respected anyone, and students were sleeping in class. What would that be like?"

"Like most parties I've gone to," Andrew said.

"Yes," Clark said. "It does sound like a lot of fun. Maybe, if that is what you want from this class – fun – maybe we should have that kind of atmosphere."

"No," Kerrie was adamant. "I want to learn algebra. I know that makes me some kind of nerd, but I'll need it next year and the year after that.'

"And the rest of your life I would argue," Clark added.

"I see what you're doing," Andrew spoke out. "You want us to say we need rules because it affects our education. We can't learn without it."

"Andrew, I don't want you to say that unless you believe it."

Andrew glared at him and turned away as he talked, "You ain't no different. You just want to trick us into saying what you want us to say." He spoke with such finality and cynicism, that everyone in class sat stunned.

Clark started to move toward Andrew, but thought better of it and moved slowly to the front of the room instead. "Andrew, I'm sorry, man. But, you are wrong about me. I really had no idea ... I had nothing in mind when I ... we started this discussion. But, I kinda like where it has ended up. It seems to me it has come to this point. Wrong behavior – bad behavior in class – is anything that comes between you and learning. I don't think you need me to play a part in that process.

"If you disrupt class, if you act disrespectful, if you sleep in class, you need to ask yourself if your behavior is helping your goal of learning. Then, you can decide what you need to do. My job is to provide feedback."

"You haven't been teaching very long, have you?"

"What? Who said that?" Clark looked around the room, but no one claimed the statement, and Clark couldn't recognize the voice or the direction of the voice. "Well, you're right. Today is my first day, and I might be … idealistic, romantic, or hopelessly unrealistic. Still, I think I want to start here and change only if I have to … if you make me. Maybe, I won't have to. We'll get through this together."

A silence followed before Carol needed further clarification. "Do we need a notebook? Do we need to bring our books to class every day? Is there a special format for homework?"

"Carol," Clark breathed a deep sigh before he began. "I don't know. Do you need a notebook to learn math? If so, you better get one. Andrew, do you need a notebook? Kerrie? Dwayne? A better question: Will you learn better with one? I will be teaching from the textbook every day. Do you need to bring it to class to read along with me? I don't know. What do you think? I don't have any format for homework. Do it on the back of your lunch bag for all I care … as long as I can read it. I don't know how you learn. You need to figure that out. I'm gonna have a hard enough time figuring out how to teach.

"I'm gonna teach most, if not all, the chapters in the book. If you can close your eyes in class, read the material at home, and make a grade that you're satisfied with, who am I to criticize your learning style? On the other hand, if you don't pay attention in class, don't do any homework, and make grades that you are not satisfied with, you might want to reassess your approach. I'll be glad to help you."

Clark sat down on his desktop, put his papers down, and leaned forward with his hands on his knees. "It seems to me that all this talk of rules is very one sided. Like everything is about rules for students. You already know what the rules are for you, but I'm the rookie. What are the rules for me? What are the rules you want me to follow?"

Silence followed.

"I guess I know how to get silence in class anytime."

Still no one said anything. Clark looked at Carol – the obvious leader in the class.

"Carol, what do you think?"

"I don't know. I've never been asked that question before. Never thought about it."

"I guess," Clark began to pace again. "My rule should be the same: Don't do anything wrong. But what is wrong for a teacher to do?"

"Don't give us any homework," Dwayne spoke out, and everyone let out a nervous laugh.

Clark looked at him and didn't laugh, but treated him as if what he said was a serious proposal. "Dwayne, that's not going to happen. I want to teach you algebra, and that's not going to happen without some homework. Besides, you wouldn't want it any other way. Let's face it: You really want to learn algebra."

"Don't give us a gazillion pages of homework every night."

Clark turned, but he couldn't see who said it. "Well, I can promise you that. I will not give you a gazillion pages of homework every night. I save my gazillion page assignments for weekends."

"Don't give us too much homework," Kerrie was the speaker.

"How much is too much?"

"I don't know," Kerrie shook her head. "Some teachers think their class is like the only one that matters; they pile on the homework like we don't have anything else to do."

Clark nodded.

A girl in the middle of the class spoke out for the first time, "It's not even that they give too much, but it's like they all give it at the same time. Every class will have a major assignment at the same time. Every class will have a major assignment or a major test the last day of a grading period."

"What's your name?" Clark asked.

"Martha."

"Thank you, Martha. I will try not to do that."

"Try. That's teacher talk for I'll do whatever I want, and you can't do anything about it," Andrew spit out his conclusion. Everyone in class inhaled and sat in silence waiting to see how Clark would respond.

Clark nodded and looked at Andrew, "Fair enough, Andrew. You have no reason to trust me. How's this: If you communicate to me that an assignment or a test is scheduled at a really bad time for you – individually or as a class – I promise I will work out a compromise due date. That will be my policy as long as I can trust you to treat me with the same kind of respect and not take advantage of me.

"Andrew, there is nothing I can do to prove to you that I mean what I say until I show you, and that will take time. You will have to see me in action. I am not going to try to talk you out of how you feel, but I hope my actions convince you before long that I can be trusted and I am not like … other teachers. I will try to earn your trust. In the meantime, I'll teach you algebra. Deal?"

Andrew nodded and the bell rang. Clark opened the door and let one class out as the next class started coming in.

He nodded to the students coming and going. He said softly to himself, "Yeah, I can do this."

Building a Boat

February 25, 1969

San Francisco, California

Grace was washing dishes at the sink when Clark came in from class. He got an apple from the refrigerator, and sat down at the table. "How's the weather?" she asked.

"It's winter in San Francisco – you know, cold enough to acknowledge the season, but not the life threatening chill of the Midwest. Wear a coat." He took a large bite of the apple.

That Grace was pregnant was just now becoming obvious to the casual observer. "Everyone would complain about the heat in Texas, but I kind of liked it." Grace talked as her hands disappeared into the water and splashed around with the dishes. "What I can't stand is the cold and wet that just soaks through you." She shrugged her shoulders. "You know you could help here … dry the dishes or something. I'm pregnant, in case you forgot."

"No, I wouldn't want to usurp your position. You know, disrespect your authority"

"You're just going to sit and watch?"

"I could sit and watch you all day."

"You probably would, too," she said with mock anger, but really a laugh in her voice.

"In fact, I can't imagine a better way to spend the rest of my life," his voice dropped in tone. "Why don't we get married?"

She dropped the dish she was holding into the water and turned toward him. She stared at him. "Please, Clark," she said. "Don't joke like that; my hormones can't take it."

"I'm not joking," he matched her stare. "Grace, will you marry me?" From his shirt pocket, he pulled a gold ring.

Reflexively, a soapy hand moved toward her eye, but she stopped herself. She only blinked. He did the speaking, "I know you think I am being flippant, but I'm not. I've thought about this for a long time. I think our getting married would be a good thing. I've got enough money. I could help you get through school. I could provide for you and the baby while we get our feet on the ground – you graduate and I get a job. It would be in the baby's best interest to have father, and I think I will be a good father. Your mother already thinks I am the father."

"She's just guessing; she doesn't know." That was all she could get out before she started to cry. She walked over to him, kneeled and buried her head in his chest, and sobbed. "These damn hormones. I never used to cry." She wiped her eyes with the dishtowel, and continued. "Clark, I can't … I just can't. It is very sweet of you, but it is for all the wrong reasons. You would be marrying the baby, not me. You won't always feel this way, you would end up hating me, and I couldn't stand that."

He nodded and stood up. He walked to the garbage can and threw the apple core into it with force. "Grace, you don't seem to have much of an opinion of me." He slapped the wall and turned toward her, "Look, I've seen a lot of things in my life. I've been to jail. I've lived on my own for several years now. I've taken more than my share of classes and read more than my share of books, I've buried my parents and, when I think about the future … seeing you standing by the sink washing dishes …

or sitting at the table … or reading in my chair … those are images that please me. They please me deeply. I want to build that boat for two. You know like in the song. I can see a future with you, but I'm not sure I want a future without you. I think you want those things, too. I guess what I'm saying is that I love you, and I think you love me, I hope you love me. I know I love you."

"Oh, Clark," she reached for his hand and held it. "I don't think either of us – especially me – really knows what any of those three words mean: I or love or you."

"You are probably right," he lowered his head. "But, I think both of us are willing to commit to helping each other grow and discover the meanings. I just think we can do that best while together – married."

She shook her head very slowly. "I think the answer has to be no."

He nodded and walked into the other room.

An hour passed before she walked into the bedroom. He was sitting on the bed reading. She sat at the edge of the bed. "I think I owe you an explanation … at least." She said. "Clark, I am just not the marrying type."

"Oh? What type is that?"

"I do not want to lose my independence. I cling to my freedom."

"Yes, I know. It defines you. It is who you are."

"Exactly! I can't believe you understand me so well."

"I do, but you," he stood up. "You insult me, deeply, and you do not understand me at all. Your ferocious nonconformity is one of the things I admire about you. I would not threaten that for anything. Do you really think that a marriage to me would smother you? I would not allow that to happen."

She shook her head, "You might not mean to, but marriage has a way of stifling relationships and closing people into boxes."

"You know this is what hurts and insults me. You've been with me these past months. How can you say this? Have I done anything that would indicate that I would do anything except nurture you? Marriage would be legally convenient for the baby and for you, and I can't see how you and I will be anything but supportive of each other."

"What if I want to move to another state for a job or if you are offered a job somewhere that I don't want to go?"

"Then, we would have a problem, and I suspect we would have to find a solution. You know, like adults often do. Do you really think I would be the kind of person who would put down my foot and say you would have to move with me because I am the husband?"

"What if I'm not ready to settle down?" Grace looked down before she continued. "What if I find … other people attractive?"

Clark nodded. "You tell me, what if I found someone else attractive? What if I went off with another girl right now – this weekend. Nothing is stopping me. There are no wedding vows. You certainly would not prevent it. What would happen?"

"I would feel hurt."

"I would feel hurt if you left me for someone else if we were married or not."

"I am not sure I can promise to not be attracted to others," she said.

"I'm not sure I would believe you if you did promise, and I'm not sure I could make such a promise. I can tell you this: I have no desire to be with anyone else right now … today."

"I feel that way, too. But, is that enough?"

He nodded. "Here's what I know, Grace. From what I have studied in psychology and what I have seen in life, and even what I have read in philosophy: Happiness exists in only one tense – present tense. The future will be built from the present, but you can only live in the present. I don't know the answers to the future, but I do know that right now I want our lives to be together. If sometime in the future, either one of us want something else, we will deal with that then."

He sat down, somehow spent from his emotional release.

She stared at him in silence for several minutes before she responded. "Build me a boat that can carry two," she sang. He joined her in harmony, "And both shall row, my love and I."

Nurturing a Legend

March 20, 2011

Red River Shore Nursing Home, Nettie, Texas

Cassandra had been working at the Red River Shore Nursing Home for six months. She loved her job.

During her training, she met nurses and aides who had become cynical and disillusioned about the clients, but she was very pleased that she saw very little of that at Red River Shore. She enjoyed her interactions with the staff as much as her interactions with the patients.

She walked into the nursing station and poured herself a cup of coffee. She stood next to Andrea and across from Kenneth. They nodded at her.

"Have you had any luck getting Mrs. Hammons to eat?" Cassandra asked. "I have tried just about everything I know, but I can't get her to eat but about three bites of her meal."

"I tried flirting with her and pretending to be interested in her grandkids, you know from the pictures, but three bites sounds about right. I don't think I got any more than that," Kenneth said as he took a deep drink of coffee.

Andrea nodded, "I think you are doing really well with Mrs. Hammons if you get her to eat at all. Most of us can't get her to take any food. I'm impressed. Really, all of the patients love you. You are really endearing yourself to them. I envy you."

Cassandra blushed, "Thank you. Gee, I hope you are right. I want so very much for them to like me. I mean, I can't do much for them but, at least, I can do that, right?"

"They know. They can tell," Kenneth said.

"Yes, they know real caring," Andrea added. "And that is what it is all about, isn't it? I really like it here because we don't seem to lose sight of that."

"Most of the time," Kenneth swallowed his coffee. "Sometimes, it is hard, you know, with one of the lumps, like … Mr. Williams. I mean, I try to talk to him, I try to get a response and nothing for weeks, then all of a sudden he starts screaming that someone is trying to kill him, and you can't get him to calm down until he … Then, he is constipated for like a month and I have to … " he gestured with both arms like digging a hole. "Two days later, he craps all over himself in the shower. And that's the only time he smiles."

Andrea and Cassandra broke into laughter. "You got to admit, it's funny," Andrea said between muffled giggles.

"You weren't there. You didn't have to clean it up." Kenneth blew through his nose.

"It's kinda funny," Cassandra tilted her head and smiled.

"All right, it's a little funny." Kenneth looked down. "What hurts so much is that I look at those pictures of Mr. Williams in his room, those war pictures. You know? When he was young."

Andrea nodded, "The ones in his uniform?"

"Yeah, one or two are on the battleground in the Pacific. I mean, he was a good-looking, healthy kid. But a kid – couldn't have been more than 18 or 19 years old and fighting in a war on the other side of the world."

"And he was a hunk … real eye candy. You know, he won some medals," Andrea added.

"Now he is such a lump," Kenneth lowered his head and stared at his coffee.

Cassandra shook her head, "He is still the same person, deep down inside … He is still there."

"I know … I know. That is the saving grace of this job, but it hurts, and sometimes it is hard and I just have to be reminded." Kenneth hung his head in shame. "Take Mrs. Wheeler, she's another example. She doesn't keep any pictures or anything in the room, and it is hard to remember the person she was."

"What do you mean?" Cassandra asked.

"You are new here, to Nettie, I mean. You've been here … how long?" Andrea wanted to know.

"Six months. I moved from Oak Cliff. You know, south of Dallas. Why?"

"Mrs. Wheeler is like a *legend* around here." Andrea put an emphasis on legend. "I am not just making an exaggeration. She is a … tell her, Kenneth."

"She isn't joking. Wheeler is … there is no other word: legendary."

Cassandra was shaken. "I've seen the new elementary school near the highway on the east side of town that's named after her."

"Well, after World War II," Andrea sat down and began the story. "She had been a nurse in the war, but probably didn't have a lot of training – you know, college wasn't as necessary during the war as it was after. The district hired her to help with shots or health records. I think it was considered a part-time job because she lacked some certification. Besides, the district was too small for a full-time nurse.

"What I'm gonna tell you is the truth and you can check it out in the administration building. There is a display case with the newspaper story and pictures and everything. It's an incredible story. One day she is in the office, and there is an explosion in the chemistry class – couple of boys goofing around. Nothing to it – except some glass beakers randomly explode and one shred severs the jugular vein of one of the boys. By the time she gets to him, he has passed out from loss of blood. She manages to stop the bleeding using ... a paper clip?" Andrea looked at Kenneth for confirmation.

"I heard it was a clamp from the chemistry lab," he said. "It doesn't really matter."

"An ambulance was called for," Andrea continued. "But, back then, an ambulance from the city would take 30 minutes at best – sometimes, more like an hour – to arrive and Mrs. Wheeler knew that the boy had lost too much blood to last that long. She figured he needed a transfusion. Do not ask me how she did it, but she rigged up a transfusion and saved the boy's life. To me the most incredible part was that she ... her own self, was the donor." Andrea just shook her head in amazement.

"Here is the amazing part. She put herself and the boy in the bed of a pickup truck and drove into the city. I mean ... she didn't drive."

Kenneth picked up the story. "The principal drove. It was his truck, and the superintendent drove ahead clearing the way. They finally found a state patrolman, who drove with the alarm on the whole way to the hospital. Everyone agreed that Mrs. Wheeler saved the boy's life."

"It was just a little something I learned in the army was all she said," Andrea shook her head. "I mean, can you imagine doing that – under any circumstance?"

"When I went through EMT training, we made reference to this incident and how dangerous what she did was, and how unsterile all the equipment was, and how we should never even think about trying something like that," Kenneth just smiled. "In other words, we should just let the kid die, I said and our instructor said 'Probably. That would be the safest thing to do.' Not to the kid, I said. Mrs. Wheeler did the only thing she could do to save the kid, and the more you know, the more you admire her decisions. I mean it took a lot of courage."

"Wow," Cassandra whistled through her teeth.

"The boy's father was on the board. The board immediately hired her as a permanent school nurse. He established the policy that she would always have a position as a school nurse in the district. Later, the father became an important politician at the state level. He made sure that any certification she lacked would be waived for her. He even made sure that she kept her position when she had the accident and became paralyzed from the waist down."

Kenneth shook his head, "That is not the ending of her story; that is just the beginning. I'm telling you, she is a legend. She touched everyone who went through this school system in the 50s and 60s. You've seen that iconic picture of her with the kid in her lap wheeling across the playground with the lightning in the background? I think Life magazine published it first."

"That was her?" Cassandra was astonished. "Everyone's seen that picture. I mean it is the ultimate ... something or other ... courage or risk."

"Yeah, that was her," Kenneth nodded. "As I understand it, there was a tornado watch, so the schoolyard was closed, and one kid took advantage of no lines on the playground. Only Mrs. Wheeler noticed the kid missing, so she went out to get him."

"Or maybe she was the only one brave enough to venture out. A tornado had been spotted," Andrea interrupted Kenneth to complete the story.

"You might be right," Kenneth continued. "There was never any real tornado danger as I understand it, but no one knew it at the time, but talk about images. Here she is, alone, with one kid in her arms, rolling across a schoolyard with the sky full of these dark, ominous clouds, and one lightning bolt in the background. The picture will bring tears to your eyes … a lump to your throat. And it was Mrs. Wheeler. She had no way of knowing that tornado's path, by the way. All she knew was that this kid was left on the playground. You gotta admire her."

"The way I remember it, I think," Cassandra said. "There was a tornado funnel in the background and the kid was an African-American."

Andrea turned directly to Cassandra, "You're very religious, right? You go to the Mount Zion Church on the east side, a mostly black church, right? Ask your minister what he thinks of Mrs. Wheeler. When the school system was integrated in the mid-60s, a lot of people were expecting trouble. But, when the first busload of kids showed up at the school, Mrs. Wheeler was there to greet them and say hello as they got off the bus. We never had any trouble and a lot of people think it was because she was always between the black kids and any troublemakers."

"My uncle had a best friend in junior high school," Kenneth poured his coffee down the drain and turned to face Cassandra. "One day, his father died suddenly from an accident at work … out of the clear blue, without a warning. The mother was devastated and went into shock, had to be hospitalized herself. Mrs. Wheeler told the boy and took him into her home for a few days until the mother got it together. I mean, she didn't have to do that. But, that was the kind of thing she did all the time. She took care of people … she nurtured people."

Suddenly, they were all startled by the ringing of the emergency bell. They turned to look at the panel: "It's coming from Mrs. Wheeler's room," Andrea said.

"I'll take care of it," Cassandra said.

"You do that – you take care of Mrs. Wheeler." Kenneth said.

- - -

Clark woke up at 4:43 a.m. He knew there was no chance he was going back to sleep no matter how hard he tried. He swung his feet over the side of the bed and sat up. He stretched and flexed his ankles and feet before he stood up. When he finally stood, he grabbed his eyeglasses from the nightstand and stretched again. He turned the light on and made the bed. He pulled a pair of underwear, a pair of gray socks, and a T-shirt from his chest of drawers. From his closet, he laid a pair of khaki pants and a light blue shirt. Then, he headed for the shower.

After the shower, he dressed slowly. Everything he did these days seemed at a slow pace – arthritis in his fingers, wrists, and knees – acute soreness everywhere, slowed him down. He looked around the room. He was in Maggie's room, or more accurately, what had been Maggie's room. Now it was his since she was in the nursing home. He stood up and looked in the mirror. He considered a tie but decided against it. It being 5:30 a.m. now, it was too early to visit her in the nursing home, and he didn't want to make breakfast and leave the dishes before he took off on the road. He grabbed his windbreaker and headed for the Waffle House on Highway 75. He could eat and still be back home before it was time to hit the road.

He was right. He was home by 6:30 a.m., still too early for visiting hours at Red River Shore. He turned on the television and watched the early morning Sunday news show from his usual perch on the recliner in front of the TV. He didn't last 15 minutes before he was asleep. When he woke up, it was 8 a.m. and he was angry at himself. He wanted to be on the highway by now. He still wanted to stop by the nursing home, and he feared it was going to make him late.

He went into the bedroom, and put on a blue blazer and grabbed a small birthday cake from the refrigerator. It was

279

slightly chilly, but the rain was more of a threat than a reality at his point. Just a typical March day in north Texas.

When he got to the nursing home, he parked and carried the birthday cake into the nurse's station. He handed the cake to Cassandra, who was getting ready to end her shift and leave for the day. "Good morning," Clark had to look down and read her nametag, "Cassandra, I brought Mrs. Wheeler a birthday cake. Please share it with the staff. I doubt that she will want much of it."

"Thank you, Mr. Bradley." Cassandra replied. "We will all appreciate it."

"How is she today?"

"She just finished her breakfast, and she is settled down," Cassandra tried to be as cheery as possible.

"Settled down? What does that mean?" Clark seemed irritated.

"Last night, she couldn't get the television remote to work right. She kept getting confused with the nurse's call button. Today, the frustration was still there. You know, there is just a lot of frustration with her limited amount of muscle control."

"I understand."

"I got her up, fed her, and tried to comfort her. She was comfortable just now and seemed to be comfortable watching TV." Cassandra looked at him. "I try Mr. Bradley. I try."

Clark comforted Cassandra as best he could, "I know you do but, sometimes, she just can't be reached."

Clark turned and walked toward Mrs. Wheeler's room. He stopped and turned back toward Cassandra, "Thanks. I really do appreciate all you do, and all you try to do."

He stopped in front of her door and braced himself. He took three deep breathes. The first sight of her was always the hardest. He knocked gently on the door, and then pushed it open.

"How many things are wrong with this picture?" he muttered under his breath. The TV was hanging from the ceiling too high for her to see from her current sitting position. It was not turned to any channel and was broadcasting only noise – random static. She held the remote rigidly with her right hand, but only the left hand had any movement, and its movement was spastic at best – up and down with no finger control at all.

Yet, every time he entered her room, the first thing his eyes would focus on were the nubs of her knees – both legs gone at the knees, bandaged only. Sometimes, there would be a hint of blood at the tip. Clark felt that the level of care that she had received correlated to the amount of blood on the knees, but he wasn't sure if that was true. He noticed that today, her knees were clean and freshly bandaged.

She weighed a good 80 pounds less than she did two years ago when she first entered Red River, but he knew that was not the staff's fault. He tried to feed her, and she did not respond to him any more than she responded to food from anyone else. She barely ate and she breathed with the help of an air tank connected with a tube in her nose. Still, spittle constantly rolled from the right side of her mouth and air bubbles formed outside the tube occasionally. Her hair was matted on one side and extremely thin on both sides. Her eyes were seldom in focus. When he talked to her, maybe one comment out of 50 would elicit something resembling a response – a blink or movement of the head, some slight indication, some slight degree of understanding, or a glimpse of awareness. Then, she would quickly revert back inside her shell. It was hard to look at her and see a person.

"Good morning," he said as cheery as he could be. He took the remote control from her hand and settled on a channel – a news channel that was covering the weather. "Looks like it is going to have a heavy rain today. I was hoping I could make the trip and be back before the rain. Doesn't look like I'm gonna make it. I'm gonna see Hope today."

She didn't blink or acknowledge him or the content of his message. "I'll be back tomorrow or the next day for sure," he said this as he patted her arm as an attempt to reassure her, but if she noticed at all, he could not see any reaction. "But, I had to come by today. You know why, don't you?" Clark reached over, caressed her hands, and made sure he had eye contact. "Today is your birthday. I had to come by and celebrate your birthday with you."

She didn't move or acknowledge his presence. She did close her eyes slightly and saliva rolled out of her mouth.

"Happy birthday, Maggie!" He interpreted her movement as some sort of awareness. "Let's see ... is this your 87th or 88th?" He looked to her for a response but there was none. "I'm pretty sure it is your 87th."

Just then, Cassandra came in to give Mrs. Wheeler some medication. The needle was injected into the IV already hooked up to her arm.

"How come she has to have her medicines through her IV?" he asked.

Cassandra smiled as she talked, "We can't really get her to swallow pills anymore, and she needs the meds to prevent another stroke. It really is the best way."

"Oh, I don't doubt that. I was just curious."

The nurse technician left and they were alone. He looked at Maggie and stared at her. There was nothing said, nothing to say. Finally, he stood up and said, "I need to be going ... you know, if I want to see Hope in time." No response. He bent down and looked into her eyes, "I wish … I don't know what I wish …" He rolled her over closer to the window so she could look out. "I know you like the rain. Maybe you'll like this view better."

He turned to leave, but before he left the room, he stopped at the garbage can and retrieved the disposable hypodermic needle from the trashcan. He walked over and kneeled in front of her, close to her face in front of her eyes. He pushed any excessive medicine out of the tube and pulled back so that there was only air in the needle. Then, he put the needle by her side next to her one mobile hand. "If you can remember what you once told me, if you muster up enough control for one last effort of will power … well … you will have a choice … one last choice." He stood up and kissed her forehead. He turned and left. By the time, he got to the car, the rain had started.

"No More Shepherd's Pie"

March 3, 1969

San Francisco, California

Clark sat down for dinner. Grace had set the plate in front of him and one in front of her. She sat down across the table. "Shepherd's pie?" Clark asked.

"Is there something wrong with it?" she asked.

"No. Not at all," Clark put his fork into the food and twisted it around. "It used to be my favorite in prison."

She jerked her head at him and looked directly his way.

"Of course, they never had as many vegetables – carrots and tomatoes. This is really good, rich, and thick," he smiled and tried to be positive.

"You were in prison for two hours," she dropped her fork into her food. "Listen, I'm only going to say this once, but if we're going to do this wedding thing tomorrow I think I should ..."

She looked down, took a deep breath, and then lifted her head, "I am not going feel guilty. I am not going to start this marriage ... all defensive. Now I know, up 'til now, you have not asked, but I think I have to tell you about the father ... who the father ..."

Clark looked at her, but only picked up a fork full of food in response.

"The truth is I don't know who the father is. I have no idea who the father is. It could be anyone of half-dozen or more guys. I don't even know names."

He lifted his head and looked at her.

"I didn't graduate high school a virgin. I had sex with my boyfriend and I liked it. I didn't do it because of low self-esteem or to try to hold him. We just did it. I didn't want to stay in Nettie. When I came to college, I was eager to be sexually active, but I wasn't stupid. I enjoyed sex. I will not apologize nor will I feel guilty. Sex was certainly not my first priority – classes were. I wanted to learn. I became politically active. I marched and protested. I really was not sexually involved my freshman year. No one interested me. There was one guy, but we only did it once, and the relationship really didn't make it through the weekend. My sophomore year, I was really active in the anti-war movement. Every weekend, there was a march somewhere.

"We started meeting the draftees coming in to the military bases; sometimes, they were coming for physical exams. I formed a group called Girls say Yes to Boys who Say No. At first, it was kind of a joke, but then, it wasn't. Guys who got off the bus and left with us were … rewarded. I literally had sex with anybody who refused the draft. It made sense to me. Make love, not war – more than a slogan. It became my lifestyle. We helped guys flunk the physical, flee to Canada, apply to be a conscientious objector – any and all of those things. I still went to class, and marched and protested. There was lots of sex. And I liked it." Her voice was filled with an air of arrogance and pride. "I just didn't plan on getting pregnant … But, I will not be shamed or judged!" She slammed her hands down on the table.

He stared at her, slowly nodded, and spoke quietly, "Could you hand me the salt?"

She stared at him, took a deep breath, and spoke more softly, more under control, "I had to tell you. You needed to know. I won't blame you if you …"

"Your shepherd's pie is the best shepherd's pie I have ever had, but it is still shepherd's pie. I really don't like shepherd's pie. If it is all right with you, I'd rather not have it again. Shepherd's pie is like beef stew that got sick or something. I'll make you beef stew like my mother use to make. In fact, I look forward to making beef stew for you for many years to come."

She was silent and simply stared at him for several minutes, stunned. "OK," she said but tears were in her eyes.

"But … no more shepherd's pie, OK?" he asked.

"OK. No more shepherd's pie."

"I really hate shepherd's pie."

"All right – no more shepherd's pie."

"Shepherd's pie – bad."

"OK. You've made your point. Enough on the shepherd's pie."

"You, I love. Shepherd's pie – not so much."

"I love you, Clark Bradley." By now, she was smiling if not laughing.

"But, no more shepherd's pie. Promise?"

"I promise."

"Can we make that part of our wedding vows?"

"I promise to love, cherish and make no more shepherd's pies?"

"That would be excellent." The next day, they were married in a simple civil ceremony. There was no mention of shepherd's pie.

Justified

March 20, 2011

Dallas, Texas roughly 70 miles from the Red River

It rained all the way into Dallas, a hard heavy rain. At times, it was difficult to see the highway. Finally, after an hour and half of driving in a steady downpour, he saw his destination. It was still raining as he looked for a parking place. There was no spot in the parking lot. Most of the congregation lived in the neighborhood and walked to church. Most of the time, the parking lot was relatively empty. But, today with the rain, the lot was full. The church served a small community inside the city, a community mostly of artists and intellectuals, an island of non-conformity in a sea of yuppies and poverty.

He took a deep breath, quickly opened the car door, and made his dash. He tried to avoid getting wet, but it was the kind of rain that drenched him before he was three feet from the car. He stepped in an ankle deep puddle of water as he darted to a back door of the church, but his foot slipped and he went down on his knees. He stepped into the hallway and quickly made his way to the back of the church to the cafeteria where everyone was gathered, sitting at the tables. He opened the door and stood silhouetted by the lights of the hallway behind him. He was the center of everyone's attention, but it was Hope who finally spoke out, "Dad! I am so glad to see you. I was afraid you weren't going to show up!"

"I'm sorry I'm so late. Did I miss your sermon? Did I miss the service, too?" he responded. "You know how much I love to hear your sermons."

She got up from behind the table at the head of the room as she was moving toward him, "Chloe! Chloe! Look who's here – Grandpa!"

288

A little 5-year old girl came running from the back of the room toward him and ran at such speed that she almost knocked him over.

"You are all wet, Grandpa!" She said. "You shouldn't be all wet ... inside the church."

"Well, you are right, what can I say?" he looked around at the room full of people, the whole congregation he guessed. "I'd rather not be all wet."

By now, Hope was there hugging him. "Oh my, you are soaked! Dad, I can't tell you how much it means to me that you came today."

"I really did try to make it earlier ... for the sermon and everything."

"There will be other sermons," she said. "As pastor, I give one every Sunday, but today is special. I'll only have one 10th anniversary. That's kind of special."

"I know. I know."

"We need to get you into some dry clothes before we do anything else." She looked around. "Do we have any extra clothes? You know, dry clothes that my Dad could put on?"

Thomas introduced himself and took Clark down the hallway. He gave him a pair of jeans, a sweatshirt, and a pair of house shoes. Thomas took all of the wet clothes and threw them into a dryer. The new clothes were too big, but Clark said he would manage and he did feel much warmer. He walked back into the dining room and joined Hope at the head table.

"Are you hungry? I bet you are starved." Hope spoke as she looked around for someone, anyone. "Can we get my dad some food?"

"I could eat," he nodded. "What have you got?"

"Shepherd's pie," Rachel said as she headed from the kitchen with a plate in her hands.

"You're kidding."

"Yeah, I've heard of your aversion to shepherd's pie."

"More of a phobia." She brought him a plate of barbecue beef. He ate as he talked to Hope. "The reception? Did I miss the celebration?"

"Yea, but you are here. That really is the important thing," Hope spoke with a sincerity in her voice that touched Clark. "We wanted to do an anniversary party right after the regular service ... I wasn't sure everyone would stay ... or want to stay for a reception in the evening. This way they get to express their support but don't have to ... you know risk getting in trouble with the church fathers."

"I understand. Actually, I have no idea what you mean. But, I know I really wanted to be here on time, but the rain ... and there was an accident on the highways ... I tried. I feel bad. I don't want you to feel that I didn't do my best to get here on time."

"You got here!" Hope spoke with a reassuring pat on his wrist. "That really is the important thing; it speaks volumes to me."

Rachel explained. "Hope and I have been together for ten years, and we have had Chloe for five, and the church administrators know about us, but still they will not officially sanction our marriage. They will let Hope be a pastor, and they will let us live our life, but they will not sanction nor officially acknowledge our relationship."

"Technically," Hope interrupted Rachel, "what we did is not holy matrimony. It has no official existence, no recognition.

It is a fantasy. My congregation knows this and still supported our efforts – our voice."

"So do I," Clark added as Chloe bounded into his lap.

"I know," Hope squeezed his hand. "That means so much to me. No one else in my hometown would be here, no one else I grew up with would be here."

"Granny would be here if she could."

"Really? You think so? I like to think so. I hope so."

"No, no. She would." Clark firmly grabbed Hope's hand. "We talked, earlier … when she could still talk. Now – not so much. She can't talk any more. The last stroke did her in as far as speech goes."

"Dad, I think her reaction hurt more than anything else … ever."

"I'm not going to lie. She had some difficulty accepting you at first. Homosexuality is something …" He shook his head. "Growing up she just never experienced or understood. She comes from an earlier time and age. She thought about it for a long time. She prayed, talked to her pastor and, ultimately, she came to accept your love for Rachel. In the final analysis, she had more faith in you than anything else. She believed in you."

"And you, Dad? Did you accept it? I mean, didn't you come from the same time? The same place?"

He nodded, "No, I'm a generation younger and I lived in San Francisco for years. Hell, I had a harder time accepting that you wanted to go to graduate school for theology and be a pastor. I thought I raised you to be a nice, sensible atheist." He grinned, and then he looked at her seriously, "Love is love, and my granddaughter could not have better parents." He hugged Chloe.

Rachel walked over and squeezed him on the shoulder. "You want some apple pie with ice cream to finish off that dinner?"

"Thanks, Rachel, and maybe some coffee." he turned his attention to Chloe. "I haven't seen you in ... so long. What is new? What have you been learning?"

Chloe began to play with a loose string on the top of his sweatshirt. "I know how to count."

"You know how to count? Really? That is amazing. Are you sure? You're not trying to fool me, are you?" he asked with a voice with mock intensity. "How high can you count?"

"I can count forever and ever. No really, I can. Want to see? One, two, three, four ..."

"Oh sure you can count like that. I mean that's kinda of cheating," he arched his eyebrows and she looked startled. "I mean, if you can count, what comes after, seven?"

"Eight," she said immediately.

"After twelve?"

"Thirteen."

"Maybe you can count." He began rubbing his chin, took a big bite of ice cream and pie. "What comes after twenty-one?"

She hesitated, and responded with a raising voice as if asking more than stating. She was entering new territory, but she was eager for the challenge. "Twenty ... two."

"How about – this is going to be a hard one." He took a long drink of the coffee as she squirmed and looked nervous. He looked around and finally looked at her with a challenging look and a deeper voice, "What comes after one hundred and thirty-two?"

She looked at him, and looked at her mother and the stared at the ceiling, then she got quiet, "One hundred and … thirty …" she dangled her fingers and swayed back and forth …" One hundred and thirty-three," she squealed.

"That is right. Boy, I can't fool you. You do know how to count and you are so smart." He lifted her up above his head, brought her down, and gave her a big bear hug. "Wait. Wait. If you are so smart, what number comes right before eleven?"

"That's easy – ten."

"How about, what number comes before ninety-four?"

"Ninety-three."

"Well, you are too smart for me. I don't guess there isn't anything about counting that you don't know. I can't think of anything," he shook his head. "Wait I've got one. I don't know anyone … well, few people smart enough to know the answer to this one: What number comes before one?"

She stared at him. She closed her eyes and looked at the ceiling. She turned her head sideways. "That's not fair … there is no number …" He was nodding his head. She could see her mother silently wording something just past Grandpa and, at first, she couldn't tell what she was saying. Suddenly, she smiled. "Zero. Zero comes before one."

"That is right. You are some kind of smart cookie. Most people don't recognize zero as a number, but you did. You are a really smart person."

"I have a question for you," she wanted to turn the tables on him. "What number comes before zero?"

"Hmm," he stroked his chin, "That is a very good question." He continued to stroke his chin and contemplate the little girl before him. "I am going to have to say … infinity. Infinity is the only number that comes before zero."

293

Chloe looked very confused and shook her head. "What is infinity?"

"Well," he started to talk but his speech was hesitant and not smooth at all. "Infinity is the end of all numbers when you count as high as can ever be counted. It is the end and the beginning."

"I don't understand."

"No one understands infinity."

Hope intervened, "That is why we go to church. Run along now and say goodnight to your friends before they leave. Let Grandpa finish his coffee." She took Chloe by the hand, and walked her to the back of the room with the rest of the children.

Clark turned toward Rachel, "You and Hope are doing an incredible job with that girl. She is so bright and charming." He just shook his head. "She is a delight, and I am so proud of her."

"Thanks. That means a lot coming from you," Rachel said. "You have no idea how much your daughter admires you, and that admiration certainly has rubbed off on me."

"Well, thank you, Rachel. I'm not gonna lie and pull any false modesty on you. I am proud of the father I have been. I think I have been a ... good father. I've tried to be there whenever she needed me and, sometimes, it wasn't easy, but do not underestimate the influence of her grandmother. Don't let the ugliness ... the disagreement of the last few years color your view of that woman. In a lot of ways, I have been Tonto to her Lone Ranger."

"I do not know what that means," Rachel said. "And I know that I do not have a complete perspective on Mrs. Wheeler. I only know her as a source of pain for Hope. You tell me that there is more to her – she is some great healer. Hope has told me that, but I all know is what I have seen. She is a source of pain for Hope. I have heard about her healing powers, but all I have seen the nights of tears her rejection has caused. I have watched Hope pray for forgiveness over and over to no avail.

"Our religion – my religion – is very special to me, and I will tell you that for the past five years my feelings toward Mrs. Wheeler are my greatest cross, my greatest burden. I have tried to find forgiveness in my heart, and I have not found it. I do not understand how someone can profess to love another, and reject her –as she did to Hope. I have tried, and I have prayed, but forgiveness has not come yet. I cannot find it in myself to forgive her. And I see my lack of forgiveness as the greatest obstacle to grace for myself. I don't know if that makes any sense to you or not."

"It does." Clark looked down and shook his head. "When Hope first came out, when she first introduced you, Maggie just couldn't handle it. It is that simple. First of all, she had been raised in a world that just … never accepted same-sex relationships. Secondly, Maggie responded out of a lifetime of disappointment. I mean, there was a context of failure in every relationship she cared about, and you were adding one more. Her husband, her daughter, and now her granddaughter? She just could not handle another disappointment as she saw it. The more she thought about it, she came around and felt differently. She came to accept Hope and you but, by then, she was in no shape to express her feelings … literally. By the time that she accepted your relationship, she had lost her legs and couldn't travel to talk to you and apologize, and she didn't know how. She had completely accepted your relationship, but she had lost her speech and most of her ability to concentrate. In moments of lucidity, she has told me how guilty she felt, and how much she wished she could turn back time and respond differently to the two of you. I think she would have liked to be here today if she could have. "

"You know, she has never even seen Chloe." Rachel spoke with a crispness in her voice.

Clark responded with softness and warmth, "And Chloe has never seen her because of me. I don't want her to see her now with her wrinkled, spastic movements, drooling with two stumps for legs, grunts for words. Nothing good could come from her visit. Chloe would only be frightened, and it is doubtful Maggie would even be aware of who she would be seeing. It is better for Chloe to learn of her great grandmother from stories and pictures. Someday, Chloe will be ready and Maggie's stories will be told to her – the good parts."

"Maybe … someday," Rachel sighed.

"After the bitterness goes away," Clark nodded.

"If it does."

"It will. It takes time."

Hope walked up, carrying Chloe. "Your clothes are dry."

He dressed in the laundry room and when he stepped out, his clothes were still wrinkled. Everyone had gone home. I guess it's time I left, too."

"Dad, why don't you stay here tonight? We have plenty of room in the parsonage – nobody is staying with us currently."

"No, thanks." He replied. "The rain has stopped, and I should be getting home."

"Why?" She looked at him playfully. "What have you got to do that is more important than eating breakfast with your granddaughter?"

They turned to leave, Hope with her arm wrapped around his arm.

"I need to check on the house." He put his arm around her as they continued to walk.

"The house will be there tomorrow; it has been standing for more than 50 years. It will survive your one-night absence."

"I want to check on Maggie. She might not."

"Is she really that bad off?"

"Yes, I think so," Clark stopped and held Hope at arm's length. "She looks like she is on death's doorstep, but I've felt that way before ... I don't think she'll survive another stroke. I don't think she wants to survive another stroke. Hope, she is bad off. I would beg you to come see her, but I don't think it would do you or her any good. She is not cognizant of her surroundings anymore. She has already left us. The rest is ... formality."

Hope pressed against his chest and wept. "You know I love her, don't you?"

"Yes, I know. And she knows, deep down. Somewhere inside, she knows."

"I've stayed away, at first because I was hurt, but then because I knew how much I hurt her, and that killed me. But I didn't want to a ... I don't know ... rub salt in her wounds. I wanted to mend things, but I couldn't see any chance ... Then, I got busy, you know living my life, too busy to try to please her, but I always wanted to tell her how much I loved her, but every time I tried, in my head, it came out how much she hurt me. I just never knew what to say to her."

"She didn't know what to say to you either, or I guess, she didn't know how to say it. But, I have enough faith in both of you that I think you would have found a way if her health had not interfered." He patted her on the back as he spoke.

Hope spoke, barely audible, "Now, you are telling me that it is too late." She sobbed into his chest.

"Maybe it is not too late. Why don't you come home with me tonight? Your room is still intact. Tomorrow morning, you can go to the hospital, and maybe you'll catch her in one of her lucid moments."

"I can't. I have a couple of important committee meetings for the church, and Chloe needs me to go to school tomorrow for a Kindergarten Step-Up Day and … and …"

Clark looked skeptical. He nodded. They both knew that she was making excuses.

"Well, Dad," she took a big gulp. "The truth is, I'm pregnant again, and my doctor would not want me to go. You remember the difficulty I had with Chloe. My doctor wants me to avoid anything too stressful and physical. He says he is not far from prescribing bed rest."

"Pregnant? That's fantastic!" Clark spun around. "You don't look pregnant. When are you due?"

"In about six months."

"Congratulations. I am so happy for you and Rachel. Suddenly, the timing for the ceremony makes sense. And that's why you wanted to talk to me alone. Do you know what it is?"

"Yeah, it's a boy."

"Have you picked a name?"

"Well, what I wanted to do … did you ever have a name picked for my brother? I wanted to use that name?"

"Nah. Well, I had one, but no one liked it, especially your mother. Don't even ask."

"Then, I guess we'll name him Clark."

Clark looked around the empty parking lot. "I would be honored, but I think maybe you should name it Meredith."

"Dad, Meredith is not a boy's name."

"Well, sure," he said. "Not yet. He would be the first. That wouldn't be so bad. I think you should think about it, though. Names are important."

"Is that why you named me Hope?"

"Absolutely, you brought hope to our lives, your mother and I. And I know your Grandmother felt that your mother was her grace in so many ways."

"We will think about it, I promise. Actually, that's why we thought of Clark; we couldn't think of a better role model. But, there is another reason I wanted to talk to you alone; a more ominous reason," her voice changed tone. "I'm scared. You live in that house all alone. You don't really *do* anything. You are about to drive home late at night all alone. Dad, I worry about you."

"What do you mean I don't do anything? I visit Maggie every other day, and I'm gonna start taking guitar lessons. I know a former student who is going to give me lessons for a reduced rate."

"Dad, I'm serious. I worry about you." She said.

"I worry about me, too. But, what would you have me do?"

"Move in with us. There is plenty of room and Chloe would love to have her grandfather around all the time."

He nodded slowly, but continued to walk until he was at his car. Then, he turned. "I have thought about it – moving in with you, or at least close to you, and I might. I might, but here's what stops me. Every time I visit Maggie, I see all these other old people, some as bad off as Maggie, some can't speak, and some can't eat, have any idea who they are, or where they are. Some are just a few years older than me. The end of life doesn't seem pretty. I mean, how many people die without any dignity? Death comes like an eraser and just erases their being. Few die with any dignity, or identity, for that matter. I don't want you to see me like that. I don't want Chloe to watch me be erased."

Hope nodded. "You know I've seen all this in my role as a pastor. We are strong. We can handle it."

It was Clark's turn to nod. "I know you can, but I can't."

A silence followed and he took the opportunity to enter the car and open the window before he spoke again, "Let me ask you a question."

"OK, shoot." She leaned against the open car window.

"Are you happy?"

"Yes," she said quickly and emphatically. "I mean nobody's life is perfect. I have challenges. I would like to have more money sometimes. Sometimes I have differences with my parishioners. There are things about this neighborhood I would change, but, overall I would say that, I am happy."

"Why?"

"Why?" She looked at him incredulously. "I have such a full life. I love someone who loves me. I have a wonderful daughter who I am thrilled to parent every day. I am expecting a new baby, who I look forward to raising with all the rewarding emotions I've had with Chloe. I have a wonderful job that is both rewarding and challenging that enables me to be fully engaged with the people in my community. It enables me to grow spiritually and psychologically, and it enables me to become significant with others. I have purpose. My life could not be more complete."

He nodded slowly and turned toward the front window. "Then, I have done my job, my primary job."

"Well, Dad, are you happy?" She was afraid of the answer.

He put the key into the ignition. "I don't think it is a relevant question. I had all those things you described. I don't know if you can ask more from life. It doesn't really matter how long it lasted – only that it once was.

"I am … content. I am at peace. I feel that I have lived a life of … value. Remember when we use to walk down the street in Nettie with Maggie. Maybe we would be shopping or going to the dentist or whatever, but all of these people would come over and greet her, everyone seemed to know her, and they all wanted to share a moment with her. Seeing her seemed to comfort them, and they wanted to tell her how they were doing and that they were happy. They all thanked her for something she gave them in grade school, some intangible gift of …I don't know…she made all of them feel important and valued. It happened less and less as more people grew up and left Nettie, and the younger kids knew her only as an administrator rather than an actual school nurse. Still, you could never escape at least one encounter with a former student."

"Yea, I remember," Hope said. "I hated it. I always felt embarrassed. Until I got in high school then…I was impressed; I thought it was pretty cool."

"Well, it is happening to me. Last week I was eating in El Fenix and a former student approached me. He introduced me to his wife and children. He told them that I was his favorite teacher in high school and that because of me he went on to college and understood math enough to get a degree in engineering. He said he owed all of his success in life to me. The fact that he was probably exaggerating my influence does not detract from how validating he made me feel. My point is that type of thing happens to me almost weekly.

"You ask me if I am happy. I think that when you are young, you measure happiness in laughter – smiles and kisses

301

and hugs, maybe, but when you get my age, there are other criteria. You measure happiness by how often you can look in the mirror and like what you see.

"All those things you described that you have – I have had them. I have had them, at different times. That I don't have them now doesn't matter. Maybe time shouldn't be viewed in a linear fashion. I mean, the really meaningful things never end. I read somewhere … somebody said … love never dies, only people do."

He paused long enough to let his words sink in to both Hope and himself before he continued, "Everyone dies, but not everyone lives. Well, I have lived. And I just don't think you can judge a life by longevity alone."

"Dad! That's beautiful! I think that might be my next sermon."

"Well," he started the car, "Feel free to quote me. Now, if I could just convince myself."

"You don't believe that? Dad, you are not that good of a liar."

"No, I really believe it … most of the time … sometimes … all of the time … occasionally. The truth is I can look myself in the mirror and feel satisfied. I have done a good job. I feel – what is the religious term – justified."

She bent down and kissed him on the forehead.

He nodded. "I'm not sure you can ask for more than that." He started the car and backed up. One last wave goodbye and he drove off.

Clark drove off thinking of Hope and how proud her mother would have been if she could have known the adult Hope. Clark had one of his typical imaginary conversations with

Grace. He saw the exit sign for Nettie right before the billboard for the Red River Inn, and he noticed the mileage marker for the actual Red River 43 miles ahead. He chuckled as he knew Grace would have. The last thing he was aware of was a bright light in the rear view mirror—almost blinding—he could hear Grace's voice softly singing "The water is wide I cannot get cross over neither have I the wings to fly...".

Not Canoe nor Kayak, but Dinghy

April 6, 1969

San Francisco, California

Grace was approaching the eighth hour of labor. The contractions were five minutes apart, but they were hardly the excruciating pain she had expected and Clark feared. She would grunt and grimace, and she would clutch Clark's hand and strain through the length of the contraction. He would ask if she wanted some medicine to relieve the pain, and she would shake her head no. Her biggest problem was the growing fatigue. She had been in the hospital labor room for three hours now with little change, but she wasn't sure how much more she could handle. The baby was, apparently in no hurry. Labor could go on like this for 24 more hours or even more. The nurse told Grace to close her eyes and try to sleep between contractions, a bit of advice that Grace put on her list of useless things people tell you at important moments.

Clark bent over and whispered in her ear, "I'm going to step out and go to the restroom. I'll be right back." He left the labor room and went down the hallway, down the stairs through the waiting room to the restroom. He walked slowly, taking deep breaths. He found watching Grace to be exhausting. He could only imagine what it was like for her. After he was finished in the restroom, he took the time to wash his hands and splash water on his face. He took several deep breaths before he started his walk back. He was not prepared for what greeted him upon his return.

Grace was almost sitting up in her bed and the noises that were coming from throat were approaching the intensity of a guttural scream, and long, loud groans … followed by panting, almost breathless, panting. "Where … have … you … been?" Then, she went into another spasm of pain and incoherent groans.

"I just went to the restroom," Clark answered bewilderedly. "Good lord! What happened?"

The nurse stepped between them, "She was stuck, so we had to break her water and induce – jump kick – the labor, in other words. We're about to take her into the delivery room."

"Grace, do you want the medicine now?"

"No! Goddamn it. I've gone this far. My kid is going to be born awake – no damn drugs!" This was followed by a long growl leading into a piercing groan. "I can do this!"

"I know you can." Clark offered his hand and she almost broke it she squeezed so hard. She cried, she groaned, but she had promised that she would not scream, and she did not although the sounds coming from her were ungodly tones.

She finally let go of Clark as they wheeled her away to the delivery room. He followed her as far as he could until the glass doors closed. He stood and watched her being rolled down the hallway. Hospital policy prevented him from being in the delivery room, and that was all that kept him from pushing through the door. He stood dumbly staring through the glass panes.

An hour, one that seemed more like seven, passed before the delivery room opened and Grace was wheeled before him toward her hospital room. She had a new baby in her arms. They entered the elevator and Clark, against hospital policy, got on the elevator with them. The nurse started to make Clark get off the elevator, but Grace would have none of it. She insisted that Clark be there on the trip to the room.

"We have a daughter," Grace whispered, barely able to speak.

"She is beautiful," his voice cracked.

"Yes, she is," Grace could barely speak after all the groaning.

"You did it – no meds."

"No meds," she repeated even as her eyes were closing.

"You did it."

She opened eyes wide enough to look at him, "No, we did it. Have you picked out a name?"

"Dinghy, I think we should name her Dinghy."

"OK." She closed her eyes. "Wait, what the hell kind of name is Dinghy?"

"I think it's perfect," Clark said. Dinghy is a small boat, you know, that will carry two … like the song."

"Clark, you are out of your mind if you think my daughter is going to be named Dinghy. Can you imagine her going to school? How the kids would tease her with the name Dinghy Bradley? No. No way. I can't believe you even thought of Dinghy."

Clark smiled. "I thought of Canoe and Kayak, but rejected them."

"Clark, it really is a sweet thought, but I think we should come up with a better, more traditional name."

"How about Hope? I think that fits, too."

"Hope is perfect. I like that." She looked at Clark. "Hope it is."

The nurse stepped in to take Hope away, "We need to finish cleaning her and giving her some eye drops. You need some sleep. We'll bring her back when she needs to be nursed."

"OK," Grace said. "I am tired." The nurse carried Hope away, and Grace turned toward Clark.

He bent over and kissed her on the forehead, "You did good. But, when we have a boy, I want to reenter the name Dinghy for consideration."

"Clark, there has never been a boy named Dinghy."

"Then he will be the first. That wouldn't be so bad."

"I can't believe you are serious with Dinghy. There is no way! I'm using my veto power on this issue. That is the most ridiculous name I have ever heard."

"Well, now you are beginning to hurt my feelings."

"We might as well give him a wooden leg at birth ... it might even qualify as child abuse."

"We'll talk later. We could always call him by his initials."

"I miss her already," she said with her eyes closed and sleep already affecting her speech.

"It is amazing how much I can love somebody who wasn't even here yesterday," he said.

"Oh, she was here, believe me. She has been here for quite a while."

"You know what I mean," he pulled up a chair and sat next to her bed. "The two most important people in my life – weren't even in my life seven months ago, and from now on, they will always be a part of me."

She smiled, and fell asleep as he held her hand. He softly hummed The Water is Wide.

"I don't do ambiguity very well."

October 16, 1968, late afternoon

On the Streets of San Francisco, California

Grace stepped out of the office building. She tugged on her raincoat, pulling it together in the front but not buttoning it. She looked at the paper in her hand—stared at the results of the test. She chose this gynecologist because he was downtown away from campus, providing privacy she thought. She came to get a prescription for birth control pills. If she was going to continue to have sex, she wanted to be sure she was protected. She was not prepared to find out that she was pregnant. She was pregnant. Last week when she first went to the doctor, she was sure there was a mistake. The test was repeated and today she got the same results. There was no mistake. She was, indeed, pregnant.

She was not sure how she found herself in this predicament. She had been very careful. She used more than one method of birth control and was always particularly careful while ovulating, but the results were what they were. She was pregnant. Dr. Kuchinsky had been very supportive; he implied that he might know the name of a doctor, a retired doctor, who specialized in cases like hers—an abortion doctor. She took his business card.

She rumpled the test results into a ball and threw them down the sewer by the curb. It looked like it might rain, so she turned her collar up and proceeded to walk the seven blocks to the restaurant at which she was going to meet Gil for a late lunch. She liked Gil a lot. She found him attractive and a great deal of fun, but she wasn't sure he was cut out to be a father. They were both about to find out.

She stepped into the restaurant which was already crowded. She looked around but couldn't see Gil. Finally after three glances around the room she saw him waving at her, sitting in a booth on the side of the room. She walked up to him, "What the hell happened to you? Your hair, your beautiful blonde hair—it's all gone! Yesterday you looked like a Norse god; today you look like an ad for Brylcreem."

He stood up and gave her a slight hug. He was wearing a navy blue blazer and khaki pants, a blue shirt and a red and blue striped tie. "Look at you," she said. "I've never seen you in anything except jeans and sweat shirts. Were you kidnapped by a fraternity? What is going on?"

He laughed and sat down, beckoning her to sit across from him. "I started without you. I hope you don't mind. I was really hungry."

"Actually, I'm very hungry, too. What's going on, Gil? Are you OK?"

"Yeah. Yeah, I am...great. How about you Grace? You OK?"

"I have had better days."

"Well, I just wanted you to know. I am dropping out of school. I'm flying home today. My dad has got me an appointment in the army reserve back home." He stared at her, looking for a reaction. "It is the best thing for me. I won't have to worry about the draft or the war or any of that shit. I mean it

310

is a sweet gig—a little basic training and then a couple of weeks a year for a few years. It is sweet."

She shook her head, "You are joining the reserve?"

He nodded.

"But…but…what about the movement? Aren't you going to protest the war?"

"Grace, Grace…that's not my battle anymore. I just wanted to make sure I didn't go."

"I thought you were against the war. I thought you cared."

"I do. I mean, I am against the war, but do you really think that you marching around and carrying some stupid sign in San Francisco is really going to make a difference? I mean, I liked protesting. It was fun…but …"

"Fun? It was *fun?*"

"I mean, really, Grace, do you take it seriously?"

"Yes, yes I do. And I thought you did, too. I thought you did."

He leaned back in the booth and crossed his arms. "I like to keep all my options open, you know what I mean? I do a lot of things to keep my options open. I am a member of a fraternity in order to make some business connections after college. I studied for tests so that I can stay in school and keep my draft exemption. I marched because it was cool, and maybe it would help keep me out of the war. Besides hippies had the best drugs, and the hottest girls, you being the prime example. I even—man I hate to admit this because it is pretty low—I punctured, you know, put some holes in the rubbers we used for sex a few times. I figured if I knocked you up, that would be a draft exemption for sure. But now I don't have to worry. And, you are not pregnant, right? So, no harm done."

"I thought I knew you. I thought I might even love you..." Grace shook her head.

"Oh Grace, don't be like that. I mean, I love you. I do love you. But I have to follow my own destiny. I have other priorities. You know I have some time before my flight...we could get a hotel room...for old time's sake...one more time."

Grace stared at him. She stood up to walk out. He nudged her back into her seat.

"Oh, don't go giving me that look. Don't get sanctimonious on me, and all self-righteous. I worked just as hard as you for the movement." He raised his hands to form quotation marks when he said movement. "I marched in as many marches; I carried as many signs. And we had a good time. We had a great thing. I found you attractive, and you have to admit you found me attractive. We've been together three, four months. But neither of us thought in terms of forever. In the future, when I think back on these days here, I will always remember you as a...wonderful part of my time, my experience. I hope you see me that way too." He finished with a big smile.

"You are such a disappointment. Gil, you are just an asshole. I thought there was more to you...but you are so superficial, I didn't see that."

"I don't know what you are talking about. I never led you on. We were never anything more than what we were: we laughed, we marched, we got stoned, we fucked. And now I have to move on. No hard feelings."

"No hard feelings." She nodded her head. "You are what you are, as trite and as shallow as that is. I'm really just disappointed in myself for not seeing that, for trusting...for letting myself see what I wanted to see rather than what was real. Well, I won't make that mistake again."

She stood again, and this time, she did walk out. On the sidewalk, she reached into her pocket and found the card for the abortion doctor. She looked at the address. She started walking in the direction. She walked and walked. She actually made it to the address of the doctor's office and turned into the hallway. She stood in the hallway for perhaps an hour before climbing the stairs to the door on the second floor of the actual office. She stood outside the door for another hour watching three women enter and four other women leave the office. All of them seemed in good physical shape, half left crying, but half left not crying. She could not make herself open the door. Eventually she left the building and walked and walked.

She spent the night walking, and sitting in the library and in the bus station and at the counter of an all-night drug store nursing a coffee with her last dime, and walking some more. The next morning she went back to the abortion doctor's office and this time she made her way into the office to talk to the secretary.

"I think I want to make an appointment," she said.

The secretary showed her into an office. Rather than sitting on the table, Grace sat on a chair when the nurse. The secretary proceeded to fill out all of the necessary forms.

Grace did not wait, "Dr. Kuchinsky referred your office to me. I am pregnant and he said you could sometimes help girls in my situation. I am single, enrolled in college and on my own. I do not want to have a baby."

The secretary looked at her and nodded.

"I cannot do pregnant right now, I just can't, but..."

"But?" The secretary spoke softly.

"But an abortion; I'm not sure I can do that either."

"It sounds like you are really ...torn. You really do not know what you want to do."

"That is exactly right. I am just not sure, and that is really a new feeling for me. It is not a feeling I'm comfortable with. I'm not the kind of person who does ambiguity very well. I usually know what I want."

"You need to be sure, whatever you decide."

Grace just sat there and nodded. "I am sure I do not want to go through with this...today."

The secretary stood and moved over close to Grace. She patted her on the shoulder. "You do not have to. If you change your mind, it will be all right to come back here. But I want you to know, that it is all right to have doubts, and it is all right to never come back here."

"Thank you. I guess I need to think and really decide what I am going to do, what I can do. What I really can do." She stood up to leave. She looked left and right as if lost.

"Where are you going?" she asked.

314

"I wish I knew."

She left the building feeling more sure but also more frightened, and yet she was also less sure and more frightened. She walked and walked in random directions in the city. It began to rain and rain. By the time she ducked into a coffee house for some shelter from the rain, she was drenched. She looked around the room and on the other side she recognized a face from some of the protest rallies, Clark Bradley.

"Everything reeks of money"

September 5, 2011 about noon

About five miles northeast of Sherman, Texas

On the Red River

With the help of directions, and the GPS on the dash, Rachel finally pulled into the Kennisons' Driveway. The house was a huge two story stone mansion on the banks of the Red River. It was on one of those streets that had a name but didn't really deserve one. The driveway was bigger and better paved than the street; the street signs were small, hand-painted and almost impossible to see.

"If you didn't know you were there, you wouldn't know how to get here," Rachel said.

"That makes absolutely no sense," a very pregnant Hope said as she tried to get out of the car and make her way to the front door.

Chloe was trailing behind twisting and looking and trying to see everything. Chloe stared up at the twenty-foot Oak door with stained glass windows. "That is the biggest door I have ever seen. Do giants live here?"

"I certainly hope not," Rachel said. She was carrying a heavy cloth book bag.

"There are no giants living here," Hope said. "Just a nice family with a little girl who doesn't have many friends and I think you will like playing with her, and I know she would like to play with you. Chloe, remember what we talked about. This girl hasn't had many friends so she could really use a friend."

"Don't worry, Mom. I know how to play with little girls. I'm an expert. I kinda am one."

They all looked at the pumpkins and bales of hay on the porch and the two scarecrows.

"Everything reeks of money," Rachel whispered.

"Are you having doubts?"

"Are you?"

"No. I talked to them; they are really sweet people; some rich people are, you know."

"Really? I have trouble relating to rich people. They all seem so...wealthy."

"Oh Rachel, the Kennisons have been coming to the church for six months, give or take. They are fine people. Don't let your past color everything."

Suddenly the door opened and the Kennisons were all there to greet and welcome them. "Hi, I'm Will, this is my wife Carol and our daughter Jill. Welcome to our house. We are so happy that you could come here today. Please come in."

Will was dressed casually in shorts, sandals and a bright golf shirt. Carol equally breezy, but Jill had on a floor length formal looking pink dress. She was barefooted and had a large ribbon in her hair. She was huddled behind her mother almost hiding, peeking out to view the visitors. The incongruity of her appearance was highlighted by the doll she was clutching in her right hand. The doll was a larger than real life infant baby doll with a cute smile and formless body, stubby legs and arms, but only one eye. Jill held on loosely to one arm.

317

Hope kneeled down and spoke to Jill, "What's your doll's name?"

"Jill. My doll's name is Jill." She spoke in a whisper.

"That's your name, too!" Chloe said. Jill seemed to pull back. "No wonder that doll is so cool. I use to have a doll sort of like that but it was really, really different. Her name was Daisy. She wasn't near as *cool* as Jill .Have you got any other dolls that I could see and maybe we could play with?"

Jill nodded her head.

"Could you show me? I mean, you know, if you want to."

Jill nodded and she walked off with Chloe headed toward her bedroom. Will and Carol looked at each other.

THAT Phone Call

March 24, 2011, 1:30 a.m.

Hope's Home in Dallas

The phone rang. Rachel woke first. "Do you want me to get it?"

"Yes, please." Hope thought for one second. "No, I'll get it. At this time of night...what time is it? 1:30, you know it is going to be for me, and it is not going to be good news."

"The wages of righteousness." Rachel said and turned over to go back to sleep

Hope reached over across the bed and picked up the phone, clicked it on and the ringing stopped. "Hope Bradley, can I help you?"

There was a long silence and then she slowly sat up in the bed. "Yes" was all she said. "I understand. Of course. I will be right there...about an hour. Thank you for calling me."

Hope turned and sat on the edge of the bed but didn't move except to put her hand to her mouth. Rachel knew immediately, "Hope, what is it? What happened?"

"You need to call Florence and get her over here to take care of Chloe. I want you to go with me." Rachel nodded and silently agreed, without hesitation. "Of course."

"Rachel, I just got THAT phone call, the one you never want to get. Dad was in a car crash. They need for me to go to the hospital in Nettie." With the last words, her voice cracked

319

and it frightened Rachel. She grabbed her mouth and found herself starting to cry, but composed herself. "He'll be all right."

"No, Rachel, you don't understand. It was THAT phone call. I've had to make them many times. They used all the proper euphemisms; they said all the right things; they need me to come up there. That's what they say when there is a death. That's why I need you to come with me. I'm pretty sure my Dad is dead."

"No, no," Rachel voice was growing into hysteria. "You do not know that. You do not know. He cannot be dead; he was just here today." She looked at Hope and saw her staring back at her. Rachel took a deep breath. "I'll call Francine; you get dressed."

"Thank you." Hope said.

"Hope, I won't let you down." Rachel said.

"I know."

Rachel walked over and hugged her, and Hope allowed herself to sigh deeply before she broke loose to hand Rachel the phone and open the closet to choose a dress.

Within a half hour they were pulling out of the driveway, Rachel at the steering wheel. The drive to Nettie was nearly silent. Rachel complimented Hope's choice of a dress, professional and maternal. Hope returned the favor. Rachel was dressed in a grey pants suit. Hope looked pregnant. Rachel looked feminine.

When they arrived at the hospital, Hope went to the emergency room desk where she was promptly introduced to the hospital chaplain. As he approached, before he could say anything, Hope raised her hand to stop him, "I am the pastor at a church in Dallas—a small non-denominational church—but I was chaplain at Parkland Hospital for three years as part of my seminary training and I completed a two-year residency program after ordination before accepting my current position. At any rate, I am aware of your nomenclature, your protocols and emergency procedures. I understand my father's condition." She stopped, took a deep breath before she continued. "Well, I may not know exactly how he is, but I assume he is either dead or technically dead and on life support. We wouldn't be standing here if he was ...only injured."

"I am sorry." The chaplain said. "He is brain dead and is currently on life support."

"How long has he been like this?"

"He was brought to the hospital around 10:30. The absence of brain activity was noted after eleven o'clock."

"That sounds about right. He left our church about 9 o'clock."

"We found his papers—his living will etc.—all were on file, but the only relative listed was his Mother-in-law, and she is not competent to make any decisions or sign any papers. It took several hours to find you."

"I understand. And you need someone to sign before you can pull him off the life support."

"As well as consent to organ donation. You father agreed to be an organ donor."

She smiled for the first time sense entering the hospital, "Of course he did. Let me have the forms. I will sign them."

"I don't want to be morbid or insensitive, but your father will save the lives of several people with his organs."

As Hope grabbed the pen and started to sign the forms, Rachel put her hand on hers and looked at her. "There is no hesitation on this. Life—he would want that to be his legacy." She said and reached out to pat Rachel on the cheek.

The chaplain took the forms and handed them to the clerk behind the desk. "Do you want a few minutes with him before..."

"Yes."

The nurses were already beginning to take the tubes from various places when Hope and Rachel pulled back the curtain and entered the area where Clark lay on his bed. They had covered his torso with a sheet and the bandages on his forehead were loosely wrapped. The band aid that held the tube in his nose was being removed.

Hope stood back. "He's not breathing," Rachel said. Hope nodded.

Hope stepped forward and held her father's hand. "Oh, Dad." That was all.

The chaplain appeared. "Would you like for me to say a prayer?"

Hope shook her head.

"Would you like to say one?" He asked.

Hope looked at the chaplain. Rachel leaned forward and whispered into his ear, "She is praying."

Hope stood by the bedside silently, holding Clark's hand with a solitary tear rolling down her cheek. Eventually the medical staff indicated that they needed to move Clark's body and Hope let go as the wheeled his bed toward the operating room. She turned and accepted Rachel's embrace; she sobbed quietly until she gathered her strength.

"We need to go."

They stopped in the waiting room. Rachel brought them some coffee. They sat there looking at each other.

"I don't know about you, but I really needed this coffee," Rachel said.

Hope nodded. "I was just thinking how much I need you; how grateful I am that you are in my life especially today."

Tears seeped out of Rachel's eyes but she wiped them with her hand. "Oh, Hope, I am so sorry. I know how much your father meant to you."

"I keep reminding myself that he will always be with me; his fingerprints are on every part of my being, of my soul. A presence like his does not end just because of death. I choose to celebrate his fingerprints... even though I miss him, I miss him already, profoundly."

She took a large drink of coffee. "But now we have to do something even more difficult. We have to go tell my Granny."

"Why?" Rachel was shaking her head. "It is not like she will understand. Why do we have to confront her? Hope I can see no good coming from you seeing her and telling her; I think..."

"It is the right thing to do. I have to do it. We'll go get some breakfast, call and check on Chloe. By then, it will be time to see Granny."

It's About Fingerprints

September 5, 2011 about 3 pm

The Kennisons' house on the Red River

"Well, that was an excellent lunch, the burgers were exceptional," Rachel said.

"Thank you. The grill does all the work, the grill and the butcher." Will said.

"I have some homemade strawberry shortcake later." Carol said as she stood and grabbed dishes off the table.

"Let me help you," Rachel said as she stood and grabbed some other plates.

"Do you always divide chores like that?" Will asked. "I don't want to embarrass you or anything, if you don't want to talk about it."

"What do you mean?" Rachel asked.

"Well, I just wondered if you do all the domestic shores, like clearing the table, while Hope has the more traditional head of the family role."

"Not really," Hope spoke out. "But right now, Rachel does more than her share because I'm about 12 months pregnant." She saw the look on Will and Carol faces. "I'm due in about two weeks; not really 12 months pregnant, it only feels that way."

Carol and Will laughed. "That's nice to know," he said.

"I'm curious." Carol said. "What does Chloe call you? I mean how does she..."

"She calls me Mom, and she calls Rachel Ma or Mommy, and no, she doesn't get confused. She hasn't asked for an explanation yet, and when she does we will explain. If other people get confused, that's really their problem."

"It has been a long time since I've eaten on a patio, and I've never eaten with such a magnificent view. The river is beautiful," Rachel said. "Beautiful is not the right word; it is majestic."

"There is something about the water, and thank you. We try to spend every week end here during the summer, and some holidays. Thanksgiving is breathtaking. Sometimes in the summer we'll travel down the river. We went all the way to Shreveport once...for the fourth of July and fireworks. That was something. Mostly we just love watching the sunset. We'll have two hours, maybe two and half."

"Where does the river go? I mean how far?" Rachel asked but Hope answered.

"It goes all the way to the gulf...eventually. It was very kind of you to invite us and let us..." Hope's voice trailed off.

"Think nothing of it." Will said.

Suddenly Jill came running out of the house with Chloe following behind. "Mommy! Mommy! Mommy!" Jill was screaming. "Can Chloe and I play with your make-up? Please! Please! Please!"

Carol looked at Hope and Rachel. "Sometimes I let Jill play with some of my make-up, although she usually doesn't seem this excited about it."

"Mommy, Chloe and I are going to put make-up on each other!"

"Well, it is up to Chloe's parents."

Hope and Rachel both nodded that it would be OK.

Chloe and Jill ran off laughing together and holding hands.

Carol turned to Will. "Jill has made a friend, she has a friend." She started to cry.

Will hugged her and turned toward Hope and Rachel, "We have been very worried about Jill. She is very different and doesn't open up to many people. We want her so much to have friends, but she just doesn't. We just want her to be normal. I can't tell you what a gift it is to see her laughing and smiling with someone."

"I was hoping your daughter would play with Jill, but I didn't really expect..."

"Chloe is kind of special in her own way," Rachel said. "She reminds me of Hope's father.

"We were so sorry to hear of your father's death. It must have been a terrible loss for you." Will said.

Hope was silent. Rachel stood behind Hope and rubbed her neck. "Mr. Bradley was a special man. He taught school for over 40 years. He left a legacy—fingerprints as Hope calls it—on the community of Nettie in very profound ways. We have had cards and notes from students from each decade he taught telling of the lasting impact on their lives both intellectually and emotionally. His first principal, Ralph Plymale, wrote from Hot Springs Village, where he has retired with his second wife and told us that Mr. Bradley saved his life."

"My dad," Hope spoke in a quiet voice, "was far too intelligent to be intolerant, and he was far too wise to be superficial; he always let me know he loved me."

Grace Is Just a Four Letter Word

March 24, 2011, 10 am

Red River Nursing Home, Nettie, Texas

Hope and Rachel entered the Red River Nursing Home. Hope approached the desk clerk, "I would like to see Margaret Wheeler, please."

"You will have to wait. Visiting time is in one hour."

"This is rather important. I am her granddaughter. I would appreciate it if you could let us see her. I have some bad news for her."

Cassandra, in the nurse's station, heard Ms. Wheeler's name. "Is anything wrong? Excuse me, I am Cassandra and I work with Ms. Wheeler quite often. I am very fond of her, actually." She offered her hand to Hope and Rachel, and they stood in the hallway shaking hands.

Hope spoke, "I am Hope Bradley, Mrs. Wheeler's granddaughter. My father passed away early this morning in a car crash on the highway."

"Mr. Bradley? Oh God, no. He was here just yesterday." Cassandra began to cry. She began to tremble and Hope put her arms around her to comfort her.

"I am sorry to bring you the news like this. You knew my father quite well?"

"He would come and take care of Ms. Wheeler often, daily sometimes. He was so gentle and kind. You couldn't help but admire him, and when I found out she was his mother-in-law...I mean, there are many people in this home and the kids don't treat their own mothers as well as he treated her. He was one of a kind. And she is so... out of it." She looked at Hope. "I don't mean to speak out of turn."

"I am a pastor and have been in situations like this many times; I understand your discomfort. Feel free to speak openly."

"Oh Miss...Bradley, Ms. Wheeler is in a bad way and she keeps getting worse. She is hardly ever lucid anymore and she has gotten to the point that when Mr. Bradley visits she won't really acknowledge him. She just stares all day and doesn't react to much of anything. I can't get her to hardly eat or smile or anything. I don't know if telling her will get through to her. I doubt that she will know who you are."

Rachel touched her shoulder, "Hope, let's leave. You do not want to remember your grandmother like this. You're not going to accomplish anything good from this."

"Miss, I'm afraid I agree. I'll tell Ms. Wheeler, but I don't think she will understand and I wouldn't want you to get all upset especially being pregnant."

"I appreciate the concern of both of you, but I owe it to him, and I owe it to her."

Cassandra nodded. "I just finished her bath and she was trying to sleep. I'll take you to her room."

They walked down the hallway and into her room.

Maggie was lying in the bed but the bed was tilted in a sitting position. She was staring but it was impossible to tell if she was staring out the window at the wall or at the silent television. Her mouth was slightly open and spittle was dripping down the corner of her lips. Hope looked at her and at first gasped. She stepped back and Rachel grasped her arm. Hope nodded and stepped forward, gently placing her hand on Maggie's, "Granny, it's me, Hope."

Maggie slowly, unresponsively turned. And then the light went on. She jerked her head and moved her lips into a smile, tears started flowing down her cheek. She tried to speak, "ow, oww, ohh, op, op op, op!"

"That's right—Hope. It is Hope."

"Op, op. Uv .. ,ue, uv ou, ov ou."

"I love you too, Granny. I love you too."

"Op...sss...oppy." Maggie shook her head. "Sss...arry."

Hope nodded for her, "I know. You are sorry, it's all right."

Then, somehow, Maggie saw Rachel and gestured for her to come closer. "Sss...ary...ov oou. Sssary." She held out her arm and Rachel received her hug and hugged her back.

Rachel stood back, "It's all right. We both love you."

Hope stepped between them and grabbed Maggie's hand. "I have bad news."

Maggie continued to smile and nod. "C..ck...d..d"

Hope nodded. "Clark died this morning."

Maggie nodded and smiled.

"She knew? How did she know? Did she know?" Cassandra asked and looked to Rachel and Hope for an answer.

Maggie smiled and nodded. "Ov...ope!"

"I love you, too," Hope said

Maggie closed her eyes, but continued to smile. Cassandra stepped in. "She really needs to sleep now. This is the most energy she has spent in months."

They walked out into the hallway. Rachel was wiping tears out of her eyes. Cassandra was shaking her head. "That was amazing. I haven't seen her that lucid in...I have never seen her that aware! It was like a miracle."

Hope took a deep breathe, and then another.

"How did she know about Mr. Bradley's death?" Cassandra said.

"Are you sure that's what she meant?" Rachel asked. "I mean she just sort of clicked."

"You were there." Cassandra was visually disturbed. "What else could she have meant? I mean, was that some kind of spiritual thing?"

Hope looked at them both, "I don't know. I'm not sure. I just know that things happen around death, and sometimes there doesn't seem to be an explanation. I wouldn't waste my time trying to explain it. It is enough for me that my father just died and my grandmother just told me she loved me." She turned to Rachel, "I need to go home and hug our daughter." Then she turned toward Cassandra, "Thank you for everything. You indeed are a wonderful nurse. Tell Granny when she wakes that we will be back soon to see her and we will bring our daughter, Chloe."

They walked out into the parking lot. Rachel got behind the steering wheel. She started the engine, but before she drove she turned to Hope. "I'm sorry, but I can't hold it in any longer." She put her head on the steering wheel and sobbed, loudly and intensely. Hope patted her on the back.

Finally, Rachel could speak. "I think I will feel that hug forever."

"I was dreading seeing her—she looked worse than I thought—but I am so glad we came, but not for the reasons I anticipated. I think she needed to see us. I think she has been clinging to life for this one last chance to see us and make right her relationship with us. I wouldn't be a bit surprised if we got home to a phone call that she had passed away."

"You think so? Really?"

"No. Probably not. But life is pretty weird sometimes, and death can be even weirder."

Rachel started the car and turned out of the parking lot. "How did you get to be so wise?"

"From my father. I got it from my father."

Clark and Grace on the Red River

September 5, 2011 about 6:30 pm, sunset

On the banks of the Red River

"Mr. Kennison I can't tell you how much this means to me," Hope said.

"Think nothing of it. We are very glad to do it. And please, call me Will."

Will brought out a small sail boat from the house, a toy actually, but a boat that would sail. It was perhaps three feet long and the sail was equally as tall. The bottom dropped down as deep as the mast stood tall. The deck was flat and sturdy. He held it up in front of the gathering—Carol, Rachel, Jill, Chloe and Hope. Rachel had the cloth book bag straining from its contents, the same one with which she had arrived.

They all walked down to the dock except Carol. "Would you please play this CD as soon as the boat is launched?" Rachel asked.

"Of course. What is it?" Carol asked.

"Mr.Plymale sent it to us. He had it made from a tape of Hope's mother. You know, it's cleaned up, scratches removed. It's Hope's mother singing."

Carol nodded.

The rest stood looking out as the sun was beginning to melt into far left side of the river. The reflection danced and gently swayed across the water. Will stood in front of Hope and presented the sail boat.

"Perfect" she said in response to Will. Hope closed her eyes, "Dear Lord, I've waited a long time to do this. I've prayed for many years, trying to find the right place, and I know this is the right place."

She turned and grabbed two urns from the bag Rachel was holding. She poured the ashes from her mother's urn into the deck of the boat and then poured her father's ashes next to her mother's. A gentle breeze scattered a few of the ashes. Will turned and put the boat in the water and gently pushed it into the middle of the river. The stream took charge and the boat gently drifted away. Carol started the CD and Grace's voice rang out clear and strong:

"The water is wide I cannot get over,

And neither have I the wings to fly

But build me a boat that can carry two,

And both shall row, my true love and I."

They all stood there on the dock, arms around each other, watching the boat sail off into the setting sun, breathing, and listening to the song.